WISH YOU WOULD

HAVEN HARBOR SERIES BOOK FOUR

LILY MILLER

ABOUT THE BOOK

It wasn't that long ago that I vowed to stay away from Holden Banks. He's stubborn, cocky, practically intolerable. And now he's my new roommate.

Suddenly, the two of us are sharing dinners, secrets, late night massages. Did I mention the guy is drop dead gorgeous? This was *not* in the plans when I moved back to Reed Point.

I know all about Holden's reputation. He's a notorious player. A heartbreaker who is way too attractive for his own good, with his smoldering smirks and piercing green eyes.

But it turns out he's also sweet and thoughtful, even taking care of me when I get sick. Maybe that's why, in a moment of weakness, I offer to be his fake date to his ex's wedding. This is starting to get complicated—and dangerous.

There's no denying the explosive chemistry between us, but we're also complete opposites in every way. I'm a free spirit, he's a Type A neat freak. I'm a romantic, he's quick to remind me he doesn't believe in love. Oh, and he's also newly celibate.

That is, until a night out with our friends and a few too many tequilas ends with me in his bed. I tell myself it's just one electrifying night and come morning, I'll forget it ever happened. But the filthy things he said to me are unforgettable.

Soon, lines are blurred, and our relationship starts to feel very real. After all, what's more real than finding out I'm pregnant with his baby?

Copyright © 2025 by Lily Miller

All rights reserved.

No part of this book may be reproduced in any form or by any electronic or mechanical means, including information storage and retrieval systems, without written permission from the author, except for the use of brief quotations in a book review.

This book is a work of fiction. Names, characters, places and incidents are products of the author's imagination or are used fictitiously. Any resemblance to actual events or locals or persons, living or dead, is entirely coincidental.

Wish You Would

Cover photo: Briquelle Kayanne, Briquelle Kayanne Photography

Cover models: Lindsey and Alex

Cover design: Kim Wilson, Kiwi Cover Design

Editing: Carolyn De Melo

PLAYLIST

ONE

I MAY BE CELIBATE, BUT I'M NOT BLIND.

Holden

The high-pitched sound of a woman's pleading echoes off the walls when I slide open the patio door and step into my best friend Tucker's house.

"What do you mean? You can't be serious! Where am I supposed to stay?"

Tucker and I just finished a 5-mile run, and I had agreed to a quick beer at his place before heading home. From the sound of it, we've interrupted something.

Tuck's wife Daisy is sitting at the kitchen counter, her chin cupped in her hands as she watches a very upset woman pace a hole in the tile floor. She holds her cell phone out in front of her, her platinum hair swinging as she shakes her head vigorously at the guy on the other end of the call.

"It's out of my control," says the man, who is on speaker. "It is what it is. It's an inconvenience for me too."

"*It is what it is?* I don't think you understand. I have nowhere else to live." She emphasizes each syllable.

Daisy waves us in, a grimace on her face as she returns

her attention to the phone call. Tucker heels off his running shoes and then crosses the kitchen to where Daisy sits, placing a kiss on her temple.

The corners of my lips quirk in a smile. Tucker is such a giant mush around his wife. I'm still trying to wrap my head around the fact that my best friend is a married man.

Daisy has been the best thing to ever happen to Tuck. They've actually known each other since birth— they even share the same birthdate—it just took 25 years or so for them to actually get together. There was always an undeniable tension in the air whenever they were in the same room, but I always assumed it was because they hated each other. It turns out the exact opposite was true, and they finally realized that. I'm happy for them, and Daisy has become one of my closest friends. But things are just different now.

Tucker and I were roommates for four years, but he moved in with Daisy when things between the two of them got serious. I'd never admit it to him, but I miss having him around the house. We used to do everything together, now I'm lucky if I see him once a week.

One by one, every one of my buddies have gotten hitched. Tuck married Daisy, Jake married Everly, Grayson married Jake's sister, Sierra. I'm the last one standing.

Watching these guys settle down has forced me to take a long, hard look at myself. There was a time not too long ago when all I was interested in was hooking up and no-strings sex. That all ended when I met Aubrey, and well, that ended in a huge fucking disaster.

So, here I am on a self-imposed detox. I'm focused on work and on myself. No one-night stands. No women, period. I'm celibate and committed to keeping it that way for the foreseeable future.

"How could this happen?" the woman wails into the phone, pulling my attention back to her.

"Is everything okay?" Tucker whispers into Daisy's hair. She shakes her head in response.

"You told me the place was newly renovated. You said it was in mint condition. Those were your exact words. *Mint condition.*"

I feel like I'm intruding. I should probably just turn around, jump in my truck and head home. I catch Tucker's eye and nod toward the door, but he waves me off. He grabs a couple of glasses from the cupboard, fills them from the tap and then hands one to me. I chug it back, realizing how thirsty I am after our run.

"I'm sorry again, ma'am," the voice says on the other side of the call. "I promise you'll be the first to know when everything is fixed. You have first dibs."

"*Wow, thanks,*" she says, sarcasm dripping from her voice. "I signed a freaking lease. I gave you a deposit." The blonde stops pacing and stands with her back to me. My gaze wanders to her heart-shaped ass. I may be celibate, but I'm not blind. "Isn't there another unit I can stay in while you work on mine?"

"I'm sorry, I'm full."

"I can't believe this."

"I will keep you up to date on the repairs. I need to go. I'm sorry again."

The line goes dead as the blonde huffs out a deep breath.

"Are you okay?" Daisy's face is sympathetic.

"No, I'm not okay." She stuffs her iPhone into her back pocket and then turns around. She looks up to me, and my heart seems to stop beating in my chest.

Emerald-green eyes. Platinum-blonde hair that falls in

waves past her shoulders, the strands so shiny they shimmer under the kitchen lights. A perfect nose, and lips that are glossed in pink and look as soft as pillows.

Goddamn... she's beautiful.

It's been a long time, but I definitely remember her. Briar Moore is hard to forget.

What is she doing back in Reed Point? Last I heard, Daisy's best friend had moved back home to Vancouver to be closer to her mom and she had no plans to return to Reed Point. That was at least a year ago.

"The apartment I just rented had a flood. The whole place is two inches deep in water. The landlord says it's unliveable." She drops her head into her hands and groans. "I was supposed to move in right away."

"Oh, Briar. I'm sorry." Daisy gets up off her stool and gives her a hug. "But we'll figure it out. You can sleep on our couch. Right, Tuck?"

Tucker chews the inside of his cheek. I know why he's hesitating. Tuck is the kind of guy who would give a friend the shirt off his back, but he and Daisy are in the middle of a major renovation. The upstairs bedrooms have been stripped down to the studs and the two of them have been sleeping on a mattress on the floor in the family room for the past month.

"I love you, Dais, but I can't crash at your place for two or three months. I have too much stuff, I have a cat. Besides, you two are newlyweds. The last thing I need is to listen to you go at it like wild animals."

Briar slumps down into a chair at the kitchen table. It's then that I notice the small crate in the corner of the room, and the orange-and-white-striped cat crouched inside. It fixes me with a lethal glare before arching its back and turning away.

"What about The Seaside?" Daisy turns to Tuck. "You can call Jake, ask him to talk to Liam. I'm sure he could get Briar a deal on a room at the hotel." Jake is a good buddy of ours, and my neighbor on Haven Harbor. He's close friends with Liam Bennett, whose family owns a boutique hotel chain that is headquartered in Reed Point.

"Dais, you're sweet," Briar says. "But one, I doubt they accept pets and two, I could never afford weeks on end at a luxury hotel... even at a discount."

Daisy frowns. "It's okay, Bri. We'll figure something out."

"Well, I could call Braxton."

Daisy fixes Briar with a pointed stare. "You are absolutely *not* calling Justin's best friend."

"Who else am I going to ask?"

"Over my dead body are you asking him."

Leaning back against the kitchen counter, I look to Tucker to see if he's following the girls' back and forth. When I catch his eye, he shrugs in response.

Who the hell are Braxton and Justin? And why is Daisy so adamant that Briar not get in touch with them?

The gorgeous blonde collapses onto the kitchen table, resting her head on her forearm with a sigh. "I know, you're right. I just don't know what else to do. The apartment is perfect. Or it *was* perfect. It's close to the beach, it has a cute little white kitchen. You saw the photos, Dais. Wasn't it perfect?"

Instead of answering, Daisy turns to me suddenly with hope in her eyes. "Holden has a spare bedroom! Maybe Briar could stay with you?"

"What?" There's no chance I heard that right.

"Your place has two bedrooms. And now that Tucker's not living there anymore..."

"But—"

"It would only be temporary," Daisy quickly continues, obviously not understanding that this is a terrible idea. "And as her former roommate, I can vouch for Briar. She's tidy, she's quiet... well, most of the time she's quiet. She's the best. I bet you'd actually enjoy her company."

I'm sure I would enjoy Briar's company, on her back for me with her long legs and her smooth, creamy skin. But that doesn't mean I want a roommate. Especially a roommate that looks like her— a girl straight out of my fantasies. Briar is Daisy's best friend, which makes her a no-go for a night of fun. Not that I can remember the last time I allowed myself to have *fun*.

"Holdey, please. She just moved back from Vancouver, and she has nowhere to stay." Daisy's expression is all sad eyes and pouty lips. I'm familiar with that look; I've seen it aimed at Tucker more than a time or two. "It wouldn't be for long."

I look to Tuck for help, but the smirk on his face tells me that he's enjoying watching me squirm. Briar's shoulders drop in frustration and her bottom lip begins to tremble. *Dammit, don't cry. Please don't cry.* I won't be able to handle it if Briar's green eyes turn glassy. When she blinks back a tear, I feel my resolve begin to crumble. When a second tear falls down her flushed cheek, I give in immediately.

"You can stay with me," I tell her. "Until your apartment is ready."

Briar wipes the tears from her cheeks as the corners of her pretty lips turn up. Damn, she is beautiful.

She drops her gaze to the cat carrier. "What about Bear?"

"The cat can come too," I say. "But I'm not a cat guy, so keep it in your room."

I'm not a cat guy is an understatement. They're not cuddly. They don't listen. They pee in a box. And worst of all, I'm deathly allergic. If this cat gets too close to me, I'll be covered in hives within five minutes.

"I'll keep her in my room. I promise. No lecture needed. And Holden—"

Briar pushes up from her chair and walks across the kitchen to where I'm standing, then wraps her arms around my neck. "Thank you."

The moment our bodies touch, tingles race over my skin. I wonder if she feels it too. She smells like sugar and lemons, and for a second my brain seems to scramble. Her ample chest is pushed against my ribcage, her small hands rub back and forth over my shoulders. Thankfully, she unwinds her arms from my body and takes a few steps backwards, putting some much-needed distance between us.

"Briar is a great cook," Daisy says, motioning towards her best friend, her eyes sparkling. "And she's really good company when she's not reading her smut books."

"They're called romance novels," Briar corrects her as she crouches in front of the cat carrier and pulls out Bear. She squishes her face into the cat's neck, scratching its ears before holding the thing out to me. The cat hisses.

"Not a cat guy, remember?" I hold my hands up in defense and take two steps backwards.

"I don't think Bear is a fan of yours either," Tucker mutters with a smug smile. I flip him off.

"Don't feel bad. She hates most people." Briar snuggles the fur ball into her chest as my eyes begin to itch at an alarming speed.

"Way to sell him, Briar," Daisy deadpans

Briar stuffs the fleabag back into the carrier as I use my T-shirt to wipe at my watery eyes.

What the hell have I gotten myself into? I just hope I can put up with living with the two of them for the next couple of months.

"I am so happy this all worked out! I know you two are going to like living together. You're the best, Holdey." Daisy squeezes my bicep. "And I love you, Briar, which means Holden is going to love you too."

"Here's hoping," Tucker mumbles with that same shit-eating grin across his face.

I try to ignore how much my best friend is enjoying watching my misery as I slowly come to terms with the fact that I won't be living alone anymore. Forget walking around in my underwear or blasting whatever music I want to on Saturday mornings. She'd better not make a mess or move any of my things around. I like things the way I like them. Neat and organized. In their place. As much as I've missed having Tuck as a roommate, I've gotten used to living on my own. By my rules only.

Fuck.

Scrubbing my hands through my hair, I try to fight off the intense feeling of regret. I came here for a fucking beer, and I'm leaving with a roommate.

"Why do you look so grumpy?" Tucker shoots me a sideways glance after the girls have gone upstairs to look at how the reno is progressing.

"Is that a serious question?"

Tucker laughs. The fucking guy laughs.

"If I knew I was going to be swindled into living with a woman I barely know, I would have stayed home."

"Oh, come on, Holdey. You've been in that house all alone for a year. She'll only be there for a few weeks. Besides, it will be good for you to have some company before you turn into a grumpy old man."

A long stretch of silence lingers between us as I stare at Tucker with my eyebrows raised.

"*A few weeks*? Try months. Thanks a lot for the help, by the way. You're supposed to be my friend. Where were you when your wife gave me her *please, Holden* eyes?"

"You've met my wife. She's the boss. I am no match for Daisy Collins."

It's true—Daisy calls the shots. Normally, I would give Tucker a hard time for handing his balls over to his wife, but I'm too distracted thinking about my new roommate.

Briar is beautiful. Stunning. Different from the rest.

Shit, I'm in trouble.

"Hey. Be nice to her, okay? She has a lot going on."

"Obviously. I'm always nice."

"No, but you are particular."

"*Particular*? What the hell does that mean?"

"It means you can be an uptight asshole sometimes," Tuck laughs.

Daisy and Briar arrive back at the kitchen before I have a chance to respond, so instead I just roll my eyes. Okay, I might be a little Type A. When Tuck and I were roommates, he learned what would set me off. He put his shoes away in the closet, he did his dishes, he didn't leave his shit lying around.

I scrub my hand over the back of my neck.

"You okay, Holdey?" Daisy asks. "Another one of your headaches?"

"Nah, I'm good. Just a little tight." I stretch my neck from side to side.

"Well, just so you know, Briar gives great massages. I'm not sure how, but she gets in deep. For being as tiny as she is, the girl can really get in there."

Fuck my life. I know what she said, but that's not what I

heard. I may be a *nice* guy, but I'm also a healthy, red-blooded 28-year-old man. I really need Daisy to stop putting thoughts in my head about Briar's hands on my body.

"You keep saying things like that and I might get a big head over here." Briar smiles.

"See, Holdey... this arrangement is going to work out well," Daisy assures me. "Nightly massages sound good to me."

Briar laughs, and it lights up her entire face. Her gold-rimmed green eyes shine, and her cheeks turn the softest shade of pink to match her lips.

Well, *damn.*

Moving her in may not be my finest idea, but it's too late now.

"So, do you have a car here?" I ask Briar. "Or do you need a ride?"

"I have my car."

"Great. I guess I'll see you at my house then," I answer, clapping Tucker on the shoulder before leaning into Daisy for a hug. "It's the first one on the right when you drive down Haven Harbor."

"Got it." She smiles, and fuck, is it gorgeous.

On the drive back to my place, I'm not surprised to find that my mood has turned to shit. Whether I like it or not, I'm getting a new roommate. And I'm going to need to learn how to keep her at an arm's length.

And I can already tell that's going to be really fucking hard.

TWO

IT SEEMED LIKE A GOOD IDEA AT THE TIME.

Briar

The song drifting through the radio is one I know by heart. The Jonas Brothers. It was playing when I met him. It's our song. At least, it used to be.

That's all it takes for my mind to return to the one thing I've been trying to avoid: Vancouver, and the guy I fell in love with there. Or maybe it was just lust.

I knew the second I saw him; we had an instant connection. I wanted to know everything about him. Every time he touched me, it felt dizzying, like I was spinning on the fastest carnival ride.

But that time in my life is behind me. As hard as it was to leave my hometown, he gave me no other choice. I had to do what was best for me. So here I am, back in Reed Point. I'll get through this, even if it means starting over. Every day seems to get a little easier. I haven't thought of him or how he humiliated me since I boarded the plane at YVR—that's one whole day. It's not much, but it's progress.

I roll down the window as I turn onto Haven Harbor, taking in the view of the ocean from the secluded street.

Stupid song. I don't want to think about him. Not today and actually, not ever again. Breathing in the salty air, I pull my car in front of the small split-level beach house that I'll be calling home for the next couple of months.

I'm still not sure how this happened. One minute I was practically homeless and the next, I'm moving in with Holden Banks. I may have been distracted by that disastrous phone call, but I definitely noticed how good he looked when he showed up at Daisy's place today. Fresh off his run, his dark hair a mess. He felt good too when I wrapped my arms around him. I didn't need to pull him into a hug, but I saw the opportunity and I took it. I wasn't going to miss the chance to feel his rock-hard body up against mine, and it didn't disappoint. I bet he has chiseled abs under his shirt. I bet his skin would feel so good under my fingertips. He probably would be great in—

"Are you coming?"

Startled, I whip my gaze out the window to find Holden standing there, staring at me expectantly. I lift a hand to shield my eyes from the blinding sun. The temperature on the dash reads 94 degrees and if it wasn't for the air conditioning in my car, I would be sweltering. A blush heats my cheeks as I swallow. "Yes, yes, I'm coming."

"Thought you might need some help with your things."

I smile. "I don't have much. Most of my stuff is still in storage."

I follow Holden to the back of my car, where I watch him pop the trunk then begin lifting my suitcases from the car.

"Let me show you inside."

"Okay, thanks." I open the car door and take Bear's crate from the back seat, then I follow Holden up the driveway to the front door. I follow him inside, slipping off my Converse before setting Bear's carrier down in the living room.

My eyes drift around my temporary new home. I immediately notice that it's spotless. Every surface is clean and dusted, everything is put perfectly in its place—though "everything" may be a misleading description.

The place is practically bare. There is a black, oversized leather chair and matching couch in the living room with a single black throw pillow. There are no knick-knacks, no family photos on the bookshelf, no artwork on the walls—none of the personal touches that make a house a home.

Is he a minimalist or something? Maybe he isn't planning on living here long? Maybe Tucker took most of the décor with him when he moved in with Daisy?

"This is nice, Holden," I say, because the house itself *is* nice. The kitchen looks like it has been renovated, and the large windows reveal a beautiful view of the beach across the street. It's just lacking character. Charm. Personality.

"Thanks." Holden picks up my suitcase and nods to the stairs. "Come on, I'll show you to your room."

Up five or six steps is the second level of the house. There is a bedroom on the right which I assume is Holden's, a bathroom on the left and then another smaller bedroom. He pushes open the door to that room and then steps aside, motioning for me to go ahead.

"We'll have to get you a bed," he says, following me into the completely empty bedroom.

"Oh. I didn't realize your spare room isn't furnished," I say, my voice echoing off the walls. "Holden, I really appreciate the offer, but I don't want you having to buy a new bed. Really, I can get a room at The Seaside."

"It's fine, Briar. We can get you one. It's just won't be today. For now, you can have my bed."

Holden looks at me, nodding like he expects me to go along with it.

"I'm not sleeping with you, Holden," I tell him, and he frowns at me in response. God, he's still so attractive when he scowls. Broody and arrogant and ruggedly handsome. Why does he have to be so hot?

"What? Why are you scowling at me?"

He shakes his head, his frown deepening. "I wasn't asking you to sleep with me, Briar. I was offering you my bed until we get you one. I can sleep on the couch."

"Oh," I say, feeling a blush creep up my cheeks. "I'm not taking your bed. *I'll* sleep on the couch." I grab the handle of my suitcase, ready to drag it back downstairs to the living room.

"You're not sleeping on the couch. You're a guest. I'll change my sheets," he says, motioning down the hall to his bedroom. "I'll be in my room for a bit catching up on emails if you need anything. Just make yourself at home. I'm going to turn in early, I need to be at work for 7."

"What do you eat in the morning?"

"Why?"

"I was thinking I'd make you breakfast."

The frown returns. "It's fine. I'll grab something on my way to the office."

"I'd just like to do something nice for you, since you've been so kind to let me stay here."

"It's fine, Briar."

"Okay, so you don't like breakfast. Got it," I say, pushing the handle of my suitcase down to the base.

I'm about to tell him again that I'm not okay with taking his bed, but he's already gone, stalking down the hallway to his bedroom, closing the door behind him a little harder than necessary.

He hates me.

Dropping my face to my palms, I squeeze my eyes shut,

regretting my decision to stay here. I should have thought this through. It seemed like a good idea at the time. Maybe I just need to give Holden a day or two to get used to having me here.

Holden and I spend the rest of the afternoon locked away in our respective bedrooms. Attempting to get my life together, I unpack my suitcase, organizing my stuff in the bedroom's small walk-in closet. I let Bear out of her carrier and watch as she explores the empty room, looking for an escape hatch. After spending an hour or so on the floor with my laptop, I stand and stretch, realizing how hungry I am. I tuck Bear back in her crate and then head down to the kitchen to make myself something to eat.

There's no sign of Holden, who must still be working upstairs in his room. I open the fridge to find it's about as empty as my new bedroom. There's a liter of milk, a bunch of energy drinks, parmesan cheese and a few apples in the crisper. The state of his pantry isn't much better—I find some pasta and a few different boxes of cereal. Does this man live on energy drinks and Cap'n Crunch?

I'll go to the grocery store tomorrow.

But for now, I can make spaghetti. I take the parmesan from the fridge and grab a small bottle of olive oil and salt and pepper from the kitchen counter.

I'm tossing the cooked pasta in a pan with a splash of olive oil when the creak of a floorboard down the hall stiffens my spine. I was hoping I wouldn't see him for the rest of tonight, but I guess a man has to eat. Especially one of Holden's size. He must be six-foot-one. Probably 200 pounds, maybe more with all that muscle. And that is exactly the reason I was hoping to avoid him.

I can't look at the man without imagining him naked. Imagining what he has going on under his clothes. Does he have chest hair? Is he hiding a 6-pack or an 8-pack under his T-shirt? How big is he? Is he long and straight or does his dick have a curve to it?

I look up from the stove to find Holden leaning against the doorframe, watching me. I feel my heartbeat kick up a notch. Why can't I just look at him like a roommate? Or Tucker and Daisy's best friend?

Because he's ridiculously hot, that's why. Too attractive for his own good. And any girl in my shoes would want to see Holden Banks naked.

"Briar." He snaps me back to reality.

Turning my attention back to the pan, I sprinkle in some parmesan and toss the noodles to coat them. "Hey."

A pair of gray joggers and a faded Reed Point University T-shirt grace his body, stretched perfectly over his pecs and broad shoulders.

God, he's perfect.

"I was going to order us takeout. You should have told me that you are hungry."

"Oh." I awkwardly shrug my shoulders. "That's okay. I made enough for both of us but if you'd rather order in, that's fine. You don't have to eat it if you don't want to."

I turn my gaze to meet his sea-green eyes and find him staring back at me with a frustrated expression. Does he just hate pasta? Or avoid carbs? His reaction catches me off guard. It's becoming crystal clear that Holden Banks isn't interested in my cooking or my company. I'm surprised by this version of him. I didn't know him very well when I last lived in Reed Point, but he always seemed so fun and charming.

"You don't need to cook for me, so we're clear, but it smells good. Thanks."

He grabs two plates from the cupboard and sets them

down next to the stove. I pile pasta onto each, and then he takes them to the table. I slide into the chair opposite his.

"Can I grab you a drink?" he asks before shovelling a heaping forkful into his mouth.

"I'm fine, thanks. Not a big energy drink girl. I'll make myself a cup of tea after dinner."

"Huh."

I pause and look at him, my fork hovering halfway to my mouth. "What's the *huh* for?"

"Nothing, I just didn't take you for a tea drinker."

"What's wrong with drinking tea?"

"Nothing," he says through a mouthful of pasta. "If you like water-flavored nothing."

I shoot him an unimpressed glare before taking a bite. "So, what you're saying is, I'm not going to find a selection of tea in your pantry?"

Holden laughs. It's the first one I've heard from him all day. "Unfortunately for you, you won't. But I have water, that's practically the same thing, right?"

"Well, that's a start." I smile, noticing the crinkle at the corners of his eyes. "What's your favorite drink?"

Holden hums, sitting back in his chair. Another frown. I immediately miss his smile. "A cold beer. Gin. A cup of coffee in the morning."

"I can't stand the taste of coffee. I'm telling you, there's nothing better than a steaming cup of peppermint tea before bed. You should try it sometime."

He shrugs. "I'll take your word for it."

Holden is cute when he's not wound so tight.

We finish our dinner in silence. Holden keeps his head down, which gives me the opportunity to sneak a few glances at him. Thick chestnut hair with a slight wave at the ends. Sharp jaw with a five o'clock shadow. Deep, green eyes.

It's strange how he's been nothing like the guy I got to know before I moved to Vancouver. Not that I knew him well, but because our best friends were dating, we were together at a few parties. He seemed playful, always up for a good time. This Holden is different. He's quiet. There's something mysterious about him.

After we eat, Holden insists on washing the dishes while I tidy the kitchen. I keep my mouth shut when he begins to clean the countertops again, going over the same surfaces I just wiped down.

"Thanks for the company," I say when there's nothing left to clean up. "I'm … um…going to have a shower."

"There are towels underneath the sink, and I changed the sheets on my bed. It's all ready for you," he says, not looking up as he scrubs at the sink. "And before you try to argue with me… don't."

"Holden—"

"I said don't." He places the sponge in its holder and then finally lifts his eyes to meet mine. My knees go weak.

"Okay," I relent, sighing in resignation. "Thank you."

He holds my stare, unwavering, before I turn to leave.

"Hey, Briar?" he calls, stopping me.

"Yeah?"

"Who's Braxton?"

My shoulders stiffen. "A friend of my ex's."

"Then who's Justin?"

"No one important. Not anymore."

"If he's not important, why won't you tell me who he is?"

I flinch, doing my best to act like talking about my ex is not a big deal. "It's a long story."

"I've got time."

His eyes hold mine as he leans back against the counter, one ankle crossed over the other. He looks relaxed in his gray sweatpants, his feet bare. But I can see the concern in his gaze. He must have picked up on the tension when I mentioned Braxton and Justin to Daisy earlier today.

Drop it. Please drop it. Holden and I shared a nice dinner together. It feels like we're beginning to get along. Talking about Justin will definitely ruin the mood. But the way he's looking at me, the way he's refusing to look away, tells me that he doesn't want to let this go. It's unnerving, but also undeniably sexy.

"Fine," I sigh. "We used to date. Back in Vancouver." The words taste sour on my tongue. "Until he decided he didn't appreciate monogamy. He just didn't bother to tell me he had moved on until I found them together on my couch."

Holden's jaw tightens, a pulse ticking below his cheek. But he doesn't speak. He just stands there, motionless, watching me as I nervously talk about my ex.

"It was humiliating. I sort of lost my mind for a little while. I keyed his car and gave all his stuff to Goodwill while he was at work. So, he got his."

Holden looks impressed. "I bet he was pissed."

"An understatement."

"He deserved it. And just so we're clear, as long as you're staying here with me, you will not be calling Justin or his friend. For anything. He doesn't deserve to talk to you. He doesn't even deserve to breathe the same air as you. Understand?"

I swallow. "Understood. Now, I need you to drop it. Please. I want to move on with my life and it's easier if I forget he ever existed."

Holden nods.

"Thanks."

I leave him in the kitchen and head back up the few stairs, grabbing a pair of shorts and tank top from my temporary closet before going to the bathroom. Talking about Justin made that old hurt return to my heart. I turn on the shower and step under the hot spray, taking slow, deep breaths until the pain subsides. I tell myself I'm fine.

Will this feeling ever go away? Every damn time I think about Justin it comes right back, strong as ever. The way he betrayed me. The way he humiliated me with the photos that were supposed to be for his eyes only.

I should have known better with a guy like him. I should have seen the warning signs; there were enough of them. For months, there was a voice in my head telling me something was off, but I ignored the red flags. I pretended we were good. God, I was good at pretending. Sometimes I swear I even believed the lies I told myself.

But never again will I allow myself to be used like that.

If Holden only knew the half of it, but he never will. I don't need to relive that humiliation.

I allow the spray to wash over my face and my shoulders until I turn off the faucet, towel off and get changed. I quietly glance down the hall to make sure Holden isn't in his bedroom. I stand outside his door, stiff and uncomfortable in the dark. Assuming he has already gone to bed on the couch in the living room, I nervously push open the door and pad into his room.

The first thing I see is his bed— it looks like a king size — with crisp white sheets and a dark gray bedspread. Not surprisingly, the room has no photos and very few personal items, but the window gives a nice view of the beach across the street. There's a dresser with a TV mounted on the wall above it and two side tables with table lamps that he must have turned on for me. That was sweet of him, I think to myself, doing my best to keep my racing heart in check. There's something so personal about being in someone's bedroom. I feel like I shouldn't be in here, but I cross the room anyways and crawl into his bed.

And that's when I notice the mug on the nightstand, filled with steaming hot water, a tea bag still steeping— peppermint tea.

I take the mug from the table and raise it to my lips, settling back into the plush pillows behind me.

Maybe Holden doesn't completely hate having me here.

THREE

YOU GOOGLED ME, DIDN'T YOU?

Holden

I wake up and reach for my phone on the coffee table, groaning when I see the time. I'm up an hour before my alarm, with a sore shoulder and a kink in my neck from what I'm pretty sure was one of the worst sleeps of my life, on a couch that I'm too tall for in a room without blackout blinds. I unfold myself from the couch, shading my eyes against the sunlight that's already pouring into the room, then fold the blanket and set it on top of my pillow. Walking quietly up the stairs, I pause outside of my closed bedroom door. Briar must still be sleeping.

I go to the guest bathroom for a shower, immediately noticing her things cluttering the countertop. This girl is messy. *Very* messy. A hairbrush, her toothpaste, makeup, a curling iron, plus a collection of bottles and cannisters of all different sizes. What the hell does she even use all this stuff for? How many beauty products does one person need?

Shaking my head, I take off my clothes and then step under the scalding spray of water, hoping it will help wake me up. I'm usually a morning person, but today my mood is as bad as the disaster all over my bathroom. I can't stand clutter. My head hurts. Daisy is going to owe me big time for this.

I'm brushing my teeth when the smell of coffee wafts through the air. Briar? She must be up. I throw on my clothes and head downstairs, ready to tell her to clean up her crap.

I enter the kitchen, immediately regretting it.

My once-pristine countertops are buried under a chaotic spread of ingredients—flour dusted across the granite, a sticky puddle of batter near the stove, and an upturned carton of eggs teetering dangerously close to the edge of the counter. The smell of something sweet fills the air.

And there's Briar, standing at the stove in one of my old T-shirts—because apparently, she has already decided my wardrobe is fair game— humming to herself as she flips pancakes.

I stand in the entryway and stare, my pulse racing so fast I wonder if it could cause a heart attack. Briar looks gorgeous. She isn't wearing a stitch of makeup, and her hair is piled on top of her head in a knot, showcasing the slope of her neck. She's wearing a pair of shorts that leave little to the imagination. Probably dangerous if I stare much longer. She's hot as fuck, the perfect example of the girl next door.

Too bad I've sworn off women.

Too bad I'm annoyed with her.

I tear my gaze away from her legs and instead look around my kitchen. It looks like a bomb went off. The mess in the bathroom is nothing compared to this. I chew on my lip to stop myself from snapping, feeling my lack of sleep and aching back. I should be grateful. Really, I should. She's only my temporary roommate, a favor to friends, and yet here she is, making me breakfast like she'd done it a hundred times before.

"Morning," I manage to say, fighting my instinct to grab a cloth and start cleaning.

Briar turns, jumping like I startled her. Her green eyes are brighter than emeralds. She's so pretty, I almost forget about the destruction she unleashed on my kitchen.

"Oh my gosh, you scared me," she says, a pair of tongs in her hand. She smiles at me in a way that can only be described as magnetic. I can't tear my eyes off her. "I hope I didn't wake you."

"I woke up early. I couldn't sleep," I say, then immediately feel bad when the happiness on her face fades. "Just a lot going on at the office this week. It's not because of the couch," I add quickly, not wanting her to feel guilty about taking my bed.

"Oh." Briar turns her attention back to the stove. "Web design, right?"

I raise a brow. "You googled me, didn't you?"

"I did not, you big goof. I remembered. Did you forget we used to hang out last year?"

"We've met before?" I tease, walking past her to the sink to pour myself a glass of water.

She laughs. "Don't pretend like you haven't missed me while I was gone."

After downing the water, I start to fill the sink with hot water so I can tackle this mess.

"What are you doing?" I feel her small hands on my shoulders, gently pushing me away from the sink. "I've got it. This will take me five minutes to clean later. Go sit down."

Five minutes? I look around the disaster zone. Is she kidding? With the state that my kitchen is in, this will take her five hours. I must side-eye her without realizing it, because she crosses her arms over her chest and shoots me a look. "The breakfast will be worth it. Now, can I pour you a cup of coffee?"

"I can get it myself, Busy Bee."

Her head tilts to the side. "Holden, would you just sit down and let me handle this? Or is that difficult for you? You know, when other people want to do things for you? It kills you to give up control, doesn't it?"

"No."

"Yes, it does."

"No, it doesn't. And why are we arguing over this?"

"Don't worry, I'm just giving you a hard time." She hands me a cup of coffee and points me in the direction of my table. I sit reluctantly and take a sip of the brew, watching as she moves around the kitchen with ease. It's as if she's lived here all her life. I would have thought she'd feel out of place, uncomfortable even, given the fact that she's been here for less than 24 hours. But she's just... graceful. I should probably hate that she's here, in my space, making a mess of things. Don't get me wrong, I don't love seeing my house in this state—I swear I can feel my right eye twitching—but I'm not angry.

But it *is* going to take some getting used to, living with someone again. Especially someone like Briar. I like my privacy. And fuck, I need to figure out how I'm going to live with her when she's dressed like that. Maybe I should ask her to wear a sweater and sweatpants—extra baggy ones—when she's lounging around the house.

"I took a chance that maybe you'd eat breakfast," she says as I watch her slide the bacon from the pan onto a plate lined with paper towel. "Do you always go into the office this early?" she asks over her shoulder. She pours pancake batter into yet another pan on the stove then sets the bowl on the counter. A trickle of the pale-yellow batter drips over the edge, pooling on the counter.

"No, it's a busy week at work. I have a presentation tomorrow with a new client we've been trying to land."

"Ah, you need to be on your game. I'm sure you will be if you're as thorough at your job as you are at keeping your house tidy."

When I don't respond, Briar turns to face me, and I'm sure she catches the look of annoyance on my face.

"I'm not judging you, Holden. Just stating the facts. You're a neat freak."

"And *you* are not."

Briar slides a heaping plate of pancakes, bacon and strawberries across the table to me and smiles.

"Wow, thanks," I tell her, looking down at my plate. The pancakes look perfect—shockingly so, considering the state of everything else. I'm being a dick. Sure, the place is a mess, but she got up early and cooked me breakfast. A delicious-looking breakfast.

"Where did you find strawberries?" I know she didn't find them in my fridge.

"I ordered a few things last night and had them delivered." She brings her plate to the table and sits down next to me. I watch her dip a strawberry into the whip cream on her plate then slide the berry between her lips. She really has the most perfect mouth.

"Yeah, I was going to go grocery shopping tonight. My fridge is pretty dismal," I admit, picking up my fork. "I'll pay you for whatever you bought today. Just let me know how much it is."

She nods, but the expression on her face tells me she isn't taking me seriously. Does this woman take anything seriously? She always seems so easygoing. Calm. Laid back. And so incredibly beautiful, it's making me oddly annoyed.

How is this ever going to work? How am I going to live with Briar for the next 60 or so days when she looks like that? Legs that rival any runway model's, soft curves and a mouth I'm already dying to kiss. That definitely won't be happening. Briar is Daisy's best friend, and I would never risk my friendship with Daisy. We've become close, bonding over *Gilmore Girls* marathons and giving Tucker the gears. Besides, a relationship and everything that goes along with it is not in the cards for me right now.

"Thank you for the tea last night." Briar looks at me over the rim of her mug, the tea bag still steeping in it. "I thought you said you didn't have any. Water-flavored nothing, right?"

I laugh. "I stand by that. I didn't have any."

"Then —"

"I went next door. I was pretty sure Everly would have some, and she did. It isn't a big deal so don't go making one out of it."

Briar smirks. "So how hard was it for you to make me that cup of tea?"

"I almost vomited."

She rolls her eyes, stabbing at another strawberry with her fork. "Next thing you know, you'll be running me a bath and massaging my feet."

"That would be a first."

Her brow lifts curiously. "A foot massage or taking a bath?"

"Both. Feet are gross and baths are a waste of time."

"You really need to learn how to relax, Holden. Live a little. You can be a little uptight, has anyone ever told you that?"

"No. I've been told I'm hard to resist. But never uptight."

Briar's lips slightly rise at the corners, and I wait for her mouth to turn into a full-blown smile. It's quickly become one of my favorite things about her.

"So I've heard," she continues. "You have quite the rep in Reed Point."

"Don't believe everything you hear," I say, brushing off the comment. I know the rumors she's talking about. I've heard them for years. But it doesn't make them true. "There are three sides to every story."

Briar looks like she's about to say something but seems to change her mind, instead lifting a forkful of whip cream and strawberries to her mouth. Sitting here at the kitchen table with her makes me realize that it's been a long time since I've shared a space with another person. Tucker moved out a year ago, and I broke up with my ex, Aubrey around the same time.

Aubrey was the first girl I had seriously dated in a long time, and I cared a lot about her. I always got the feeling that Tucker and the guys didn't really get our connection, but when it was just the two of us, we had a lot of fun. But after 18 months or so, we started having problems. She wanted to talk about our future, about marriage and kids, and I didn't feel ready for that. I'm not even sure if I want to be a father. The tension between us grew and we were arguing over things that didn't matter, nit-picking each other constantly. Over time, I could feel her pulling away from me, and in response to that I started pushing her away.

For a while, I wondered if I should have fought harder to save the relationship, but when things between us got diffi-cult I took that as a sign it wasn't meant to be. The writing was on the wall, and I didn't want to drag it out any longer and make it harder for both of us.

Looking back, I believe it was the right decision, but ending things with Aubrey still messed me up. She took it pretty hard, and it broke my heart to hurt her like that. It felt like yet another relationship that I couldn't make work. So, for the last year, I've sworn off relationships. I've sworn off hookups. I've starved myself of intimacy over the last 12 months. And I'm not ready to open myself back up.

Silence stretches between us for a minute as we both continue to eat our breakfast, until I motion to her plate with my fork. "You're not hungry?"

"I'm not much of a breakfast person."

"Not even bacon? No one can hate bacon."

"Relax, Mr. Clean. Just eat. And no, not even bacon. I hate all pork."

"Then what do you eat in the morning?"

"I don't. Why is that so hard to believe?"

"It just is." I shrug, taking a bite, and dammit, it is good. Annoyingly good. "What about eggs?"

"Gross."

"Sausage?"

"Nope."

"A breakfast burrito?"

"Dis-gust-ing," she says, drawing the word out. "Are you done now?"

"Nope." I pop the *p*. "Breakfast is an important meal. You should eat something."

"I like fruit," she says, sucking whip cream off her finger. Jesus, she needs to stop doing that. "I'll eat the rest of my strawberries to make you happy."

Is she not starving by lunch? I want to ask her more questions, but we've shared enough over the last 24 hours. I'm also in a rush to get to work.

"Okay, got it, no breakfast." I smile, and it occurs to me that I've done that a lot more than usual since Briar showed up. Maybe it's the food or the way she looks in my kitchen—barefoot and comfortable, like she belongs here. I stand up and start to clear the dishes from the table, reminding myself that this is only temporary.

"I've got it, Holden." Briar snatches my empty plate from my hand and my skin heats from the brief contact. Why the fuck am I having this reaction to her? I have to get this under control if I'm going to survive this roommate arrangement.

"How about I clean up the kitchen, and you stop bugging me about my eating habits?"

"You mean your disdain for breakfast."

"Forget it," she groans at me as she stacks our plates in the dishwasher. Those damn shorts. They rise up a little when she bends over.

"Fine, I won't bug you, Bee."

"But you're calling me Bee. I think that could be considered bugging me."

"You never stop. You earned the nickname. You've looked like a busy bee all morning buzzing around my kitchen." I shrug. "But no more breakfast jokes, and I won't fight you on the clean-up this time. Deal?"

She nods, then holds out her hand, intending for me to shake it. When my hand wraps around hers, the heat I felt earlier returns, skating up my spine. Briar's eyes move to my mouth. Her gaze stays there, just for a second, but it's long enough for me to notice.

Our hands stay joined in the space between us for a long moment before I finally drop her hand and take a step back. Does she feel the attraction too? If I was a betting man, I'd say yes.

Not that long ago, I would have given into the temptation to kiss her, but I made a promise to myself, and I intend on keeping it. I will take care of the sexual frustration myself, like I've been doing for months. Since Aubrey.

So, I clear my throat, reluctantly taking another step back until there's enough distance between us that I can't smell her body wash. A scent that I want on my clothes, all over my sheets.

Fuck. More distance. Go to work. Now.

"I need to get going," I say, grabbing my keys from the counter. "There's a spare house key for you by the door."

Briar blinks, drops her gaze to the floor before recovering. "Thank you."

"I'll see you when I get home from work. I'll order dinner tonight. Nothing with eggs."

Briar's face lights up in amusement. "Sounds like a date."

My heart stops. "It's not a date, Briar. It's we-both-have-to-eat-dinner-so-we-might-as-well-eat-together."

She grins. "It's a date."

Fuck me. It's hard to tell whether she's being serious or not. She never seems to be serious about anything. So then why is Briar looking at me like that? Like she's excited for our *date*. That is not happening.

Having breakfast with her was a mistake. No more meals with Briar Moore. I am not looking for a relationship and I can't run the risk of leading her on. The only reason she's even here is because I agreed to do Daisy and her a favor. End of story.

Ignoring the grin that is still plastered on her face, I turn and walk toward the front door as fast as I can. "Thanks again for the breakfast," I call as I slip into my shoes, which are placed neatly in the entryway.

"You're welcome!" She stands in the center of my

kitchen, right where I left her. And as fucked up as I feel about my morning with her, I can't help but think that I really like the way she looks in my home.

FOUR

I'M PRETTY SURE HE HATES ME.

Briar

"So?"

"Soooo, what?"

"How has it been living with Holden?"

"Well, I'm pretty sure he hates me. So, not so great."

Honestly, the man can be so hot and cold. One minute, he's making me tea before bed and the next, he's growling at me for being too messy.

Daisy stops searching through the rack of vintage coats and looks at me with a shocked expression on her face. "What? That can't be true. Holden doesn't hate anyone. He's the nicest guy on the planet."

"Daisy," I sigh. "Believe it. It's true. Don't get me wrong, I'm grateful he's letting me stay with him, but to be honest he's a bit of a pill."

Daisy cocks her head at me. "What did you do to him?"

"Excuse me, *what*? I didn't do anything. I've been there for *one* day. How bad could I be?"

We're thrifting at one of our favorite little local stores, something Daisy and I have been doing together for years.

The thrill of the thrift is a very real thing. It's that exhilarating feeling when you find that perfect pair of vintage Levi's, a slip dress from the 40s or that handmade one-of-a-kind piece.

"I've lived with Holden," Daisy reminds me. She spent most nights at Tucker's place before moving into the house they're in now, so she knows Holden pretty well. "I consider myself an expert on the man. Sure, he can be a little anal, but he's a really good guy. He probably just needs some time to get used to having a roommate again. I know after he broke up with Aubrey, he seemed a little... lost."

"Lost?" I look through the racks, trying to keep my tone uninterested.

"I don't know. It's his story to tell, but Tucker said he's on a self-imposed detox. No women. No hooking up."

I feel my brow shoot up. "Okay, maybe he isn't looking for another relationship, but I'm *sure* he must be getting action."

Daisy shrugs her shoulders. "It's just what I've been told. But I haven't seen him with a girl in a very long time. It's such a shame. A guy like Holden is a catch. I'm still curious what went down between him and Aubrey. Something had to have happened for Holden to swear off women, but he's never said."

"Hmm," I murmur, breathing in deeply, taking in the earthy scent of vintage coats I'm searching through. I seriously love thrifting.

"Briar, just get to know him. Talk to him. He has an interesting family. Wait until he tells you about his mom." Daisy's eyes go wide. "Speaking of... how's *your* mom? Have you talked to her since you've been back?'

I smile. "Yeah, she's good. So much better than two years ago. Other than missing me, she's acting like herself again."

"I love that for her. I can't imagine what it feels like to lose the love of your life, and so unexpectedly like that."

Sighing, I stop my search for a moment. "My stepdad was a great guy. It isn't fair."

"Briar, for what it's worth, I think it was good for all of you that you moved back home. But I'm also happy that you're back."

I smile at her but feel my mood sober. My family is small, and they all live in Vancouver, B.C., where I was born and raised. My older brother, Lucas, lives a few blocks from my mom, and my grandma and grandpa and my mom's twin sister all live about a 10-minute drive away. I've always been close to them. Growing up, that little extended family made up for the fact that my dad abandoned us when my brother and I were just toddlers. That was 21 years ago. I haven't seen him since.

My mom says I'm better for it.

Four years after my dad walked out, my mother married my stepdad, Jeff. He treated her so well, and he really put the work in and made my brother and I feel like we were his. We were all heartbroken when he died suddenly of a heart attack a couple of years ago, but it was hardest on my mom. It was clear that she was really struggling, so I decided to move back home to Vancouver.

It wasn't an easy decision to make. I had a great life in Reed Point. My friends were here, and I had a dream job as the director of sales and marketing for a big cheese company headquartered on the east coast. And the truth is, I left Vancouver in the first place for a reason.

Justin.

I had known that I needed to put some distance between us. Our relationship had become horribly toxic. I chose Reed Point because my mom and stepdad had brought us here on a vacation when we were teenagers, and I fell in love with the place. The people, the small-town feel, the beautiful beaches. So, I packed what I could fit into one suitcase and moved to Reed Point with no real plan. I ended up building a life here. I got a student visa, enrolled at Reed Point University, where I met Daisy, and earned my marketing degree.

Moving away from my family had come with a cost—missing them. But I didn't have to deal with Justin, and over time I found real happiness in Reed Point. Looking back, it was the best choice I've ever made.

So, the decision to return to Vancouver, to my old life and to the same area code as Justin, wasn't easy. But my family needed me.

Thankfully, with time, my mom started to heal. When she was ready, I encouraged her to reconnect with friends she'd pulled away from in the year after my stepdad's death and to get back to doing the things that used to make her happy. She still lives with the heartache of losing the man she loved, but eventually she started to seem like herself again.

Unfortunately, while I was back in Vancouver I had a setback and found myself back with Justin. He promised me he had changed, that he'd spent time working on himself while I was living in Reed Point. I believed him. I moved in with him, happy to be out of my mom's house but not too far away from her. The idea of having my old life back, our old group of friends, was exciting. It all blew up in my face a few months later when I found him on my couch, naked, with another woman. And that was just the tip of the iceberg. I lost it. It was my mom who insisted I return to Reed Point. She could tell I was struggling being in the same city as my ex, and she told me it was time to get back to living.

So here I am, back in the place I've learned to call home. When I contacted my former boss, he offered me my old position back. I found a great apartment—at least, I thought I did, until the landlord pulled the rug out from under me. Holden really came to the rescue on that one. I don't know what I would have done if he hadn't stepped up and offered me a place to stay.

"I'm happy to be back too, Dais. I missed you," I tell her before yanking a hanger off the rack in front of me. On it is a jet-black fur coat, the color of ink. "Not trying to change the subject, but you *have* to see this jacket."

I take the coat off the rack and quickly throw it over my shoulders. It's hip-length, soft with short, flat fur. It screams Hollywood glam. I pose in front of the large mirror on the shop's wall.

"Someone is going to throw paint on you," Daisy laughs, moving to stand behind me so she can see my reflection. "That's hardcore. Even for you."

"You can relax, it's fake."

"Thank god. I didn't want to have to call PETA on you."

I ignore her, turning from side-to-side as I admire the coat. I'm imagining it with a short black dress, heels, my hair pulled back into a slick bun.

"If only you had a man who you could wear it for," Daisy teases. "Nothing on underneath." She smirks mischievously. "It would be so hot. Okay, I changed my mind. You need the jacket."

"The whole store can hear you, Dais," I laugh, slipping off the jacket and sliding it back onto the hanger. I reluctantly return it to the rack, then wander over to the home goods section, where I spot some frames and a pair of throw pillows that would look perfect on Holden's couch. I pick up a pillow to check the price.

"Those are pretty," Daisy says with an approving nod. "For your new place?"

"I was thinking for Holden's. The place feels like a prison. I've never seen such an empty space in my life."

Daisy's eyebrows pinch together. "I get that you want to make Holden's house feel homier, but something tells me florals and pastels aren't his style."

I shrug. "He'll get used to it."

From the corner of my eye, I can see Daisy's shoulders shake with silent laughter. She's right, of course. Holden will probably faint when he sees these pillows propped against his dull, black couch. But they'll liven up the place, make his house feel more like a home. Besides, maybe he'll appreciate the effort. It bothers me when someone doesn't like me, and I can't quite shake the feeling that Holden falls into that category. Maybe this will help me win him over. I grab a blanket, a table lamp, and a candle for his empty coffee table and bring it all to the checkout. On my way home I'll pick up some flowers.

"I wish I was a fly on the wall when he sees all this stuff tonight," Daisy says, shaking her head as I tap my debit card against the machine. "I'm sure Holden is going to *love* what you do with his place."

"Are you gaslighting me right now?" I tilt my head to one side, eyeing Daisy.

"Never." She smirks at me, her eyes sparkling.

"Daisy, I changed my mind," I say suddenly, dropping my shopping bag to the floor at her feet. "I'm getting the fur."

"I knew you would," she calls after me as I head back to the racks to grab it. "You should try it out on Holden."

That might be the best idea my girl Daisy has ever had.

I'M A BALL OF NERVES WHEN I HEAR HOLDEN WALK THROUGH the door after work. I'm sitting on the couch reading a romance book, wearing a pair of shorts and a thrifted T-shirt I've cut to fall off one shoulder when he steps into the living room, a takeout bag in his hand.

I dog-ear my page and put the book down on the coffee table, taking in Holden. God, he's beautiful. And so effortlessly sexy. He does look a little tired, probably from sleeping on a couch that is way too small for a guy his size, but that doesn't stop my heart from thundering in my chest.

"Hi." His green eyes find mine as the corner of his mouth tips up in a small smile.

My pulse rate skips.

But his smile is quickly replaced by a frown as his eyes move around the living room, taking in the décor changes—*improvements*—that I made this afternoon. That frown. It shouldn't be so sexy.

I keep my eyes on him, waiting for his reaction. He's wearing the same crisp white button-down and gray dress pants he had on when he left this morning, the cuffs of his sleeves rolled up his forearms.

Never in my life have I noticed a man's forearms. Until now. Smooth bronze skin with a light dusting of arm hair, his muscles tight and sinewy.

"What happened to my house?" His voice is gravelly, with an edge to it.

"Do you like it? I went shopping with Daisy."

I watch his eyes track the room again. The throw pillows on the couch. The picture frames on his bookshelf—still empty, I figured I'd let him pick the photos—next to the cactus and the fern, the humungous three-wick candle on the center of the coffee table. My personal favorite is the chunky, knit yellow blanket draped over the arm of his couch.

"You'd better be able to return this stuff. I hope you didn't take the tags off."

He puts the bag of takeout on the coffee table, then turns to me, looking annoyed. His eyes track down the length of me before jerking away to the living room again.

A flash of heat covers my skin. I like his eyes on me. Something about the way he looks at me makes me feel appreciated. Admired. It's been a long time since I've been looked at that way.

Trying to ignore the fact that I'm turned on, I get up and walk past him to the kitchen.

"Where are you going?" he asks me with tension in his voice.

"I'm getting us plates and cutlery. Do you want to eat in the living room?"

"I want to finish our conversation. Briar... this stuff needs to go."

"Give it a few days. It will grow on you," I holler from the kitchen. "Did you see the blanket? It's Merino wool. It's so soft and cozy."

"It's 90 degrees outside, Briar. Why the hell do I need a blanket?" he asks before sneezing.

I roll my eyes. Would it kill the guy to say thank you? Geesh.

"Are you really upset over this?" I ask, returning to the living room with the plates and cutlery. I can feel his eyes on me as I set everything down on the coffee table. I turn to meet his gaze, and notice how his chestnut hair, which was perfectly styled a minute ago, is now tousled and messy from running his hands through it. His brows are furrowed, his eyes are red.

"I'm not upset, Briar. Do I look upset?"

"Holden, there's a vein in your neck that looks like it's ready to explode and your eyes are bloodshot, so yes, you look upset."

"Did you have Bear out here?"

"Just for a second, but I kept her in my arms. I swear. Why?"

His expression softens. "Look, let's just eat before it gets cold. I grabbed dinner from my favorite Greek place. Chicken souvlaki, salad, tzatziki and rice."

"Sounds amazing. I love Greek. Thank you!" I say, happy that he appears to be willing to let the argument go.

I settle into the couch while he opts for the floor, stretching out one long leg. My gaze traces his movements as he opens the takeout containers. He's still frowning, and my heart does this weird fluttery thing at the sight of it.

"I can take everything back tomorrow," I tell him, softly. "I'm sorry that you hate it."

Holden grumbles from across the table. "I don't hate it. It was just... a lot to come home to. It's fine. I'll get used to it. Here. Eat while it's hot."

He hands me a plate full of food then makes one for himself.

"Thanks."

He pops the lid back on the container and takes a bite of chicken before he gestures to my book where I left it on the coffee table. "You're reading a book with a naked dude on the cover. Is this one of your smut books Daisy was talking about?"

I snatch the book from the table, hiding it on the couch

next to me. "It's not smut. It's *romance*. And every man should read it. You could learn a thing or two."

Holden laughs, his eyebrows wing. "There is nothing I need to learn. I could probably write the sex scenes myself."

Heat rushes to my cheeks. Just like that, I'm imaging Holden naked in bed with one of his groupies. I bet he knows how to make a woman scream with just his big hands. I bet sex with Holden is beyond incredible. *Stop it, Briar.* Stop thinking about having sex with your new roommate.

But then another thought pops into my head. Daisy said that Holden wasn't hooking up with anyone, but I'm not sure I believe that. What if he were to bring some girl home one night? It *is* his house, he can do what he wants. Jealousy claws at my belly, so I push that thought out of my brain and change the subject.

"Tell me something about yourself."

He looks up from his plate. "What?"

"Tell me something about yourself," I repeat. "If we're going to do this roommate thing, we're going to need to be friends."

He gives me a once-over as I take a bite of my chicken.

"Just humor me, Holden." I poke him in the arm.

He stays quiet for a moment. "Okay," he says finally. "I hate New Year's. You?"

"Wait a second." I put my fork down on my plate. "Why do you hate New Year's?"

He shrugs his broad shoulders. "Because I love Christmas, and New Year's Eve is like the nail in the coffin to the holiday season. It's so depressing."

I try and fail to hide the smile on my face. I'm not sure what answer I was expecting, but it wasn't this. Doesn't everyone love New Year's Eve? It was always a big deal in my house growing up.

I think about the parties my mom and stepdad used to throw for us. My mom would buy decorations, party hats and those annoying horns that we would blow all at once when the clock turned to midnight. We also had an extra reason to celebrate December 31st in our house: it was the day my stepdad legally adopted my brother and me.

I wonder if Holden doesn't celebrate New Year's Eve at all. Does he stay home by himself while his friends are all out celebrating?

Why does that thought make me so sad?

I want to ask him, but I swallow down the question, deciding to keep the conversation light. After being so on and off with me over the last 24 hours, he's finally relaxing a little. I want to keep it that way.

"I bet you like Thanksgiving then."

"My second favorite holiday." He shoots me a glance. He does a frowny sort of thing as I chuckle. "It's the lead-up to Christmas. Plus, there's the dinner: turkey, stuffing, potatoes. What's not to love?"

"I can't argue there."

Holden studies me for a moment, then tips his chin up. "Your turn, Bee," he says, and my stomach plunges. Hearing him use the nickname makes me feel giddy.

"Unpopular opinion, but I hate ice cream."

He looks appalled. "How can you hate ice cream?"

"I just do. It's cold and messy and makes my teeth hurt."

"If I had to bet, I'd say you're among one percent of people on the planet who hate ice cream."

"It's overrated."

He raises a brow in curiosity. "Then what do Canadians eat for dessert?"

"I'm from Vancouver, not Mars," I laugh. "We like what all North Americans like."

"Just not the number one rated dessert in North America."

"Are you always this annoying?" My mouth curves into a smirk.

"Only with you."

"Tell me another," I say.

He pokes at his chicken. "I'm scared of spiders."

"I'm scared of clowns."

"Yeah, I get that," he nods. "Why are they so creepy?"

A small smile tugs at the corners of his mouth and my skin pebbles with goosebumps. I'm still trying to figure out why my body reacts to him the way it does.

I continue to ask Holden questions, wanting to know as much as I can about him, hanging on his every word even though, so far, our questions have been mostly surface-level. But with every passing second, I fight the urge to go deeper.

As we finish picking at our dinners, I learn that Holden's favorite movie is *Shawshank Redemption*, he prefers mustard over ketchup, and he has one brother who is four years younger than him.

When we're both done eating, he reaches across the table and picks up my empty plate, stacking it on top of his. "It's your turn," he reminds me, eyebrows raised.

I drop my chin in my hand, thinking. "I don't believe in fate," I tell him.

He wipes his face with a napkin and nods. "You're a determinist."

"It's hot, right?" I say, stretching to nudge him with my foot.

He's still not smiling—not fully anyways—as he leans back on his palms, his long legs stretched underneath the coffee table. He is devastating. Cocky and beautiful and absolutely killing me with his green eyes.

"How 'bout soulmates?" he asks.

"Nope. I don't believe in them either."

"Why not?"

"I think the idea of a soulmate sounds really romantic, but I find it hard to believe that there is only one person on this planet for me in a population of 8 billion. What if my 'soulmate' lives in Antarctica or Zanzibar?"

He cocks his head as he studies me. "What about Tucker and Daisy? They're the perfect example. Or Jake and Everly. She got it wrong the first time when she married her dickhead ex-husband, but she found her soulmate when she met Jake by chance at Catch 21. Hell, Grayson found his soulmate in Sierra when she moved in next door to him."

I shrug my shoulders.

"What's that shrug for?"

"Sorry to break it to you, but your soulmate doesn't exist."

He seems to think on that for a moment. I'm surprised at this. Holden believes in soulmates. That's unexpected... and hot. "You think I'm being harsh, don't you?"

"You can say anything you want."

"I sorta have a bad habit of doing that. My mom always taught my brother and I to speak our minds."

His expression softens. "You seem like you're close to your mom."

"I am. She's been through a lot. My dad walked out on us when I was four and never came back."

"Jesus, what an asshole. I'm sorry, Briar."

"Oh, don't be." I wave it off. "I never really knew him, and I've never had the desire to. I got lucky when my mom married my stepdad. He adopted my brother and me."

"I didn't know you were adopted. Well, by your stepdad, I mean."

"I guess I never talk about it. As far as I'm concerned, Jeff is my dad. I don't remember anything about my bio-dad, and that's just fine with me."

Holden leans back, his gaze drifting to where my T-shirt has slipped down my arm, exposing my shoulder. He lingers there for a brief moment, an appreciative look in his eyes. Another burst of warmth spreads up my spine. I like the way Holden looks at me.

"You feel like someone whose parents are still together," I tell him.

He tilts his head to the ceiling. "I would need a drink or 10 to talk about my parents."

"Beer or wine?" I ask, taking the cue and standing up from the couch.

"Briar, I need to work tomorrow. And you are sitting on my bed. Shouldn't you go check on Bear or something?"

"One drink. Don't worry, we won't make it a late night."

I catch him glance at my shorts, then his gaze travels down my legs. He blinks then slides a hand through the short strands of his hair.

He sighs. "Fine. But only one."

Trying to ignore his appreciative stare, I walk into the kitchen and grab two beers from the fridge. He's sprawled across the couch now, and I settle back into my spot at one end.

"The pillows are so you're more comfortable," I note, motioning to the pile of throw pillows he's moved to the floor.

"They take up too much space."

I roll my eyes as I drape the thrift store blanket over my legs. Holden is a lot. My body tingles just from being this close to him, and don't get me started on how it feels to have his eyes on my body. But we're both emotionally unavailable. After everything that happened with Justin, the last thing I need is to get myself entangled with a guy I barely know—a guy I need to live with for the foreseeable future. That would be a *very* bad idea. Right now, I just need to take some time to work on myself.

"So, why does talking about your parents make you want to drink?"

Holden groans softly, and I can't help but smile. He takes a long pull of his beer.

"My mother was married to my father, but now my mother is married to a woman." He clears his throat. "Try to follow along."

He settles further into the couch and looks up at the ceiling for several seconds. "My mother and my father are still best friends. The three of them are just... weird."

That's not what I expected. "Wow, sounds like a very modern family."

Holden nods. "I'm fairly certain that my mom is in love with them both. She invites my dad to every holiday and family party. Her wife goes along with it. Sometimes it feels like they're a throuple."

"And how are you with it all?"

He takes a sip of his beer, his eyes softening. "My brother and I could care less that my mom's with a woman, but it can get a little weird when she acts like she's married to them both."

Okay, I'm kind of liking that his mom and dad are so progressive. And Holden's easy acceptance of his mom's marriage to a woman makes him that much hotter.

I take a long sip of my beer, grimacing as it goes down.

"What's that face for?" he asks.

"I hate beer."

"Then what's your poison?"

"Tequila."

"Trouble. Isn't that what makes people's clothes come off?"

"Feed me tequila and find out."

Heart racing, my eyes stay glued to his. I didn't mean for that to come out so flirty, but I don't regret it. I'm not taking it back.

"I'm tipsy," I declare.

"Noted... it doesn't take much," Holden deadpans.

"So... we should probably get some sleep."

"Yeah, umm... we should," he says, nodding. He stretches his neck, tilting his head down toward one shoulder and then to the other.

"Does your neck hurt? I feel bad. That's all my fault."

"Don't worry about it. It's just a stiff neck. I'll live."

I must be tipsier than I realized, because what I say next surprises even me: "You can sleep with me. Your bed is huge, I'll never even know you're there."

He looks at me like I'm crazy. "Pretty sure you ripped my head off last night when you thought I was trying to sleep with you."

"I didn't rip your head off. Look, sleep on the couch if you want. It's your neck. But I'm offering to share the bed with you."

Hesitating, I can see him thinking it over. "You won't try anything with me if I do?"

"Holden!" I pick up one of the thrifted cushions from the floor and toss it at him.

He half-smiles. "Are you sure?"

"I offered, didn't I?" I hug my knees to my chest.

"You're drunk, Bee."

I like it when he calls me Bee.

"So are you."

"I am definitely not drunk." He scrubs his fingers through the stubble of his jaw. "You promise to stay on your side of the bed?"

"It's not me we're going to have to worry about."

Holden looks at me for a moment longer, then seems to make up his mind. He stands, takes our empty bottles to the kitchen and then returns, pausing at the bottom of the stairs.

"Ready?" he asks.

"As I'll ever be," I tell him, smiling. I follow him up the stairs to his bedroom. He flicks on the light, stands at the foot of his bed and turns to face me.

"Which side of the bed do you want, Bee?"

I must be out of my mind because the way he's looking at me with that little smile on his lips, his deep green eyes crinkling with mischief, it's going to take everything in me to stay on my side of the bed.

FIVE

THE POOR GUY THINKS HE'S GETTING LUCKY.

H olden

Goddamn this woman.

I shouldn't be sharing a bed with her.

Briar's hair is down and she's wearing those goddamn tiny shorts again, the ones she likes to kill me with, and a shirt that falls off one shoulder.

No makeup and she's still more beautiful than any woman I've ever seen. Did I also mention she isn't wearing a fucking bra? Fuck my life.

What am I doing? What are *we* doing? I am so turned on right now, I can barely draw a breath. This is a very bad idea.

Briar and I spent the last four hours sitting in my living room eating takeout and talking, and I swear it was the best night I've had in as long as I can remember. And she looked good too, curled up on my couch, her toned legs tucked underneath her.

Conversations were never like that with Aubrey. She liked to talk about the shows she was watching or her latest purchase. They were more surface-level, which is fine, I guess. But Briar really let me in, and I allowed her to see a little of me too. We have chemistry. My heart pounds in my chest when our eyes lock, and when she smiles, I'm fucking gone. I spent half of the night imagining Briar naked. I bet she has the most perfect body under her T-shirt and short shorts. I bet she'd fit perfectly in my arms. When I'm around Briar, it takes a conscious effort not to touch her. I feel this pull to her. Maybe, instead of ignoring the spark I feel between us, I should make a move. Show her my cards. But it's hard to know if Briar feels the same way. She's always so calm, so cool; it's difficult to read her.

No. I swore off women for a reason. Yet another failed relationship is the last thing I need right now. But I can't deny that I like having her here, in my bed, next to me.

"Your bed is like heaven," she murmurs, snuggling into the mattress. I admire the curve of her shoulder, her blonde hair fanned out over my bed sheets as she lets out a sigh that goes straight to my cock.

I bite the inside of my cheek, willing my dick to behave. I can't blame it. The most beautiful girl I have ever seen is in my bed wearing next to nothing. The poor guy thinks he's getting lucky.

I stare at the ceiling and inhale deeply, noticing the way the sugary scent of Briar already fills my bedroom. Bergamot and citrus. Turning my head to her side of the bed, my heart races when I see the way the shape of her body is illuminated by the dull glow of a streetlamp outside. Her back is to me, one shoulder fully exposed. It takes every ounce of my willpower not to touch her. I always want to touch her.

She turns suddenly so that she's facing me, her eyes finding mine. It's dark, but I've already memorized the shade. My new favorite color.

"What's your biggest fear, Holden?" she asks quietly. "No wrong answers."

"Anyone ever accuse you of being nosy?" I answer, trying to skirt the question.

"Maybe once or twice. I prefer *curious,* though. You should see my Google history."

"I'm not sure I'm ready for that. I'm sure it's wildly entertaining."

She giggles. "I try whenever I can to exceed expectations."

I laugh too. There's a beat of silence between us before Briar speaks again. "I'm scared of people not liking me. Is that the dumbest thing you've ever heard? I'm impulsive, and emotional. I think it can be a lot for some people."

I look back at the ceiling because looking at Briar right now feels like too much and too little all at the same time. "No, it's not the dumbest thing. Not even close."

God, the urge to wrap her up in my arms and pull her into my chest is almost more than I can handle. To show her that *I* like her. To make her understand that anyone lucky enough to spend five minutes with her would like her.

"Briar?"

"Yeah?"

"You're also funny. And smart. And beautiful." I can feel her smiling next to me, but I force myself to keep my eyes on the ceiling.

"According to Justin, I'm hard to handle," she says. "He always said I was too much."

"Fuck him, Briar. The guy is an insecure asshole. I want you to forget everything he ever said to you. You're perfect the way you are."

I feel the weight of the bed shift when she rolls to her back, her position mirroring mine. "What's yours, Holden? Do you have a greatest fear?"

I stare at a shaft of light that stretches across the ceiling, a thunderbolt against the shadowed stucco.

"I'm afraid of flying," I tell her. "I don't admit that to too many people. A 28-year-old man who's afraid to get into an airplane? It's embarrassing as hell."

I hold my breath in anticipation of her reaction. But instead of laughing or cracking a joke, she reaches her hand over the space between us, then gives my forearm a gentle squeeze. "That's a legitimate fear. I know there are plenty of people who feel the same way. Can I ask you if it's because something happened?"

I should have known she would ask questions. I'm already learning that Briar is one of the most inquisitive people I've ever met. I honestly can't remember the last time I told the story. Even in my family we never talked about it much, but I can still remember the way my mom bawled for weeks. I've sometimes wondered—if we *did* talk about it, would I still struggle so much with this fear?

Briar has left her hand on my arm, and she gives it another soft squeeze encouraging me on.

"My grandparents died in a plane crash when I was in grade 6. They were on vacation, visiting the Grand Canyon. They booked a plane tour. It was supposed to be a 45-minute flight. But something went wrong. They crashed into the canyon."

"I'm so sorry, Holden. That is awful."

"Don't be sorry, it's not your fault. Besides, it was a long time ago."

"I know," she says. "I'm still sorry."

"Thanks."

I feel her small hand cover mine in the center of the bed that we share, and we lie here together, not speaking, staring at the thunderbolt on the ceiling overhead.

"I had a good night tonight, Bee," I say, feeling a little vulnerable, heart racing. I hope she did too.

But the room is silent. I chance a glance at Briar and find her eyes closed, her lips parted slightly, chest rising and falling as she sleeps.

She's beautiful.

Then I close my eyes and wait for my breathing to return to its normal rhythm, and eventually I fall asleep too.

My hand in hers.

It's still there seven hours later when I rise with the sun.

MY CELL PHONE RINGS ON MY DESK, PULLING MY FOCUS AWAY from my computer. The screen flashes with my mom's number, which immediately seems strange. She doesn't often call me at work.

I could use the distraction. I've been staring at my monitor most of the day, thinking about how much I liked having Briar in my bed. Yes, dammit, I wanted to kiss her. Hell, I wanted to do a lot more than that. She was still asleep when I slipped out of the house this morning. Careful not to wake her, I had a shower in my ensuite, got dressed, and made myself a cup of coffee. Before I left the house, I took a mug out of the cupboard and dropped a peppermint tea bag in it, leaving it on the counter for her.

I scrub a hand across my face, picking up the phone on the third ring. "Hey, Mom."

"Hi honey. Sorry to call you at work. Do you have a minute?"

"For you, always. What's up?"

"I'm guessing you haven't checked your mailbox in the past couple of days?"

I'm lucky if I check the thing once a week. "I haven't. Why?"

My mom exhales. "Amy is getting married. She's inviting the whole family to the wedding... including you."

I pause. "Why would she invite me?"

Amy Nichols is my girlfriend from high school. We dated in our junior and senior years, until she broke up with me—and broke my heart in the process—after graduation.

"I think she was trying to be nice. Our families have been friends for years, I'm sure she didn't want to invite everyone but you. You know... rock the boat."

"Right. I'm not gonna go, Mom." Maybe that makes me an asshole. It's not that it would bother me to see her get married. I was pretty devastated when she dumped me, but that was years ago. I closed that chapter in my life a long time ago. But I don't think I need to witness her wedding. I picture myself, still single and sitting with my parents, while my ex-girlfriend starts her happily ever after. It's a depressing image.

Amy and I made sense back then. She was the first girl I dated. We'd known each other most of our lives. Our parents were best friends. She was pretty and smart, easygoing but also determined. A lot like Briar, now that I think about it. I loved her, but that was so many years ago. When I think about her now, all it conjures up is a feeling of nostalgia.

I've only had two real relationships in my life—the first was with Amy, and the second was with Aubrey. Both got serious fast, and both crashed and burned. It's not that I'm afraid of commitment, I just think maybe I'm not cut out for love.

"You have time to think about it, honey," my mom says. "The wedding isn't happening until the fall."

"It's a hard no, Mom."

"Okay. At least send the RSVP back, okay?"

"I do have manners, Mom," I remind her. "I gotta run. I have a stop to make on my way home from work."

"What are you up to, sweetheart?" She must be home alone. My mom has always been very social. I think she's afraid of silence. It might be one of the reasons she left Dad. He's quieter, more comfortable on his own.

"I need to order furniture, Mom."

"Oh, that's nice. Do you want my help? I can meet you wherever you're going."

"Nah, I'm fine. Thanks for the offer, though." She is definitely alone.

"What are you looking for?"

I sigh. "I need a bed and a side table. Maybe a dresser."

"How come? You getting another roommate?"

"I sorta already have one. She's a friend of Daisy and Tucker's."

"*She*?"

Shit, I shouldn't have let that slip. Here we go with the 20 questions. "Yes, Mom. *She*. But it's not like that. She needed a place to stay. It's only for a few months."

"Is she pretty?"

Fuck. "Yes, very."

"Single?"

I feel my eyes roll. "Single."

"Ooh, Barb and your dad are going to love this. Will you bring her to dinner next weekend?"

"Mom. Don't make this a thing."

"I think *you* should make this a thing."

Shaking my head, I blow out a breath. "I'll talk to you later, Mom."

"Love you, Holdey."

"Love you too."

I arrive home a few hours later to find Briar in the kitchen. She's leaned over the counter, scrolling through something on her phone. A bolt of lust hits me in the chest like it always does when she's around.

She looks up and a smile spreads across her face when she sees me.

"Hey, welcome home," she says, grabbing something from the counter, holding it up, still grinning. "This looks fun!"

In her hand is a cream-colored envelope tied with a satin bow, my name scrawled across the front in gold script.

SIX

THE OFFER STANDS

Holden

I change out of my work clothes into a pair of basketball shorts and a gray T-shirt, aware of the fact that Briar is waiting for me downstairs. I'll have to tell her about the invitation, it would seem strange if I didn't. I don't know why the thought makes me so nervous. I know that Briar won't just let it go—she'll probably want to know all about Amy, and I'd rather not have to explain to her what a train wreck I am when it comes to relationships.

I'm probably worrying too much. Briar is an understanding person, that much was clear that night when we talked about my parents and their unconventional relationship.

Taking a quick look in the mirror, I run a hand through my hair and then head back downstairs. I grab a beer from the refrigerator and sit on a barstool, while Briar leans against the kitchen counter across from me. It feels too far away. I liked it better last night, when she was only inches from me in my bed, her hand in mine.

"How was your day?" she asks, a sweet smile on her face.

"Mine was good. How was yours?"

"Nothing exciting. I go back to work soon, so I ran a few errands today. I picked up your mail." Briar motions to the pile on the counter in front of me, the invitation sitting on the top. "Looks like you're invited to a wedding."

I sigh. "Yeah. I won't be going," I answer, slipping the satin bow from the invite. Did Amy hand deliver every invitation? Why does that not surprise me?

"An ex-girlfriend?"

"You guessed it." I look down at the invite. *You are cordially invited to the wedding of Preston Stephens and Amy Nichols.* She's marrying a guy named *Preston.*

"Sooo, how come you're boycotting—" Briar leans over the counter between us, reading the invitation. "Amy's wedding?"

"I'm not boycotting her wedding. I just don't want to go. I think it's a bit weird she even invited me, to be honest. But our families are close friends. It still feels weird."

"Bad breakup, huh?"

"I guess." I shrug. "She just loved her new life more than she loved me."

Briar scrunches her nose like she's thinking on that.

"We were young. She didn't want to be tied down in college," I explain. "Wanted to sow her oats and all that shit." I leave out the part where I pushed Amy away first when I started to sense she didn't want to be tied down to her high school boyfriend.

Briar leans in with her forearms on the counter, dropping her voice. "She gave up a good thing when she let you go, Holden. It's her loss."

Briar's face is inches from mine, and her faint scent of bergamot hits me. Her green eyes seem to search every part of my face, making me breathless. She doesn't move, and something fills the air between us. I watch her mouth part and her gaze drops to my lips, lingering there before her eyes return to mine. I want to kiss her. I want to know what it feels like to have her mouth on mine. My mind spins. I lean in a little closer, my body seeming to move all on its own... and the timer on the stove goes off.

Briar blinks, straightening her spine as she takes a step back. "That's dinner. I better... uh... get that before it burns."

I watch as she pushes back from the counter, turning towards the stove. Maybe this intense attraction I feel isn't just one-sided. That thought makes my pulse race.

"Can I help you with anything?"

Briar pulls a pan out of the stove. "I've got it."

"You sure?" I slip off the stool, stepping behind her, so close that her back almost brushes against my chest. So close, I can feel the heat radiating from her skin, smell the sugary scent of her shampoo. "I'll get us plates." I reach around her to the cupboard above her head, trapping her against the counter, my hip brushing the curve of her lower back. I hear her breath hitch when my arm rises over her head, landing on the cupboard's shelf, crowding every inch of her personal space.

Briar's breathing is shallow. My own breath is trapped in my throat being this close to her.

The doorbell rings, breaking the tension that has suddenly filled the room. I immediately take a step back while Briar places her palms on the counter taking a deep, fortifying breath. I leave her in the kitchen while I walk to the door. Only when I'm in the hallway, away from the pull of Briar, do I exhale, looking up at the ceiling. *Of course, someone has to be ringing my doorbell at this exact moment.*

I pull open the door to find Jake standing on the doorstep.

"Hey, man."

"Hey." I watch Jake's eyes wander over my shoulder into my kitchen, where I'm sure he can see Briar. "Sorry, needed a quick favor but maybe it's not a good time?"

"Nah, it's fine. What's up?"

"Hey, Jake. It's good to see you," Briar says, appearing in the entryway. "How's Everly and the kids?"

"Everyone is good, thanks." Jake grins. "Ev said she'd like to invite you over for dinner. Welcome you to the neighborhood."

Fuck my life. Jake is loving this right now. He's playing it up; he knows he's under my skin.

"That would be nice. I'd love that." Briar nods her head and smiles. "I'll leave you guys to it while I finish up with dinner."

When Briar disappears back into the kitchen, Jake smirks at me and I shoot him a death glare in response. I motion him out to the porch, where I join him, shutting the door behind me. "What do you want, Jake? Or did you just come over here to torture me?"

He laughs. "I need help moving a couch and a dresser." He's wearing a shit-eating grin. Asshole. "So, Tucker was telling me Briar moved in. How's that working for you?"

"I can tell you're enjoying this, but you can cool your jets. She needed a place to stay, that's it. Daisy practically forced her on me."

"I should send you a gift basket for the hardship you're having to endure. Are you going to make it, buddy?" Jake mocks me. "It must be so tough living with a woman who looks like Briar. And she's cooking for you too? What a tragedy."

"Fuck off." I shoot him a glare. "The moving, can it wait until after I eat dinner?"

The fucker laughs as he turns and heads back towards the driveway. "It can wait."

I go back inside and find Briar still in the kitchen. The table is set but the rest of the kitchen is a complete disaster. Dirty bowls. Used spoons. Condiments from the fridge cluttering the counter.

I always clean the kitchen before I sit down for dinner. It's the way I like it. But Briar has taken the time to cook for me, so I overlook the mess and sit down beside her.

She glances at me quickly as I pick up my fork. I can tell she has something on her mind. It's the first time since she moved in that she seems nervous around me and it's cute as hell. It's sexy too.

"Anything on your mind?" I ask.

She shuffles her broccoli around on her plate. "I was just thinking about the wedding invite."

This again?

She scans my face, then clears her throat, her eyes softening. "You've got a plus one. You could bring a date; make her see what she's missing."

"And who would I bring, Bee? I'm single."

"You could bring...I don't know... maybe me?"

Her cheeks pinken. Briar wears every emotion on her face. It's something I like about her. A lot.

"I'm not trying to push. But you said yourself that you're over her. Why not go to the wedding and prove it? We can pretend that we're a happy couple, really play it up. It could be fun."

"Are you saying you want to be my fake date?"

Briar grins. "What would you say if I was?"

"No."

Her shoulders drop. I expect her to leave it, but I should know better than that by now. Instead, Briar turns her body to face me, studying me with a determined, playful look in her eyes. It's unnerving—and wildly sexy. Briar is so full of life. She's always up for anything.

She locks eyes with me. "The offer stands, Holden. At least think about it."

Be smart, Holden. You need to be smart. Saying yes to Briar's proposition would *not* be smart. Still, some part of me wants to say yes to her. Maybe Briar has a point. If I avoid going, Amy might think I'm not over her.

"Briar?"

She's chewing her bottom lip. "Yeah?"

"You'd wanna go to a wedding where you wouldn't know anybody?"

"I'd know you," she says. "Besides, it's not about that. It's about doing something nice for you. And I think we would have fun! A fancy dinner. Free drinks. As long as I stay away from the tequila, we'll be fine."

She rests her chin in her hand and smirks at me, her blonde hair falling in soft waves around her face. I can't help the smile that tips at the corners of my mouth.

"And you'd have no problem pretending we're a couple?"

"You act like it would be a chore, Holden. I mean, look at you... you're not exactly a 2."

I nearly choke on a potato. "Not a 2, hey?"

"Nope."

"Then....?"

She taps her index finger to her chin two or three times as if she's thinking on it. "A solid 6."

I laugh, rolling my eyes. "Bee, you're a ball buster. Give me time, I'll grow on you."

She tips her head back in a laugh, and I feel it in my chest. The sound is pure Briar: bright, impulsive, infectious.

Realization hits me. I have a crush on her.

I should hide in my room for the next couple of months until she moves out. Except I think it might be too late. I can't get her out of my head.

"I'll think about it, Bee," I say, then add, "Oh, and I went shopping after work. I ordered you a bed. It will be here by the end of the week."

"Thanks, Holden. I don't know what I'd do without you."

"It's no problem."

Getting up from my chair, I take our plates to the sink and do the dishes while she works on her laptop at the breakfast bar. When the kitchen is clean, I tell Briar I'm going over to Jake's.

Everly is putting baby West to bed when I get to their house so Jake and I tackle the move as quickly and quietly as we can. That works for me—less chance for him to take any more shots about my new living arrangements with Briar. We move the bedroom furniture without too much trouble, but it's still warm out and Jake and Everly don't have air conditioning in their place so there's a sheen of sweat on my skin by the time we're done.

It's quiet downstairs when I get back to my house; no sign of Briar in the kitchen or living room. Needing a shower, I head to my bedroom. My eyes land on my bed, and I can't help but wonder where I'll be sleeping tonight. Will I be back on the couch or next to Briar? I know where I want to be sleeping.

Smart, Holden. Remember, be smart.

Removing my phone from my back pocket, I toss it on the dresser, then I pull the hem of my T-shirt over my head. A noise from the hallway draws my attention, and I turn to find Briar standing just outside the open bedroom door. Her eyes are glued to my torso, her mouth slightly open.

"Oh, hi," I say, enjoying the feeling of having her eyes on me a little too much.

Her cheeks turn pink, and she tears her gaze away, walking to the nightstand on the side of the bed that has become hers. "Hi. Sorry, um, I didn't realize you were back. I was just grabbing my book."

"Just got home two minutes ago. I'm going to have a quick shower," I tell her, standing in place, noticing the way my bare chest seems to be making her feel frazzled. I run a hand over my stomach just to drive her crazy.

"Don't let me stop you," she says with a slight crack to her voice, her eyes lifting to meet mine. "I'm going to read my book for a bit, then I thought I'd watch a movie if you want to join me?"

I nod. "Sounds good," I tell her, but she's already headed out the door like the bedroom is on fire.

"I MADE US POPCORN," BRIAR ANNOUNCES WHEN I WALK INTO the living room after my shower. I look around the house that until just a few days ago was mine alone. Briar's strawberry-embroidered slippers have been kicked off in the middle of the room, a hair scrunchie sits on the side table next to the couch. And then there's the stack of romance novels with half-naked dudes on the cover that are now sitting on my side table. Those have to go. I can just hear the shit the guys would say if they ever saw them. I would never live it down.

Briar shifts her legs so there's room for me on one end of the couch, and I sink down into it. Feeling my head throb, I rub my temples with my fingertips.

"Are you okay?" Briar's voice is laced with concern.

I nod and force a smile, not wanting her to worry. "It's nothing. I just have a headache. I get them all the time and I hate taking pills, so I just try to ride them out."

"Have you had that checked out?"

"Yes, Bee. I'm not dying. They seem to run in my family. My dad gets them too."

"Maybe I can help? I give good massages."

My heart races at the thought of having Briar's hands on my body. I start to tell her again that I'm fine, but she's already up off the couch and pushing the coffee table towards the center of the room.

"Sit on the floor, Holden."

"What are you doing?"

"I'm going to massage your neck muscles and it's easier if you're on the floor, so I have some leverage."

"Briar—"

As she approaches, my eyes lower to take in her mostly bare body: her toned legs on display under an oversized T-shirt. Her smooth skin the color of bronze from the sun. Is she even wearing shorts under that thing?

I lower myself to the floor and feel my cheeks flood with heat as she climbs onto the couch behind me. As she spreads her legs wide and guides my back in between her parted thighs, my mouth goes dry. I want to run my hands up her calves then over her knees and up her thighs until they reach the hem of her T-shirt. I want to find out what she's wearing under that damn shirt.

But as soon as Briar moves an inch closer, her petite body closing in on me, the swoosh of my heartbeat pounds in my ears, bringing me back to the moment. My eyes squeeze shut and then Briar's hands are on me. Every bit of her is crowding every inch of me and it feels so good.

My breathing seems to stop entirely as I bend my head forward and relax into her touch.

"I found the knot that's causing you the pain," she says as she pulls down the neck of my T-shirt and her hands drift over my bare skin. "No wonder you have a headache. You are wound so tight. This knot is huge."

I wince when her hand applies pressure on the bundle of muscles in my right shoulder blade.

"Relax, Holden. Just breathe until it loosens."

I do exactly that, closing my eyes, stretching my head to the side. A moan slips past my lips as she continues to rub the same spot in tiny circles.

"This would be easier if you weren't wearing your shirt."

"You want me to take off my shirt?"

"It would be easier."

Taking in a stuttering breath, I grab the fabric at the neck with one hand and pull the shirt over my head, dropping it on the floor next to me. I feel her warm hands return to my shoulders but this time when they do, my skin erupts in a shiver. My muscles tense.

"Relax, Holden."

I do as she says, swallowing the nerves that have risen in my throat. I relax my shoulders, loving the way her fingers feel on my skin, the sound of her voice, the way I'm notched in between her legs.

Her fingers ease up on the knot, drifting over my shoulder blades, up my neck then down my spine. They travel further down to my lower back, and when she reaches the band of my shorts, a soft sigh escapes my mouth.

"That's better. Does it feel good?"

"So good," I tell her, a mixture of relaxation and exhilaration flowing through my veins. "My headache is almost gone."

"Good. See, I told you I'm good at this."

Of course she is. Briar seems to be good at everything. She's successful, people love her, she can even cook. Not to mention she's effortlessly stunning. Maybe that's why she has very quickly gotten under my skin.

It feels strange, really. The first day she moved in, I was annoyed. I didn't want her here and I wasn't exactly subtle about the fact that her stuff strewn around everywhere got on my nerves. She felt like a hurricane, but even in her storm, however small and fierce she is, not even an oak tree could stand tall against her.

Ironically, it feels like in the midst of her storm, I feel a calmness.

I've never felt this way before. Is it just Briar and her pretty smile, or is it the pent-up sexual frustration after not allowing myself to be touched by a woman for a full year?

I didn't think I missed that type of connection, the intimacy of being with another person... until now. Until Briar walked into my life and turned it upside down.

"Are you going to Catch 21 this weekend?" she says suddenly, distracting my focus from the feel of her skin against mine.

"I'll be there. You?" I ask.

Grayson booked the patio at our usual spot in Reed Point. Everyone has been so busy lately with kids and summer vacations— including him and Sierra, with baby Sadie who turns one in the fall— so I'm looking forward to catching up, having a nice dinner and a few drinks with friends. Catch 21 is one of the town's swankiest restaurants, with live music and a small space for dancing. We all plan on taking Ubers so we can have a good time.

"I plan on it," she answers. "Daisy and Tucker invited

me." I can't deny that it makes me happy that she'll be there with me and my friends.

"Do you live at the gym, Holden? You are all muscle."

Briar's soft hands rub wide circles over my shoulder. "I work out. They have a decent gym at my office."

She hums, her hands moving to the back of my neck. "I need to get back into the gym now that I'm back home. Remember when you and Tucker and Daisy and I played pickleball? That was fun. We should do that again."

How could I forget? The image of Briar in her lime-green sports bra and short white skirt have been imprinted on my brain ever since. Her skirt was so short you could see the tiny pair of bootie shorts she was wearing underneath.

Yeah, these thoughts are not going to help the hard-on I've been trying to control all night from being this close to her. There is literally not a single part of Briar that doesn't turn me on. The scent of her skin. Her pouty bottom lip. Every curve of her body. Her presence. The way she lives in the moment.

When her fingernails gently scrape over my skin, the last bit of my restraint breaks. I quickly stand, taking a step away from her parted legs. If I stay here any longer, my dick will be as hard as stone and impossible to hide.

"Holden? Are you okay?"

"I'm fine," I say, quickly excusing myself to the bathroom before I do something I can't take back.

Shutting the bathroom door, I lean against the counter and take a shaky breath. With every minute that ticks by, I feel that pull toward Briar growing stronger. I stay there for a few more minutes, giving myself time to gather my thoughts. Finally, I open the bathroom door and return to the living room. Briar is standing now, and when I enter the room, she looks at me with concern.

"Are you okay?" she asks again, chewing on her lower lip.

"I'm fine." I wave it off.

Briar's expression tells me she's not buying it. She's probably trying to understand why I suddenly bolted from the room, and I can't blame her. The room goes silent, all but the sound of my heart beating rapidly behind my ribs.

Nothing happened between us tonight, I remind myself. But Briar has never had her hands on my bare skin before, and I haven't felt the touch of a woman in a very long time, so it doesn't feel like it was nothing.

"I'm going to check on Bear then I think I'm going to turn in. Maybe read a chapter or two," she says, clutching the book in her hand to her chest like a shield.

"Okay, I can sleep on the —"

"In your bed with me," Briar says, cutting me off mid-sentence. "It's only a few more days. What would be the point of the massage if you're just going to sleep on the couch again? Kinda defeats the purpose. Plus, I've gotten used to having you next to me. I like it."

She holds my gaze with her sparkling eyes, refusing to look at my bare chest.

There's a beat of silence between us.

And another.

I couldn't look away if I tried.

Briar clears her throat, takes a small step toward me. "Holden, have you thought about my offer?"

I swallow. "The fake date?"

"Yeah."

"Possibly."

"I might look like a mind reader, but I'm actually not," Briar jokes, relieving the pressure a bit. "So, is it a yes or a no?"

This girl is a ball buster, but it's working. Her insistence is wearing me down.

I sigh. "My answer is yes."

Excitement flashes in her emerald-green eyes before she gives me one of those smiles that just about knocks me off my feet. She claps her hands together. "Yes! This is going to be so much fun. Okay, so who is going to be at this wedding? Anyone you know?"

"I know my parents will be there, and my stepmom. They're close with Amy's family still. Why?" I narrow my eyes, wondering what's going on in her head.

"Well, we can't just show up together out of the blue and tell your family we're a couple. If we're going to pull this off, we have to be convincing. So, there will need to be a fake date or two first."

I nod with a laugh. I can't believe I'm going to go through with this. "Okay. In that case, Briar, will you be my fake girlfriend?"

"I thought you'd never ask!" she squeals. "Yes, muffin. My answer is yes! I will be your fake girlfriend."

"Muffin?"

"Yes, babe. We're going to need cute nicknames for one another if we're going to be the cutest couple Reed Point has ever seen."

"I draw the line at muffin, and the cutest couple in Reed Point? You're taking this way too far."

"Not far enough, cupcake," she smirks. "It might not be obvious, but when I commit to something, I give it 100 percent."

I snort. "Oh, it's obvious. I'm getting the message loud and clear."

I haven't known Briar for long but what I have discovered is that she says what's on her mind. She's fearless. Determined. And a lot of fucking fun.

I can't believe I've agreed to this plan of hers, but if I'm honest, I'm looking forward to this fake relationship already.

"We're going to have to kiss if we're going to pull this off. You realize that right?"

Adrenaline rushes through my veins. "Don't worry, Bee, that won't be necessary. I've never been into PDA. Anyone who knows me, knows that."

"Holden. I'm not saying we make out like two horny teenagers, but a peck on my temple, or on my lips, *is* going to be necessary if we're going to convince anyone."

"Sure. I'll kiss your forehead. You can kiss my cheek."

"Holden Banks. Are you really that much of a prude that you won't fake kiss me on my mouth?"

Her gaze is pinned to mine, our faces only inches apart. It's almost as if she's daring me to make a move. It would be all too easy to take just one more step closer to her and seal my lips to hers.

It suddenly feels like we're the only two people on this earth.

"Holden, if you pretend kissed me right now, I'd kiss you back," she says softly.

"You don't think that would be a bad idea?" I whisper.

The corners of her mouth tilt upward. "Definitely not."

My cock stiffens as I think about closing the distance between us and sweeping my lips over hers. It takes everything in me to keep from taking her face in my hands and devouring her the way I've been longing to do.

Briar's breath turns shallow when I drop my eyes to her full, pink lips. Her mouth is parted, her eyes hooded. I have never been more turned on in my life and I haven't even touched her.

But I want to. Badly.

There are only a few inches of space between us, and my cock is now almost fully hard behind the confines of my shorts. My pulse races, my body in overdrive at the thought of finally getting a taste of Briar. But I have a feeling that a kiss won't be close to being enough.

With a tilt of her head, Briar studies me attentively. It's difficult to stand steady under the intensity of her gaze.

"Think of it as a practise kiss for when we need to kiss in public," she says in a soft voice. "We need to be believable."

She doesn't move. Briar doesn't flinch.

Olive skin. Full, pink lips. My eyes slowly return to her mouth, and I find myself scraping my teeth gently over my bottom lip.

"Briar," I say, my voice coming out like a feral growl. "Put down your book."

"Why?" she whispers.

She hands the book to me, and I immediately drop it to the floor, taking the last step towards her.

"Because I'm going to kiss you."

She doesn't waver or shy away.

I can't hold back any longer. I give in. I take her face in my hands, and I kiss her. A slow, lingering kiss. Simple. Soft and languid. Chaste and lingering, but my body still somehow erupts in a shiver.

Once she realizes what is happening, she goes up on her toes and flattens her hands against my pecs.

I'm kissing Briar.

Briar is kissing me back.

It's only when we need air to breathe that we pull away.

My hands still holding her face, Briar's eyes sparkle before they go wide as if she's realized what just happened.

The feeling is mutual. I'm still coming to terms with it myself.

"Wow." She rolls her lips together like she's savoring the wetness from the kiss. "I think we're going to be okay at this."

Shock is painted all over her face as she lowers her heels to the floor, but she doesn't break eye contact.

"The best fake kiss of my life," I admit.

Her eyes close for a beat. "Holden, I know that didn't mean anything. I know it was just practise, but... you can kiss me like that anytime you want. Anywhere."

Nervously, she tucks her blonde hair behind her ear. Dammit, I love when she shows me this side of her. It's so fucking hot when she's vulnerable. "I... I'm going to check on Bear. I'll come to bed soon."

I nod, watching her walk down the hall then I turn in the opposite direction to the kitchen to make her a cup of tea.

That's when I realize how easy it would be to fall for this girl.

SEVEN

THE BEST FAKE DATE I'VE EVER BEEN ON

Holden

I was eight when my teacher noticed I had a talent for drawing. She had asked the class to draw their dream home for an art project, and I drew a whole damn city. I got an A on the assignment and after that I took as many art and design classes I could all the way through school.

I've always had a creative mind, and I've always loved technology. So, I figured if I focused on web design, it would be the best of both worlds.

After high school, I took a part-time job as a server at a bar to make money while I worked towards a diploma in New Media and Web Design in college. As soon as I graduated, I got an entry level job at the company I still work for now. It's a great place to work, I get to be creative and utilize technology to solve visual problems. But my end goal is to start my own company one day. My buddy Nick, who I work with, and I have talked about going in as partners.

That dream is still a ways off. Right now, we're just busy making plans for tonight. Our boss got us tickets to a Reed

Point Outlaws pre-season college football game. Technically, it's a work event—they're calling it "team building"—but the reality is, it's a free game and most of us are die-hard Outlaws fans. No one from the office is complaining they *have* to go.

Nick's wife Zoe also works with us—they met at work. She's hilarious as hell, is always changing her hair color from one wild shade to another, and always has an insane story from her weekend. The story of how they hooked up is also insane. Let's just say it involves a blind date, an "incident" with the Reed Point police, and many follow-up meetings with HR.

"Are you bringing a date, Holden?" Zoe asks, leaning against my desk, sipping what is probably her fourth coffee of the day.

"I wasn't planning on it."

"But you could?" Her eyes widen as she fishes for info. "Sounds like you're seeing someone. Is this new? Spill the beans, Banks."

I look to Nick for help, but he just raises his hands. "You're on your own, man. Good luck."

The game invite was extended to spouses and girlfriends too, but I am one of only a few who are going solo. I've gotten used to being the third wheel, but it's always a bit awkward.

This time around, it has occurred to me that now that I have a girlfriend—albeit a pretend one—I could technically bring someone along. I have no doubt Briar would be up for it if I asked her. Besides, if we're going to start fake dating, we might as well start now.

"I'm seeing someone, but it's new," I lie. "Her name is Briar."

"I love this. Are you going to tell us more?" Zoe leans closer to me, anxious for details.

"She's a few years younger than me, she's Canadian, and... she recently became my roommate."

Zoe whistles through her teeth. "Dating your roommate? Scandalous."

I wrinkle my brows. "You married your co-worker."

Nick laughs. "Holden has a point. Don't be judgey."

Zoe narrows her eyes at her husband then returns her attention to me. "I really need to meet this Briar. Please bring her to the game."

Nick nods. "I agree, Holden. Bring her. Need I remind you that you and Shirley from admin are the only people going without a date? And I love Shirley, but she's like 60, dude."

"Thanks. I'm well aware."

"Yup, you should invite Briar. You know she would be welcome," Zoe adds.

I weigh my options. This is probably the point where I should put a stop to this silly charade before it blows up in my face. But there's no denying I want to hang out with Briar. She makes everything more fun.

"I'll ask her and get back to you."

A little while later on my lunch break, I dig out my phone and send Briar a text.

Me: Outlaws game tonight. Wanna come with your hot fake boyfriend?

Briar: Who is this and how did you get my number?

Me: Funny. It's your better half and I got your number from Daisy. So, what do you say?

Briar: I've never said no to football. It's a date.

Me: A fake date.

Briar: Whatever

I shake my head at my phone. This is such a bad idea.

Me: Oh, and it's a team-building night for my work.

Briar: You should probably have mentioned that before you invited me.

Me: Too late. You said yes.

Briar: I've been bamboozled.

BRIAR AND I STAND AT THE TOP OF OUR SECTION OVERLOOKING the green and gold college football field. Our seats are in row 4 behind the Outlaws, but before we walk down to meet the group, I want to check in with her.

I reach for her hip, giving her side a pinch. "Nervous?"

"Not at all. I'm excited to meet your work friends."

"Nerves of steel," I say, smirking.

She shrugs. "One thing about me, Holden: I'm always up for meeting new people. Also, I'm never going to say no to free popcorn." She pauses, eyebrows raised. "The popcorn *is* free, right?"

I laugh. "As much as you want."

"Perfect! Plus, I plan on asking your co-workers for all the dirt on you."

I roll my eyes. "Behave, wild one."

She snorts. "I'll behave if you throw in some free candy too. Is it a deal, fake boyfriend?"

"I think I can spring for that. Are you ready? Should we go?"

"Ready, but you should probably hold my hand, Holden, if we're going to pretend we're in love."

I playfully roll my eyes at her again before looking her up and down, admiring her outfit. She's wearing an Outlaws jersey, a pair of boyfriend jeans, and an Outlaws baseball cap, her lips painted the prettiest shade of pale pink.

Her cheeks flush when she catches me checking her out. I smile, happy with myself for being the one to make her blush. She is the perfect combination of cute and sexy. She's out of my league, but I'm not going to be the one to point it out.

Briar and I are the last ones to arrive to our seats and right before we do, she tugs on the bill of my baseball cap. "We're going to put on a show for your friends. You better act like you like me."

I squeeze her hand, already used to the way it feels in mine. "The thing is, I do like you, Busy Bee. Don't you forget it."

With a smile, I flip my hat so it's backwards then I kiss her on the cheek. She melts into my side, going all in with the public display of affection. For a moment, I wished I kissed her on the lips instead.

"Banks, what up?" Nick calls from the center of the row.

I pull Briar along to where the team is sitting, introducing her to the group. Most wave and call out a hello, but

Zoe immediately jumps to her feet and greets Briar with a tight hug.

"You can sit with me! Nick is too focused on the game, he never talks to me," she says, motioning to the empty chair beside hers. I say hello to a couple of people one row up and then sit on the other side of Briar, who is already deep in conversation with Zoe about the game and the lineup.

"I love your commitment to the Outlaws." Nick points at her jersey. "Do you come to a lot of games?"

Briar leans into my side, putting her hand on my inner thigh. She's really playing this girlfriend thing up, so I raise my arm and wrap it around her back, so it rests on her shoulder.

"I do. I'm a big fan. My best friend married their head coach, Tucker Collins, so she's always asking me to come to games with her."

"How lucky are you?" Zoe adds. "Is that how you met Holden?"

"It is." Briar's eyes lift to mine. We talked about this earlier, what we would say if people asked how we met. We figured we'd just go with the truth. "We spent some time together last year, then I moved back home to Vancouver for a year. It's a long story, but when I returned, the adorable apartment I had leased was under two inches of water. Holden was kind enough to let me move in with him."

"Holden's your knight in shining armor. This already sounds straight out of a romance novel." Zoe beams.

"Briar loves those things. There are stacks of them taking up space in my living room. I'm not sure I'll ever get used to the shirtless guys."

"Okay, I'm definitely making a point of asking you for a recommendation. I love to read. You can tell me your favorites." Zoe rubs her palms together. "I'm going to need to get your phone number before the game is over."

Apparently, my fake girlfriend and my co-worker are going to be friends after tonight. I didn't see that one coming. I'm also not surprised. Briar is likeable. She's funny and smart, enthusiastic and outgoing. It's impossible not to like her. If the time comes that I ever want to date again, I'd want a girl just like her.

THE GAME ENDS WITH A WIN FOR THE OUTLAWS, 24-14. Before leaving, we gather on top of the concourse saying our goodbyes to the group. Zoe and Briar have their cell phones out and are exchanging phone numbers while Nick and I talk about the insane play that our quarterback called.

Briar had made an impression on my friends, but she made an impression on me too. She went out of her way to talk to everyone at the game and everyone loved her. It felt good to have a girl as fun and hot as my fake girlfriend on my arm.

Her ex-boyfriend was an absolute idiot for not treating her right. It blows my mind how any guy would let a woman like her get away. She's the perfect mix of chaos and sunshine. I should probably send him an expensive bottle of scotch for fucking things up with her. His loss was my gain. It brought Briar into my life— even if we'll just be friends after all of this is over. Fuck, I hope we can remain friends after the wedding, after we stage our fake breakup. After today, I know I like having her around.

"She's cool, man." Nick elbows me gently in the side. "You're different with her than with the last one. You're less uptight. There's less—"

"Arguing?"

"Yeah, that," Nick laughs. "I think this one's going to make you work your ass off. She's going to keep you on your toes."

My stomach twists. Nick doesn't have any idea how right he is. Briar has been busting my balls since the moment she moved in. I don't see that changing anytime soon if ever. The crazy thing is, I'm kind of liking it.

After the girls have finished their conversation, they walk over to join Nick and me. He tugs his wife into his side, so I do the same to Briar. Briar nuzzles in close, flattening a palm over my abs, her other arm wrapping around my lower back. I dip down and roll my chin against her hair, liking the feel of her little body pressed against mine.

Too bad it's just pretend.

"You guys have been so nice. Thank you for welcoming me today." Briar lets go of me to hug both of them.

"We hope to see a lot more of you." Before they turn to go, Zoe flashes me an enthusiastic thumbs up while Briar isn't looking.

"I had fun!" Briar lets go of my hand as we approach my truck.

"I had a lot of fun."

She smiles. "It's always a good time, it seems, when we're together."

"Temporarily together."

"I know, Holden. You don't have to worry. I won't ask you to propose to me at the end of this."

"You wouldn't have to ask me. You are a cool chick, Bee. You deserve a guy who will treat you like the incredible catch you are." I reach for the handle, opening her door, helping her inside. "Thanks for making tonight so fun."

"Thank you for asking me. That was the best fake date

I've ever been on. I will be hoping you invite me to all future team-building events."

She smiles. My heart rate skips.

Team-building events only happen twice a year, so Briar and I will no longer be "together" when the next one rolls around. I know I'm going to miss having her with me when all of this is over.

I shut her truck door, walking slower than usual around the hood.

I need to be careful, to keep Briar at a distance. She won't be in my life for long, at least not like this. Once the wedding is over, our fake relationship will be too. Besides, she has been hurt enough as it is by her ex-boyfriend.

I can't be the one to hurt her again.

EIGHT

PRETTY SURE I SAW AN 8-PACK

Briar

"I've gotta run, Mom," I say, getting out of my car. "I just pulled into the parking lot. Thanks for calling. I'll let you know how today goes."

Ending the call on my cell, I walk towards a familiar office building 15 minutes outside of Reed Point. It's my first day back at my old job and I'll spend most of it onboarding. The plan is to meet with my boss to sign paperwork then meet with HR before having lunch with my new team.

I'm excited to be back to work, but it doesn't stop a heavy sigh escaping my throat when I walk through the doors of Rossi Cheese. It's hard to stay focused when there's a reel of Holden Banks images playing on repeat in my brain.

This past week with Holden had been an interesting one to say the least.

We went on our first fake date and it only made me eager for another one. He's so easy to hang out with. His friends are cool and uncomplicated. I found myself staring at him, wondering how this was the same man who seemed so flustered around me when I first moved in. I'm also having a very hard time forgetting what he looks like without a shirt.

When I found him shirtless in his bedroom, it was hard to turn and walk away. My fingertips were aching to trace every hard muscle of his body. The man looks more like an underwear model than a web designer who works in an office. Holden Banks can put any athlete or celebrity to shame. Defined pecs and a flat stomach with a light dusting of dark hair leading to the waistband of his shorts. I tried my best not to stare, but I am pretty sure I saw an 8-pack.

Then when I actually did get to touch him, to massage his stiff muscles, it took every ounce of strength in me not to climb him like a tree. He's hard and sculpted. Long, lean muscles perfected from hours in the gym.

And then there's the kiss.

The kiss.

I still can't believe I asked him to kiss me.

I dust a finger over my mouth remembering what it felt like to be kissed by Holden. I already know I will never forget it. I swear time stood still. It was easily the best kiss of my life.

It was worlds apart from what it was like between Justin and me. There were never sparks when he touched me, not like there are with Holden. I never broke into a full body chill when we kissed. I used to think he was the one, but one soft, closed-mouth kiss with Holden has changed all of that.

Justin may not have been the one for me, but I have to remind myself that Holden isn't either.

I've known guys like Holden. Guys who have a list of girls a mile long, who go through them like they're candy. Getting mixed up with him would be a terrible idea, and yet, I can't seem to help myself from imagining it. Even worse than that? I fantasize about it at night while he's laying right next to me. I know better than to go for a guy like him. And I won't sleep around. When you sleep with someone you give up your power. And I'm not interested in doing that ever again.

It's taken me time and a lot of soul searching to realize I didn't deserve what Justin did to me.

He broke me.

He destroyed my self-worth, but it's starting to feel like I could leave that time in my life behind. I'm feeling stronger. I'm happier. I like being me.

Having great, genuine friends in Reed Point helps. In addition to the few college friends I've stayed in touch with, Daisy and Tucker's close-knit group have all welcomed me with open arms. As much as I love Vancouver, Reed Point feels like home now. And now that I'm back here, I feel like it's going to be my year. I channel that energy as I take the elevator to my boss's office.

I'm pushing the button for the fifth floor when my phone buzzes with a message.

> Holden: It's family dinner at my mom's next week. Probably a good time to start faking our relationship around the family.

I quickly type out a response before the elevator doors open.

> Briar: This will be fun. I can't wait to see how they take it when they find out you're already living with your new girlfriend. That won't be awkward. *crazy face emoji*

Holden: My mom left my dad for another woman and the three of them go for dim sum together every Friday night. Nothing is awkward to them.

Briar: Shut up. Do they really?

Holden: Yes, Bee, they do.

Briar: They are the coolest. Okay, I'm in. Can't wait to meet them, muffin :)

Holden: Call me that again and you won't like what happens.

Briar: Ooh, I love it when you're mean.

I chuckle at my screen before shoving my phone into my bag just as the elevator doors open. The text exchange shouldn't put an extra pep in my step when I walk down the hall to my new office.

But who am I kidding?

That is exactly what Holden Banks does to me.

I'VE CURLED MY HAIR INTO LOOSE WAVES THAT HANG JUST PAST my shoulders. I went for a smoky eye, a little blush and a light pink lip gloss. It's more makeup than I usually wear but I've always liked to get dressed up. I check myself out in the mirror to make sure nothing is missing. The fuchsia pink dress I'm wearing hugs my curves and ends mid-thigh. The strappy black heels that fasten around my ankle give me three extra inches. I kind of like the idea of being a little taller next to Holden's 6'1" frame.

I'm excited for tonight's dinner at Catch 21. I feel happier than I have in a long time, and I want to celebrate that.

The sound of a loud sneeze and then another draws my attention as I stand in front of the full-length mirror in Holden's spare bedroom. Grabbing my clutch, I walk down the few stairs to the living room where I find Holden sitting on the couch with his phone in his hand, dressed and ready to go.

He stands when he sees me. My eyes roam over him from head to toe. I'm used to seeing Holden in shorts and a T-shirt or a pair of joggers while he's lounging around the house. Don't get me wrong, he looks sexy as hell in casual clothing, but nothing compares to him looking like *this*. He's wearing a black button-down dress shirt that highlights his toned physique, paired with dark-gray slacks that fit him to a T. A bolt of lust hits me square in the chest.

It's when my gaze finally lands on his face that I start to worry. His eyes are red and watery again, like they have been most of the week.

"Gorgeous, Bee," he says, his voice low and gritty, like sandpaper. Heat seeps into my cheeks.

"You look handsome, Holden. You clean up," I say, taking a few steps closer, settling my palm on his forehead "But are you feeling, okay? I heard you sneeze, and your eyes are watering."

A grin tugs at his lips. "I didn't realize you're a doctor."

"I can't be concerned about my boyfriend?"

"I am not your boyfriend."

"Not with an attitude like that, you're not," I coo, taking a step back.

"It's nothing. I'm fine." He waves it off then holds up his phone. "I ordered us an Uber. The app says the car will be here in five minutes. If it's not enough time for you, I'll ask the driver to wait."

My eyes widen a fraction. It's a small thing, him being so patient, but it matters to me. Justin would have thrown a fit if I wasn't ready on time. I would have had to listen to him yell at me for the entire drive to the restaurant, dying of embarrassment the entire time.

"I'm good, Holden. Thank you."

It takes me a second to unglue my eyes from him, to shake off the effect of seeing him all dressed up. When I finally do, he ushers me out the door and into the waiting car. My pulse races the entire ride to the restaurant from having him so close to me. Rugged, handsome, playboy Holden who I can't seem to stop fantasizing about. It's a relief when we arrive at the restaurant. We find our friends out on the patio, the first round of drinks just being delivered by the server.

Grayson and Sierra spot us first and come over to pull us into the group, where Jake, Everly, Daisy, and Tucker are waiting.

"Holdey, my man." Tuck stands up and crushes Holden in a bro-hug. It's impossible not to smile at their friendship. You can tell they've known each other for a very long time. These days, they are both successful—not to mention incredibly handsome—men, but when the two of them are together, it's not hard to imagine what they must have been like as teenagers, running around Reed Point causing trouble together.

"I miss you, man. Didn't see you at Jake's on Wednesday. Where have you been this week?"

I know the answer to that question because he's been with me every night after coming home from work. But was he supposed to be at Jake's? And if so, why didn't he go?

"Yeah, it's been a busy week. I'll make it next time."

Weird. But I don't have time to unpack Holden's comment when Everly greets me with a tight hug.

We spend the next several minutes hugging our friends and ordering drinks, and as I move around the table I can feel Holden looking at me. A couple of times our eyes meet, and he shoots me that signature smirk. When it's time to take our seats, I feel his hand on the small of my back as he guides me to the table.

"Let me," he smiles, pulling out my chair. As I slide into the seat, I feel the weight of everyone's attention on us. I didn't realize until now that everyone else here is married. Holden and I are the only single ones in the friend group, but to any outsider we would probably look a lot like a couple too. I glance at Daisy beside me and find her staring at me with eyes as wide as saucers.

"What's going on over there?" Sierra asks, and I silently thank her for the distraction. She points to the corner of the patio, where a photographer is perched with his camera aimed at a couple eating dinner.

"Is that Miles Bennett?" Everly asks. "Oh my god, it is... he's with Rylee."

The entire world knows who Miles Bennet is. He's one of Hollywood's biggest movie stars and Reed Point's claim to fame. He was born and raised here along with his two brothers and younger sister, Jules, who also happens to be best friends with Sierra. Their family owns the Seaside Hotel chain, a very upscale brand of boutique hotels on the east coast. Miles met his wife Rylee—"America's sweetheart," according to the tabloids—on set when she was working as a PA. They got married a few years ago and have a few kids now. Miles usually isn't bothered by too many paparazzi when he's here in Reed Point, but he's been doing a lot of press for a big action movie he has coming out, so I guess the press is paying more attention than usual.

"Sierra, you know him. Can you introduce us all?" Everly asks, looking completely starstruck.

"I'll let them eat first and then I'll go say hi. Okay, what's everyone getting for dinner?"

The table quiets as everyone looks through the extensive menu, and I use the lull in conversation to appreciate the stunning view. The restaurant itself is gorgeous, with a white marble bar, pale pink suede booths and ornate jellyfish-inspired glass chandeliers. But it's the covered patio less than 50 feet from the ocean on the edge of the busiest beach in the city that makes Catch 21 so special.

The air is warm, the patio is packed with people enjoying a perfect summer night, and when the sun goes down, the space will glow under pretty strands of string lights.

The waitress hurries off with our orders just as the band begins to play a string of cover songs and most of us, now on our second round of drinks, start to sing along. The chat around the table is easy and fun, and by the time we've finished our dinners we're all a little buzzed.

"So, Briar. It's good to see you back," Jake says, one arm draped across Everly's shoulders. "I hope my bro Holden has rolled out the welcome mat."

"Obviously," Holden pipes up. "Ask Tucker. I'm a great roommate."

"You were, buddy," Tuck agrees before taking a sip of his gin and tonic. "Questionable taste in TV and O.C.D. that's a little out of control, but other than that you were a dream."

I watch as Holden shakes his head, fighting a grin.

"I can confirm. Great roommate. No notes." I nod in his

direction. "I'm not sure what I would have done without him. Well, I do know... I would have been homeless."

"Have you talked to your landlord about your place?" Grayson asks from across the table.

I nod my head. "I spoke to him briefly today. He's been dealing with the insurance company all week and he finally got that part settled. He said he has guys going in on Monday to start the job."

"I guess it's progress," Grayson says.

"It is. And until then, I have a great place to stay."

"Did you ever buy furniture for my old room or are you making Briar sleep on the floor?" Tucker jokes, leaning forward to look down the table at Holden.

"It arrived today. I need to put it all together this weekend."

"You've been stuck with the couch, Briar?" Jake asks innocently enough. Daisy, on the other hand, is shooting me a look that says, *inquiring minds wanna know.*

"Holden gave me his bed," I answer for him, patting his bicep.

"No big deal, just some minor spinal damage," he teases, rubbing the side of his neck. When Holden's gaze shifts to me, I flick him an amused look. His lips quirk up in response. It's kind of cute.

Tucker laughs. "I've slept on that couch. I feel your pain."

"You should get Briar to massage it out for you. Her hands are like magic." Daisy flashes a knowing smirk as she leans one elbow on the table, resting her chin in her palm.

I take a long sip of the tequila sunrise Holden ordered for me. My skin heats as I wonder if Holden is going to tell the table that I've already done that. Something in me hopes he doesn't. The massage wasn't sexual in any way, but the physical contact did feel like it may have been the start of something. I mean, that night *did* end in a kiss.

"I'll remember that," he responds coolly as I exhale from behind my glass. I want to throw my arms around him right here and now for being so discreet—for not kissing and telling, literally.

As our waitress shows up to clear away our empty plates, Holden catches my eye. I feel like I can't breathe when he winks, then holds my gaze in a lingering, heated stare. The longer our eyes stay glued to one another's, the more everything and everyone else in the room fades away.

This man... he's confident, but still charming and sweet. I wish I wasn't so ridiculously attracted to him, but there's no denying that I am.

The conversation shifts to Tucker and his reno just as Holden's hand falls to my thigh under the table. He does it so nonchalantly, like it's no big deal, when in fact, every nerve in my body feels like it's about to short-circuit. He runs his warm hand back and forth as the conversation continues around us.

The feel of his skin against mine draws my gaze to him, but he doesn't look in my direction or give the slightest acknowledgement that his hand on my thigh is driving me wild. He laughs at something Tucker said, but I have completely lost track of the story. All I can think about is how I wouldn't mind if Holden moved his hand closer to the hem of my dress. Then even further.

Have I craved this, to be touched by Holden? The answer is yes. But I'm also confused. Holden touching me like this is completely unexpected. I don't know where his head is at. He frowns at me one minute and is kissing me in the hallway the next. I have whiplash from the mixed signals.

Skin flaming, I turn my attention to the waitress and the

round of shots she's handing out, courtesy of Grayson. It's only when Holden reaches for the shot glass that he removes his hand from my thigh, and I miss it instantly.

"Here's to a night we'll never remember with the friends we'll never forget." Grayson raises his glass in the air.

I throw back the tequila, the liquor a welcome burn as it slides down my throat. After everything that has happened tonight—Holden's lingering gazes, his hand on my leg—I'm feeling unnerved. My brain only gets hazier when he leans into my side and whispers, "Looks like I'm about to find out what happens to my girlfriend when she drinks tequila."

I study him. The alcohol has loosened my inhibitions. "So, I'm your girlfriend now?" I ask him.

"Isn't that what we agreed to?"

I watch his expression darken, the freckle under his left eye pulling my attention away for just a second before my gaze drifts to his mouth.

I'm feeling a buzz from the alcohol, which is why I take things one step further. "I wanna hear you call me your girlfriend again."

He starts to say something, but the sound of Tucker's chair sliding back over the concrete patio interrupts the moment.

Tucker pulls Daisy on to the dance floor and the rest of our friends follow soon after. It doesn't take long for the small dance floor to be full of swirling bodies. I watch my friends move to the sounds of 90s songs with a smile on my face and happiness in my heart, feeling grateful to have this group of people in my life.

I feel Holden stretch his arm across the back of my chair. If I knew what was good for me, I wouldn't melt back into him. I wouldn't inch even closer. But that's exactly what I do.

It feels good.

It feels right.

I feel safe.

And while the tequila may have something to do with the warm feeling that is spreading through my body, I know it's a lot more than that.

"Do you wish you were dancing?" Holden murmurs in a low, lazy tone.

I turn my head to the side, looking at him under the fringe of my lashes. "I'm pretty happy right here where I am."

His eyes widen, and I see the flash of heat in them. Butterflies come to life in my stomach. When is that going to stop happening? I keep thinking that the more time I spend with him, the sooner these fluttery feelings will dissipate, but if anything, the opposite is happening. They seem to only be intensifying.

"Like something you see?" he asks, eyebrows raised.

I roll my eyes. "I was just appreciating the view... of the *restaurant*."

He laughs, and something about it is incredibly sexy. I'm trying not to overthink things but the way he's looking at me with that smirk and those twinkling green eyes has me off balance.

"Nice try. You were staring at me, Bee. And I think you were liking what you see."

My eyes narrow. "Was not."

Holden leans into me, so close that the woodsy scent of his cologne just about makes me forget my own name. "Tell your boyfriend what you were thinking about when you were checking him out."

It's my turn to push his buttons. So that's exactly what I do when I decide to tell him exactly what I was thinking. "The way you are with your friends is so damn hot."

"What else?"

The arm he has wrapped around me tightens as I swivel in my seat so that I'm facing him. His eyes sear into mine, heavy with heat and appreciation. His other hand rises to my face, sweeping my hair behind my ear. The feeling of his fingertips sends a shiver of desire through me. When his gaze dips to my mouth, I feel a spark of electricity between my thighs.

"I was thinking I like it when you touch me."

"Funny... I like touching you."

"Have you thought about doing more?"

"Bee, the things I've thought about doing to you should be illegal."

I bite my lip at the same time my eyes go wide. So, he does want me just as much as I want him.

"I don't understand what's going on between the two of us." As soon as the words leave my lips, I feel a mixture of relief and trepidation. Holden has been so hard to read. "Tell me what you're really thinking, Holden."

"I'm thinking that pink is my new favorite color."

"So that means you like my dress?"

"Hmm."

A grin takes over my entire face. "Holden?"

"Yeah."

"We've slept in the same bed every night this week and you haven't tried anything, not once. I figured you weren't attracted to me."

Eyes still on me, he doesn't hesitate. "I think you're the most beautiful woman I've ever seen and..." he pauses. I watch his Adam's apple as he swallows.

"And what, Holden?"

"And I'm not sure that anyone has ever turned me on the way that you do."

My cheeks flame. It feels good to finally hear him admit his attraction to me. But where do we go from here?

"Bee, I am so attracted to you, but—"

"I'm not looking to start anything serious either," I interrupt.

I know it could be complicated with Holden, but for one night, I'd like to feel wanted. I'd like to give in to the need that I've felt coursing through my veins for this man ever since I moved in with him.

One night.

A few hours of no-strings-attached sex.

We can have a little fun, get it out of our systems, and then go back to the way things were. I'm pretty sure Holden would want the same thing.

"Briar." He lets out a frustrated groan. "You aren't making this easy for me. Just so you know, if you want—"

Behind us, a throat clears. The tension between us suddenly snaps and we pull away to see Grayson is back at the table.

"Hey. Sierra is talking to Miles and Rylee. They're getting ready to go so she wanted to catch them before they left."

Gray lowers himself into his chair and picks up his half-empty glass. I inch my body away from Holden's just slightly, taking the opportunity to take a deep breath as he chats with Grayson. A few minutes later, the rest of the group returns to the table, bringing Miles and Rylee to join us for a photo.

We all move to one side of the table and Everly passes her phone to the waitress so she can snap a picture. I'm back nestled into Holden's side for the photo, trying to hide the goosebumps that have erupted over my skin. The kiss Holden and I shared this week did nothing to temper the lust running rampant in my body. If anything, it only makes me want him more. And after tonight, all I can think about is how good his lips felt against mine and how badly I want to feel that again.

My nipples pebble under my dress.

Relax, Briar. This is not the time and place to be this turned on.

The music thumps from the crowded dance floor as our group settles back in around the table. Holden is soon deep in conversation with Tucker and Jake, so I take the opportunity to escape to the bathroom to clear my head.

Staring at my reflection in the mirror, I take a deep breath. Whatever this is between Holden and I, it's starting to feel dangerous. What are we doing? I didn't move back to Reed Point to start a relationship. Especially not with my roommate.

I have to get out of here.

I dig out my cell phone to send a text to Daisy to tell her I'm suddenly not feeling well and am taking an Uber home. Then I slip out into the restaurant, bee-lining it for the door.

I make it as far as the hostess stand before a big hand circles my waist. He pulls me towards him, desire pooling in his green eyes. "I was worried about you, Bee. Everything okay?"

No, everything is not okay.

Holden has made it clear he's not looking for a relationship right now, and neither am I. I've learned the hard way that loving someone is a weakness. You open up your heart only to have it crushed, then you convince yourself that they didn't really mean to hurt you and pick up the pieces after they've left. I've made excuses for a man before—over and over—and I swore to myself I wouldn't do it again. I'm working on myself. But the temptation to spend one steamy night with Holden is overwhelming, and it only intensifies when he inches a little closer, his hand on my waist drawing me to him.

I need to tilt my chin to look him in the eyes.

Not smart.

When my eyes meet his, every doubt in my mind and every sound from the restaurant fades until it's just the two of us.

"I'm fine," I tell him.

"Aren't you having fun?"

"I'm having a great time." Especially with him. "I just needed a minute to think."

"Were you going to leave without saying goodbye to our friends?"

"Our friends are still partying."

Holden turns me in his arms, so my back is against his chest. His breath tickles the side of my cheek, and every inch of my skin comes alive, including the space between my thighs. "So let them," he says, his voice shallow and gravely. "I'd like to take my girlfriend home."

NINE

Briar

The house is dark except for the lamp that Holden left on in the living room. It's also quiet. As quiet as it was in the back of the Uber on our way home from Catch 21.

The liquor is wearing off and I think we're both very aware of the flirting that went on between us all night.

My mind is all over the place. What did Holden mean when he said *I'd like to take my girlfriend home?* I mean, is there any other way to interpret that? Especially with the way he was looking at me when he said it. But then we got into the car, and he didn't so much as look at me once for the entire drive home. This man is going to be the death of me.

Holden rolls up his sleeves as he walks into the kitchen and flicks on the light. "Want a nightcap?"

"What do you have in mind?"

I know what's on *my* mind, and it has nothing to do with a nightcap. I'm thinking about his hand on my knee under the table, his breath on my neck, how we eye-fucked the life out of each other all night. Is Holden having the same thoughts? I'm desperate to know, but I refuse to ask him. Instead, I have withdrawn. Hooking up with Holden would be playing with fire.

"An old fashioned? Or I can make you a cup of tea."

"Tea sounds perfect." I think we've established that alcohol can get us into trouble.

Holden fills the kettle and places it on the stove and then pours himself a tumbler of whiskey on the rocks.

"It's so peaceful here at night," I say, hopping up on the counter, watching him drop a tea bag in a mug for me.

"I don't know how Tucker was ever able to leave Haven Harbor," he says. "I'm not sure I ever could."

"You're renting this house, right?"

"I am, but I'm hoping I'll be able to purchase it one day. The lady that owns it has said for a while that she's thinking about selling. I told her I'd be interested when she does."

The kettle starts to whistle so Holden turns off the burner and fills the mug then brings it to me. His hand brushes against mine as I take it from him, and even that is enough to spark a response in me.

The guy is hot. That's the only reason I react to him this way. That doesn't mean we have intense sexual chemistry. It doesn't mean I want anything more to happen between us. If I tell myself that enough times, maybe I'll start to believe it.

"Thanks," I say, letting the cup warm my hands. "I hope it works out. The house would be a great investment."

Holden takes a few steps back and leans against the counter, one ankle crossed over the other, looking totally at ease. He takes a long sip from his glass.

"Tell me where you'd want to go if you weren't afraid of flying."

He arches a brow, setting the whiskey down on the counter next to him. "You and your questions."

I shrug. "I'm curious about my boyfriend."

A smirk toys at his lips. "Okay, fine. I've always wanted to go to Disneyland."

"Disneyland?" I repeat, trying to suppress a laugh.

"Why do you look so surprised?"

"I don't know. I guess I thought you'd say Hawaii or Mexico. Disneyland wasn't even a blip on my radar."

Holden's cheeks pinken and I wonder if it's the alcohol or the admission.

"You've never been?" I ask before cautiously taking a sip of my tea.

"My parents took me when I was eight and my brother was four. I don't remember a thing. Then the accident happened, and my family never got on a plane again."

I nod, his words tugging at my heart. I hate what they must have all gone through.

"Don't look so sad, Bee," he murmurs. "You're too pretty to frown."

"I'm not frowning," I tell him, flashing him a grin, feeling the tension return to the space between us.

"See... now that's better." His gaze drops to my mouth. "Can I tell you what I'm thinking?"

"Yes."

"I can't forget about that kiss."

I swallow carefully. "I thought I was the only one."

"I've thought about it at least every five minutes of every day since I kissed you in the hallway. It stalks me in my dreams. I can't get it off my mind."

"While I was lying in your bed next to you?"

"Then too."

"It was a great kiss," I whisper right before he pushes off from the counter and steps towards me so there's only a foot of distance between us. He takes the mug from my hands and sets it on the counter next to me. The butterflies in my stomach take flight.

Our eyes are pinned to one another's, and I can see the need pooling in his. I want to reach for him and pull him into my arms, but I don't. I nibble on my lower lip instead, gathering the courage to take this one step further even though I know I shouldn't. "Can I tell you what *I'm* thinking?"

A grin tips the corners of his mouth. "I'm all ears."

"I wanna know why you walked over here."

"Here?" he asks, closing the last bit of distance between us so that we're almost touching.

I nod.

"I want to kiss you, Bee."

His eyes are locked on mine, and there's desire swirling in his green irises, the same emotion I feel in my chest.

Holden reaches for me, his hands moving to my waist, my hands moving to his muscular thighs. All I can think is how badly I want him to kiss me, to feel his mouth move against mine. But looking at Holden, there is a tiny voice that warns me I should stop this right now before it goes any further.

But then his hands thread through my hair as he leans in closer. "I'm going to kiss you—like really kiss you this time— and I'm going to make sure it is the best kiss of your life."

His mouth parts before his lips softly brush over mine. *Yes.*

I don't know how this man has this much power over me, but I need to get Holden out of my system. I don't care if I can only have him for a little while.

My eyes close, and before I can register what is happening, he crushes his lips to mine, kissing me deeply. My arms move around his neck as I kiss him back, tasting the whiskey and mint on his tongue. My god, *yes*. Holden can kiss. He wasn't lying when he said this would be the best kiss of my life. It is, and then some, and he's only just got started.

He lets out a soft groan before delving deeper with his tongue as his hand slides around to the back of my neck. He controls the kiss. I savor the moment. Then his tongue sweeps over every inch of my mouth, licking every corner, and I'm melting into him.

I know I should stop. I know this is a terrible idea, but I only kiss him harder as he grinds his erection against my center. Holden has me caged in with his thighs between my spread legs and his chest pressed against mine. His hand grips the back of my neck as he deepens the kiss. He doesn't stop until we both need to come up for air, until my entire body tingles with heat and the space between my thighs aches to be touched. We both moan into the kiss as we break apart.

"Tell me to stop," he demands.

"I can't," I breathe, sealing my lips back to his.

Holden keeps kissing me, ravishing my mouth, as his grasp on the back of my neck tightens and his eager mouth prowls mine.

Now is when we *should* stop, say goodnight, and go to sleep in separate rooms, but instead my hands roam through his thick hair then down his shoulders to his back, enjoying the way his body fits against mine.

"Briar." His fingers trail down the slope of my throat before he kisses a path along my jaw then down the column of my neck. "I've wanted this for so long."

He sucks on my neck until I whimper, until a throb pulses between my legs. My heartbeat thumps behind my ribcage as Holden sucks and licks every inch of my neck. But as good as his mouth feels, it's not enough. I want more.

"Holden." I fist his T-shirt. "Yes. Please. More."

"I'll give you whatever you want, Bee," he murmurs against my ear before sucking the lobe into his mouth.

My head slowly falls back in pure ecstasy when he licks the shell of my ear. "Yes."

"I want you, Briar. So fucking badly."

"Then take me."

He pulls back, and his eyes meet mine. I see the question in them, asking me if I'm sure. I nod. When I seal my lips to his in a confident kiss, he picks me up and carries me to his bedroom.

Holden lays me out on his comforter in the dimly lit room then moves to stand at the foot of the bed. The silvery light coming through the window illuminates the movement of his hands as he works on the buttons of his shirt. He tosses the fabric to the floor, giving me an incredible view of his pecs and his abs, and oh yes, it *is* an 8-pack.

How does anyone look like that and not work out for a living? Solid, cut muscles with the perfect amount of chest hair; a dusting between his firm pecs and a trail that leads all the way to the waistband of his pants.

"Holden, I need to touch you," I say, shimmying up the bed until my head is on the pillow.

"Any idea how hot it is when you ask me for what you want?"

He crawls over me until he captures my lips in a needy kiss. My hands wander over the hard plains of his back, needing to feel his skin against mine. Needing him as close to me as I can get him. I want our clothes gone. My pulse thrums with heat when he nudges my thighs apart and settles between my legs.

He breaks the kiss, his fingers wandering to the strap on my shoulder. "This dress, Bee. You're perfect. I've been fighting a hard-on all night."

Holden's fingers tug at the zipper at the side of my dress then he slips the straps from my shoulders, slowly stripping the fuchsia ribbons down my arms. I watch his eyes widen in appreciation as he eases the fabric over my breasts, realizing I'm not wearing a bra. He keeps going, sliding the dress over my hips and then tossing it to the floor alongside his shirt.

This is how I want every night to end while I'm living in his house. I want him to carry me to his room, watch him as he strips for me and then takes me out of every scrap of my clothing before he fucks me senseless.

"Damn, Briar." His eyes move from my black lace thong to my abdomen before settling on my chest. He bends and sucks my nipple into his mouth. My back arches into him, savoring the tremble of my skin as his tongue licks and sucks and flicks at the sensitive peak. He sucks harder. I moan. His fingers pinch. I shudder. While Holden torments both of my breasts, I squirm underneath him, releasing a series of groans.

It. Feels. So. Good.

"More of that. Yes," I plead, and he does what I want, licking and sucking.

I grip the strands of his hair as my pelvis rocks into his, seeking the friction I so badly need to relieve the ache between my legs. I don't need to see it to know that Holden is hard. I can feel the length of him graze my clit every time his erection rolls over me.

"You need to take these off," I tell him as my hands press against the belt on his jeans.

His mouth pops off my nipple and he sits back on his

knees. He smiles down at me, my fake boyfriend who I have fantasized about for days, agonizing over how badly I wanted him.

His hands lower to his belt buckle. My god, I am going to lose it. I've wondered what he looks like under his clothes. My tongue slides over my lower lip, an overwhelming need sparking to life inside of me.

"Briar, I need to know exactly what you want so you're comfortable with me and you enjoy this."

"I want you. So much. I told you, Holden, take me. I'm yours tonight to do anything you want with."

Slowly his buckle is undone, then the button on his jeans, followed by the hiss of the zipper. He pushes his pants down his legs, kicking them to the floor.

Without thinking I reach for him, tracing my fingers over every dip of his abs as he patiently watches me. My body aches to feel him, the length of him, the weight of him in my hands.

"Love your hands on me," he groans. "Goddamn, I've been dreaming about this. Of you and me. Naked. The things we do in my dreams, Briar. I bet you're fucking perfect under that lace, aren't you, beautiful?"

His eyes shut and his head falls back as my palm covers the length of his erection over his boxer briefs.

"Jesus, Bee, please take me out," he pleads. "I need you to touch it."

I giggle at the sound of him begging, then I give him what he wants. Sitting up, I dip my hand under the waistband of his boxers, feeling the dusting of coarse hair just above his erection and circling his hard cock with my hand.

His breath hitches. Holden bites down on his bottom lip, trying to keep it together, every muscle in his torso pulled taut. "Wrap your hand around it and tug," he begs. "Please."

My hand wraps around the silky-smooth skin of his width as my index finger grazes over the slit gathering a bead of liquid. Then I tug his boxers down to his thighs, watching his cock spring free.

Everything inside of me turns feral. Holden Banks is undoubtably beautiful, there is no question, and so is the package he is working with. He's long and thick with one protruding vein down the center of his shaft leading to a perfect mushroom-shaped tip. The patch of dark hair that surrounds it is short and groomed.

"I am hard as fucking stone for you," he grits out. "I bet you're soaking wet for me."

I swallow, knowing the answer is yes. He confirms it when he dips his hand under the lace and swipes a finger through my slit.

"Drenched for me, Bee. Such a good girl."

My cheeks burn. Why do I like hearing him call me that so much?

I take hold of him again, gripping him tighter, running my hand up and down his shaft then giving the head a little attention. He's leaking at the tip, so I swipe my thumb over his crown, coating my hand before spreading the moisture over his shaft. He pushes his hips forward into my hand, groaning at the feel.

"That feels so good." His eyes squeeze shut, his body tensing. "I love it when you rub the head."

Holden is coming apart, his breathing shallow. I give him three more long tugs before he's pulling away when I get him too close.

"I'm not ready for this to be over yet." His hands wrap around to my ass, pulling me into him, kneading and massaging both cheeks in his hands. His bare chest presses against my skin, and he holds me there while his mouth expertly works mine. "It's my turn to make you feel good."

His fingers toy with the lace triangle of my thong as he kisses me, sucking on my bottom lip. The moment his fingers begin to slip the lace over my hips, I'm practically begging for him to touch me.

He eases me back on to the bed, licking and kissing a path down my body. "This is when you tell me what you like."

I gently drag my fingers through his hair. "I've never been asked that before."

"I plan on ruining you for all men."

"I'd like to see you try."

He smirks, then presses a kiss right below my belly button. "That is a dare I will happily accept." I can see in his eyes that he's looking forward to the challenge, and I'm looking forward to seeing how he delivers. It has been far too long since I've orgasmed without the help of a battery-operated toy.

Holden chuckles with an arrogant smile on his lips right before spreading my legs wide. Then his tongue licks a long, achingly slow line through my seam.

I moan his name.

"Yes, beautiful. Do you want more?"

"Please."

"You're cute when you act all polite."

"I'm not trying to be polite."

He adds a finger. "I like it when you're bossy too."

I moan, arching my back. "That was hardly bossy."

"No, baby, it wasn't. But you can be, and it's such a fucking turn on."

"Less talking and more action, please."

Holden chuckles against my opening before spreading

me even wider. He's feasting on me, running his tongue from my opening to my clit, not letting up.

He fucks me with his fingers as he sucks on the bundle of nerves then circles it, changing the rhythm until I'm writhing against his mouth.

I drop my hands to his hair to anchor him in place, so close to coming undone. He doesn't stop, keeping the pace, licking me faster and fingering me until an illicit moan falls from my lips.

My muscles contract around his fingers and my legs tremble as my orgasm tears through me. He finally lets up and crawls over my spent body, nestling his hard cock between my legs.

His hand reaches for my face, brushing my hair behind my ear. "Feel good?"

"I think you know the answer to that." I cup his cheek, bringing his mouth to mine. He laughs then smiles into the kiss, and it might be the sweetest thing I've ever seen. "And by the looks of it, you enjoyed yourself too."

"I did. You taste like heaven."

"I guess I should find out if you taste just as good."

"As you wish," he says, moving beside me to his knees, stroking his cock as I open for him. "Stick out your tongue and put my cock in your mouth."

Holden inches forward, tapping the tip of his thick erection against my tongue and I don't hesitate, sucking on his crown before I take him as far as I can to the back of my throat. He groans as his head falls back, holding the base of his cock in his hand. "Dammit, Bee. Your mouth is perfect."

I pop off him, wrapping my hand around the base and stroking him. "This isn't easy. You're big." I take him in my mouth again.

"I'll like whatever your mouth does to my cock. You're sucking me so good."

He pulls out then slides himself back in, fucking my face in long, even strokes. Holden is large. It's the width just as much as the length. Thick and veiny, with tight, full balls.

I watch him, his eyes pinned to my lips where my mouth is full of his length. I massage his balls, trying to make him lose his mind, and when I get him close, he pulls out.

"Feel good?" I ask, with a smug smirk on my face.

He laughs. "You know the answer to that. I liked it as much as you liked it when I went down on you and feasted on your pretty pussy."

"So sure of yourself," I say, stretching my arms above my head.

"I am. Now, do you want to come on my cock, pretty girl?"

I smirk. "I thought you were never going to ask."

TEN

EYES ON MINE, PRETTY GIRL

Holden

I have never been as hyped-up in my damn life as I am right now, kneeling between Briar's parted thighs, her naked body spread over my bed, waiting for me to fuck her.

Briar is fucking perfect. Her tits, two perfect handfuls with pale pink nipples that are already hard and her hips, the perfect curve of smooth, bronze skin. My eyes roam over every inch of her, memorizing her body as my cock throbs in my hand.

There is no way I will be able to fuck Briar once and get her out of my system; I know that now. That makes this dangerous. But fuck me, I can't stop.

I lost control of this the minute Briar stepped out of the bedroom in that fuchsia pink minidress and those three-inch heels, her hair cascading over her delicate shoulders. She managed to throw my world off its axis in less than 30 seconds. Game over. I didn't stand a chance.

She moans when I slide my dick over her clit. "Holden, please start doing what you promised me you would."

"I always keep my promises, babe. But let me play first." I tease her opening again with the head of my cock.

"Holden!" she answers immediately.

"I love it when you scream my name."

"I'd like to be screaming your name while your dick is inside me."

I laugh at that. "Your impatience is so fucking hot."

She reaches between her legs for my cock.

"You sure, Bee, that you want this?"

"I swear, Holden, if you don't stop talking and start fucking me, we're going to have a problem."

I smirk. "I think someone needs my cock. Luckily, I need to fuck you just as badly."

Briar's eyes focus on my erection, so I give it a tug, fisting my shaft. "You're huge, Holden. I'm scared you're not going to fit."

"We'll make it fit. I'll go slow," I say, reaching for the nightstand to dig out a condom. Once I'm suited up, I settle into the V of her hips, my hands bracing her thighs.

I line the head of my cock up with her drenched entrance, toying with her at first before slowly pushing inside.

She's so damn tight.

And hot.

I'm never going to last once I'm buried deep inside her body. I lean forward on my palms over her as I push a little further, until I'm about halfway in, pressing an open-mouth kiss to her lips.

What's better? Tasting every inch of her body and feeling her come on my tongue? Or sinking into her tight, wet heat? I can't decide. One thing I know for sure is I want to make her come again, which is what I plan on doing next.

I close my eyes, gritting my teeth as I try to control

myself. I pray I don't bust my nut the second I'm all the way in because she feels better than anything I've ever experienced. It's not easy. She fits me like she was made for me.

It's so tempting to fuck her into this mattress until she's chanting my name, but I restrain myself. I'm not sure what I thought she would feel like, but I know it wasn't anywhere close to this.

"I'm going to go a little deeper, Bee. Can you handle it?"

She mewls. It's the sweetest sound. Her lips part and her eyes flutter closed. "Yes, like that, yes."

"Eyes on mine, pretty girl. I want you to remember who's fucking you."

Her hands splay on either side of my jaw, pulling my face towards her so she can kiss me. I groan against her lips when I'm filling her completely. I nearly come on the spot, balls drawing up into my body, cock throbbing.

My pulse strums a steady beat under my skin as I begin to pump my hips and thrust my length inside her body. My pelvis pushes against her pelvis. My balls tighten, wanting to release.

"Look at you taking me so good, baby, clenching my cock like a vice."

Her eyes are pointed to where we're joined, watching my shaft slide in and out of her. "Look at us, Bee. It's fucking perfect. You look so hot taking my dick like a good girl. Look at how drenched you are for me."

"So good. So, so good," she says, her fingernails scraping down my shoulders as I move my hips.

"We fit perfectly together. So fucking perfect."

I probably shouldn't have admitted that, but I'm not thinking straight. I can't think at all. It's quite possible my brain exploded as soon as I felt her walls tighten around my cock.

Briar tilts her hips until I'm hitting the right spot, and I know she's close. I'm on the verge too so I slow my pace a little trying to hold on to my last shreds of control. It's almost too much, trying to hold off my impending orgasm. And when she reaches between her thighs and massages my balls, I almost shoot like a rocket. I'm a ball man, I love when they're played with.

Go slow, take your time, I tell myself in my head, wanting to draw this out as long as I can.

If I can only have her one time in my life, I want to make sure neither of us ever forget it. I want to ruin her for all guys after me. The same way all women will be ruined for me.

I regain my composure and begin to rock my hips into her, reaching down between her legs and swirling my thumb over her clit. Her inner walls clench around my cock, and the feeling of it ignites a spark in my body. Her breath hitches and her body tenses. She's right there on the edge. She just needs a little more.

"Hold on, beautiful. I'm going to make you see stars."

With short, quick movements, I glide in and out of her tight body until the pleasure is so great, I'm biting the inside of my cheek so I don't come like a teenager. Her body shudders as she chants my name over and over, as she soars over the edge, riding out her release. It's the most beautiful thing I've ever seen.

It's only when her wet, tight channel is squeezing the life out of my cock, that I come with a moan and pour into the condom, draining my balls. Every muscle is trembling through my release; it feels like I've left my body. It takes minutes for the aftershocks to subside, and when they do and my muscles relax, I collapse on top of her, and we both lie there until our breathing evens out.

Fuck. That was the most intense orgasm of my life.

We're both destroyed. I stay inside her as she clings to me, my face nuzzled in her neck. I can feel her heartbeat against mine as our chests heave, but we stay tangled together, neither one of us wanting to move.

I only pull out when I soften, rolling onto my back, taking her with me. I kiss the top of her head, and this time when my lips brush over her hair it feels sweet and gentle.

"Don't move. I'll be right back," I tell her, walking to the bathroom to get rid of the condom.

When I climb back in bed, I breathe a sigh of relief that she's still there. It makes no sense. I know that this isn't going anywhere. We're both too messed up from our pasts. Knowing that this is probably the only time I will be with her makes my heart clench. If only things were different.

I move her face into the crook of my neck and inhale her scent, then softly stroke her hair. Her naked body snuggles into my side.

"Briar," I murmur into her hair. "Do you think it's a bad idea if we fall asleep like this? Just tonight, and then tomorrow we can go back to normal."

"I think it's fine," she sighs into my chest. "I'm your fake girlfriend. You don't have to worry."

"Worry about what?"

"About falling in love. Catching feelings. You don't have to worry."

My stomach bottoms to the tips of my toes. I know what this is but damn if her words don't sting. Briar's hand rests on my chest as she exhales a long breath into my neck, and I tighten my arms around her.

And I fall asleep hungry for more.

I'M NOT SURPRISED WHEN I WAKE UP THE NEXT MORNING alone.

It's Sunday morning and the time on my phone reads 8:00 a.m. I don't remember her having to be anywhere today. I rub a hand over my face, wondering how she's feeling after last night. Does she have regrets? Is that why she slipped out of bed so early? Or maybe she was just trying to avoid the awkward morning-after-sex conversation.

Not much seems to ruffle Briar's feathers. But maybe a one-night stand is all it takes.

I smile, my mind filling with thoughts of Briar and visions of watching her come last night. Is she replaying the night in her mind like I am? Is she already considering a repeat because I know for damn sure I want more. Maybe I'll cook her dinner tonight and see where things could lead. I laugh to myself, realizing that I'm obsessing about Briar.

But we need to talk. If we're going to live together, we need to have an open and honest conversation about what happens next.

I had more fun last night than I've had in a very long time. Dinner with Briar was incredible. We laughed, we flirted; the chemistry between the two of us was electric. I was able to be myself around a woman and that is something I haven't felt in… forever.

Briar intrigues me. She caught my eye from the minute we met, and my fascination with the girl has only grown stronger. I don't know exactly what her ex-boyfriend did to her, but I know enough to know that he hurt her. Badly. And I can't understand how anyone could be a prick to one of the sweetest women I've ever met. The guy must be a giant asshole. He's lucky he lives in another country. If he shows up around here looking for her, the violence raging through my veins will not be able to be contained.

Being around Briar—her spontaneity and bubbly personality—makes me feel lighter. There are people who make you happy by simply being in their presence and she is that for me.

It terrifies me how badly I want a repeat of last night. My god, I've never had sex like that in my life. It was mind-shattering. Life-changing. I thought I had experienced great chemistry before, but nothing even comes close to how I felt with Briar last night.

My body craved her, *I* craved her. It wasn't even 10 minutes after pulling out of her that I wanted her again. After the first time, I was addicted. After three rounds, I was insatiable.

It hadn't been all that difficult for me to go an entire year without intimacy with another woman, but one night with Briar is all it took to make me want more.

Maybe she'd agree to one more time. Maybe she'd agree to more? If there is anyone who could bring me out of my celibacy for good, it's her. Fuck me, this girl has gotten to me. I can already tell I'm getting too attached to Briar and that is exactly what I promised myself I wouldn't do. There's no point letting this go any further when I know there's no hope for a future.

Why am I such a disaster when it comes to relationships? I let out a frustrated groan before dragging myself out of bed, brushing my teeth and throwing on a pair of shorts.

Maybe a cup of coffee will help me see things clearer. I tell myself it doesn't matter if Briar is here or not, but when I step into the kitchen and see her sitting at the bar sipping a cup of tea, I instantly smile.

Her hair is a blonde, wild mess on top of her head and she's wearing my T-shirt slung over her tiny frame. She startles when she notices me, and Bear, who had been sitting on her lap, leaps out of her arms and onto the floor.

"Oh no! I'm sorry!" She springs from her stool, chasing Bear into the living room.

I lean against the counter and watch as she tries to wrangle the cat into her arms. When she finally gets a hold of her, she strokes the thing behind its ears then presses a kiss to the top of its head. "I'm sorry, Holden," she says, grimacing. "I didn't mean for that to happen."

I press my lips together, preparing for the sneeze that I already feel coming my way.

"Oh god, you're mad. I'm sorry. It won't happen again."

"I'm not mad." I hold up a hand as the sneeze finally barrels out of me.

"You're sneezing again. And your eyes are red. Holden, are you okay?"

She crosses the room to where I'm standing, Bear still in her arms. When she's a few inches away, I sneeze again.

"I'm fine." Or I will be once I take my allergy meds. And once she gets that damn cat away from me.

Briar looks from the cat to me, her eyes widening. "Holden Banks, are you allergic to Bear?"

I bite my lip. "Maybe."

Briar's jaw drops. "What!" She playfully taps my chest. "Why on earth would you allow me to move in with you if you're allergic to cats?"

I shrug, opening the cupboard and reaching for my Claritin. "You needed a place to stay."

"Have you been taking medication this entire time?" I shrug again. "You have got to be kidding me."

"This is why I didn't tell you," I say, filling a glass from the tap and swallowing the tiny pill. "I knew you'd make a bigger deal out of it than what it is."

"A bigger deal? Holden, you have been drugging yourself so I can live with you. It's a big deal."

"A little dramatic, don't you think?" She's so fucking cute. "Not even a little."

I raise my hand, holding my index finger an inch from my thumb. "Just a little."

Briar hands me a plate heaped with powdered sugar-topped French toast and bacon. "I made you this. I'm going to put Bear back in my bedroom before you drop dead from anaphylactic shock."

I roll my eyes as I watch her walk away, then turn my attention to the gigantic mess she's made in my kitchen. As usual, it's like she took a wrecking ball to the place. But on the other hand, she took the time to make me breakfast. A breakfast she won't eat. She's always busy doing nice things for the people in her life, including me. Busy Bee. The nickname suits her. And if you ask me, I think it's growing on her.

A few minutes later, she returns to the kitchen but stops near the doorway. I feel her eyes on me as I eat breakfast.

I look up from my phone and catch her staring, then raise my eyebrows at her. "Do you want me to put on a shirt, Bee?"

"You know, not everyone likes guys who are all muscle-y."

"But you do," I say with a smirk.

"I'm never looking at your muscles again," she huffs.

She takes the seat next to me, looking over my shoulder when I laugh at something on my phone. "What's so funny?"

"It's just my mom," I explain. "She's obsessed with Reddit. She's constantly sending me the weirdest shit."

"What? Show me."

She leans towards me, and I am suddenly hyper-aware of the place where her arm presses against mine. I clear my throat.

I tilt my screen to show her the post my mom sent me. It's a picture of a middle-aged woman doing a deep lunge in a sequin bodysuit, along with the caption, "Dance like the rest of the world can fuck right off."

Briar coughs out a laugh. "I don't know your mom, but I like her already."

"She sends me this stuff every single day," I tell her, shaking my head. "But yeah, she's pretty great."

Briar smiles, but it doesn't quite reach her eyes. She dips the teabag in and out of her mug, not looking at me. She seems nervous, and I can't help but wonder if she's regretting what happened between us last night.

Shit.

"So, we should probably talk." I swallow. "I haven't had a woman in my bed in a year."

"Since Aubrey."

I nod and inhale deeply. "Yes."

"What happened between you two?"

"It's a long story."

"We have all morning."

Briar watches me, waiting for my response.

I sigh. "She wanted to get married and have kids."

She arches her eyebrows. "And you didn't?"

"No."

"So, what happened?"

"Eventually, I ended things. She felt like I strung her along, wasted her time. I didn't mean to, but I hurt her."

"And you haven't dated since then?"

"No."

"Why not? People break up all the time, but they don't usually swear off dating because of it."

I consider this. I've never really talked to anyone about this, not even the guys. But for some reason, I want to be totally honest with Briar.

"I can't give a woman what she wants. Most want a ring, and a house with a white picket fence and kids. And I don't. That kind of makes me undatable."

As soon as the words leave my mouth, I want to take them all back. I want to tell her I could try for her. I want to tell her that I've never felt sparks the way I do when I kiss her. That my house has never felt more like a home than it has this past week. Even with all her mess, the brightly colored pillows, the blanket I don't need, the plants that I know will be dead as soon as she moves out. I want to tell her that I like having her here with me. That I like *her*.

But despite these feelings, deep down I'm still the same guy I always have been. In the end, I would still let her down. So, I stay silent, waiting for Briar to say something.

"Maybe if you found the right person, you'd change your mind," she says gently. "Love has a way of making you do crazy things."

I let her words sink in. There's something about the way Briar makes me feel that has me hoping that I won't be alone forever. Maybe I could make someone happy one day. That's a thought I haven't let myself believe in a long time.

"Maybe." I let out a deep breath, feeling like I'm having a hard time trying to explain myself. "It's just... look at my parents. They got married and had two kids only to decide they didn't want to be married to each other. What was the point? Over 50 percent of relationships end in divorce."

"And some don't. There's always a chance you'll find the one and live happily ever after."

"You never know. Maybe I'll change my mind."

"I hope you do," she says.

"But I'm pretty positive that I don't want kids."

Before I can say anything more, Briar takes a deep breath, like she's gathering her courage. "Holden, listen," she says, twisting her hands in her lap. "I had a great night with you last night, but it can't happen again. We're roommates. We have the same friends now. I'm not looking to date someone. When I'm ready, I want to... find my person, you know? Get married and start a family. I want everything you don't."

The muscle in my jaw flexes as my chest aches a little in my chest. This is the way it has to be. The only way. Hell, I knew this before I kissed her in the kitchen last night. She's right. It's better to end it here before we ruin a friendship, before we ruin the dynamics of our entire friend group.

"We're still friends, right? And I'll still be your fake girlfriend, but I don't think it's smart for us to fool around. We'll have to be somewhat affectionate in public, but when we're at home, we need to keep some distance."

I nod, even though my stomach is in knots and I'm not totally sure what she said. I spaced out after she told me last night could never happen again.

"Good." She wraps an arm around my back and drops her head on my shoulder, signalling that the awkward conversation is now done.

"I'm going to go take a shower," she says, stifling a yawn as she slides off her chair. "I need to wake up."

I nod and watch her walk out of the room. We were up for hours last night. I think we're both feeling pretty tired. I scrub both hands over my face. This is such a mess. I never should have had sex with Briar. How did I think I could be intimate with her and then just go back to living together as roommates and nothing more?

The ache in my chest doubles in intensity as I walk to the front door and lace up my sneakers to go for a run. I desperately need to put some distance between me and Briar.

ELEVEN

I GUESS WE WERE THAT OBVIOUS

Briar

I screwed up.

Why did I sleep with Holden?

That is the question that has been running through my head on repeat since I woke up in Holden's bed this morning.

He was still asleep when I slipped out from under the covers and crept to the kitchen. I made a cup of tea, but it didn't help keep my mind from replaying the mind-blowing sex I had with Holden last night. Needing a distraction, I decided to make breakfast and was just finishing up with the French toast and bacon when Holden finally appeared in the doorway, shirtless and with the sexiest case of bedhead I've ever seen.

I wanted to let breakfast get cold, to walk him right back into the bedroom and go for a round four. *Oh my god.* Did we really have sex three times? And the craziest part was that he was somehow able to bring me to orgasm three times too.

The barista at Dream Bean, my usual weekend spot,

calls out my order, bringing me back to the present. Grabbing my green tea lemonade, I head outside in the direction of the beach. I need to clear my head, and I'm hoping a walk and the ocean air will do the trick.

I've gotten all of 10 steps when I hear my name. I wince when I see Daisy and Everly headed towards me. Any other day I would be thrilled to see them, but I'm certainly not in the right frame of mind to talk to anyone after the morning I've had. But there's no point trying to avoid them now, so I do my best to put a smile on my face and fake it.

"Hey, Briar. Long time no see," Everly jokes as Daisy wraps her arms around me in a tight hug.

I laugh when she plants a kiss on my cheek. "What are you two up to?"

"You would know if you looked at your phone. I texted you twice." Daisy keeps her pointed gaze on me. "So, how did last night go?"

"What do you mean?" I ask, hoping I sound more innocent than I feel. Did she notice Holden and I flirting last night? Would Holden have told Tucker what happened when we got home? *Oh god.* Does she know that I had sex with her husband's best friend? Would she care?

"You were looking pretty close with Holden last night."

I guess we were *that* obvious. I shouldn't be surprised that our friends are talking about it. Trying my best to look unaffected by her comment, I lift a shoulder. "We both probably drank a little too much. I think we all did."

"Are you as hungover as I am?" Everly asks, and I mentally thank her for redirecting the conversation.

"I've definitely felt better."

"Me too," Everly says. "It was a rough morning so when Jake offered to stay home with the kids so I could grab a coffee with Daisy, I didn't argue. I might need two cups."

"Can you join us?" Daisy asks.

"I would love to, but I'm exhausted. I'm going to go home and have a nap."

"With Holden?" Daisy raises her eyebrows.

"No, not with Holden. Sorry to disappoint."

"The only one who should be disappointed is you," Daisy teases. "You should be hitting that."

I shake my head at my best friend. "Not dating, remember? Neither is he."

I haven't seen or spoken to Holden since I left him in the kitchen this morning. When I finished getting ready after my shower, he was gone. It's not like we had anything to talk about. We had already said everything that needed to be said, but still the conversation felt so awkward. And then to find out he was just... gone, it kind of stung.

"Mmm hmm," Daisy says with a twinkle in her eye before Everly interjects, saving me yet again. "I'm actually happy that I ran into you today, Briar. I wanted to welcome you to Haven Harbor by having you and Holden for dinner, and Daisy and Tucker and Sierra and Gray too. I was thinking maybe next weekend if you're free?"

A bead of sweat trickles down my spine. Summer this year in Reed Point has been suffocating. For nearly two weeks, the temperature has hit record levels. So hot that if you walked barefoot on the concrete, you'd get third degree burns. But it's possible I'm in a sweat for a different reason.

I'm not sure having dinner with Holden at Jake and Everly's is a good idea. Distance seems like the better choice. Then I remember that I already agreed to go to his parents' house tomorrow night. *Shit.* The universe is clearly testing me.

Rather than say no to Everly and run the risk of

appearing rude, I say, "That sounds lovely. I'll talk to Holden and see if he's free and get back to you."

"You two haven't synched your calendars yet?" Daisy asks.

I roll my eyes. She is not going to let up on this.

WHEN I ARRIVE BACK AT THE HOUSE, THE PLACE IS DARK, AND Holden is nowhere to be seen. I kick off my shoes and drop my bag by the door, then go up the stairs to see how Bear is doing. The door to Holden's room is open, so I peek inside, but there's no sign of him there either.

Heading to the spare room, I flick on the light to find the most beautiful bedroom I've ever seen. There is a queen size bed with a light gray fabric headboard and white comforter in the center of the room. It's covered with pillows in grays and soft pinks with crisp white bedsheets tucked neatly into the bed frame. There's a pretty white nightstand with a lamp on the far side and a matching dresser against the wall. Bear is curled up in the center of the bed and all I want to do is curl up beside her and never leave.

The room is a dream. And Holden put this all together for me.

The poor guy was probably suffering from having to be in the same room as my cat for a few hours, but knowing Holden the way I do now, that wouldn't have stopped him. He is thoughtful and kind and puts others before himself. Someone who likes to make the people he cares about happy. And I love that about him.

I feel tears prick at my eyes as I sit down and sink into the bedding. Justin never cared about me. He never cared enough to even ask me how my day was, never mind doing something like this. He gave me nothing while he took everything from me over the years. It took me a long time to see that, but now it's crystal clear. My friendship with Holden makes me feel cared for and appreciated. He makes me feel comfortable and safe enough to share how I really feel. My heart nearly explodes when I lie in this gorgeous new room... or at least it feels that way from the fullness in my chest. Holden didn't need to do any of this—just letting me stay at his house was generous enough; even if he'd just given me the couch to crash on, I would have been grateful. But he did all of this to make me feel at home, and it's the most thoughtful thing any man has ever done for me.

I'm not used to people doing nice things for me, and I don't quite know how to process it. Justin really messed me up, and I wish I was able to just get past it. I cared about him, and he hurt me in the worst way. For a long time, I've wondered if I'd ever really be able to trust a man again.

Sitting up against the pillows with Bear in my lap, I send Holden a text to thank him.

> Briar: My new room is beautiful, Holden. I feel terrible I wasn't around to help you.

I wait a few minutes and there's no response, so I change into my pajamas and get ready for bed. As I climb under the crisp new sheet, a notification from Holden pops up on my screen and I swipe the device to life.

> Holden: Don't feel bad. It didn't take me long to put it together.

> Briar: Thank you for being so generous. I hope Bear didn't give you too much trouble.

> Holden: You don't need to thank me. You do need to have a talk with your cat though. I think she hates me.

> Briar: Bear doesn't hate anyone. Give her time to warm up to you.

I stare at the screen, wanting to know where he is and what he's doing on a Saturday night. Since I moved in, we've gone to bed every night together and something about being here without him feels different... and wrong.

I set my phone to do not disturb, double check my alarm for tomorrow, and then sink into the most comfortable bed I've ever slept in. Pulling the soft sheets up to my chin, I breathe in their fresh laundry scent, which makes me realize that Holden must have washed everything before he made my bed. For some reason, that makes my heart swell a little bit more.

I'm exhausted, but I find myself lying wide awake, thoughts of Holden running through my head.

Stop thinking about Holden, stop thinking about Holden, stop thinking about Holden.

As I finally feel myself start to settle into sleep, another thought crosses my mind: I love my new bed, but it's not Holden's and that fact makes me incredibly sad.

"YOU REALLY DON'T HAVE TO DO THIS," HOLDEN TELLS ME again as he opens the passenger door of his truck, and I slide onto the leather seat.

"Are you kidding? After what you've told me about your parents so far, I wouldn't miss it for the world," I insist. "Besides, I plan on getting the dirt on you. You know, childhood photo albums, most embarrassing teenager moments. All the good stuff."

We're going to his parents' house for dinner like I promised. If we're going to sell the whole fake girlfriend thing at the wedding, we need to start now. And I actually am looking forward to it. Holden talks so highly of his mom and dad that I can't wait to meet them. I'm also looking forward to meeting Barb, his mom's wife.

But if I'm honest with myself, I'm most excited to be spending time with Holden, who I haven't seen or talked to since our talk yesterday morning.

I missed our morning chat over breakfast today. I missed dinner around the coffee table last night. And I missed falling asleep in his bed listening to the soft sounds of his breathing. I realize it has only been a day and a half, but I'm pretty sure he has been avoiding me. And the truth is, I hate it. I've missed him. I miss being with him, talking to him, riling him up. I've missed the way I feel, the tingle on my skin, whenever he's around. But I like him so much that I'm not prepared to let casual sex ruin our friendship.

"Not even a little bit nervous?" Holden asks, putting on his seatbelt. I glance at his profile, noticing the way his back is rigid, the tick in his jaw. He's trying to act like everything is fine, but it's not; something is definitely off. I wonder if it has anything to do with our talk yesterday or it's something else. Did I hurt him when I said I wasn't looking for anything long-term? But Holden isn't looking for a relationship either. Having sex was a random, impulsive decision after we both had a few too many drinks. He agreed with me that it shouldn't happen again so there's no reason why that would upset him.

Why does everything have to be so complicated? I hate that being hurt by our exes has affected us both.

"Why would I be nervous?" I ask.

"I don't know."

"Meeting new people is fun. I like learning about other people's lives. It can bring new perspectives and teach you new things. And they made *you*, so they must be cool," I tell him. All of that is true, but there is part of me that feels bad about the way I'm meeting his family. Holden and I are lying to them, and deep down that feels wrong.

Holden is quiet as he starts his F-150, then backs his truck out of the driveway.

"Holden, are you okay?"

"I'm fine. Why wouldn't I be okay?"

"You just seem quiet. It feels like there's distance between us. We're friends. If there is something wrong, I hope you would tell me."

I really wish he would tell me what is bothering him. We were doing so well—getting along, having fun—and now it feels like we're back to square one.

I take a breath when he doesn't respond right away. He has that frown again across his face, the one that he had when I first moved in with him, and I wish I could kiss it away.

"There's nothing to tell you."

There is definitely something on his mind, but I feel like I already know him well enough to know not to push him. Especially right before dinner at his parents' place.

I *am* wondering how the heck we're supposed to fake being in a relationship in front of his family when he's barely speaking to me. But there isn't time to figure that out, because 5 minutes later we're pulling up in front of his mom's house.

Donna and Barb live in a small, cream-colored house in one of Reed Point's older neighborhoods. The grass is perfectly green, which is impressive considering the heat wave we've been having, and there are two pots on either side of the front door overflowing with purple and pink flowers.

Holden opens my door and offers me a hand out of his truck. Apparently even when he is actively avoiding me, he's still a perfect gentleman.

When we get to the doorstep, Holden rings the bell and I can hear the voices inside getting louder as someone approaches the door. A moment later, a woman with Holden's deep green eyes and smile greets us.

"Hi baby, I'm so glad you could come!" She hugs her son tightly, then quickly turns her attention to me. "And you must be Briar. I'm Donna, Holden's mom. He told me you are beautiful, but I wasn't expecting drop-dead gorgeous. Barbie, you need to see Briar."

He told his mom that he thinks I'm beautiful? He talked to her about me?

I am still wrapping my head around this when Barb appears in the foyer and pulls Holden into a hug before turning to me. She clasps my hand in both of hers as she introduces herself, a wide smile on her face. Soon we're being ushered into the air-conditioned living room where his dad is waiting for us.

"Look at her! So pretty. Isn't she beautiful?" Donna says to Holden.

"She is." Holden's eyes lock on mine. A shiver skates over my skin. All I have to do is look at Holden and my body reacts in some sort of primal way.

"Holden, my boy," his dad says, giving his son a bro-hug before looking at me with kind eyes. "I'm David, Holden's dad, it's nice to meet you. Holden tells us you're from Canada?"

"I am. Born and raised in British Columbia, about 45 minutes outside of Vancouver," I tell them, taking a seat on the couch next to Holden. "It's beautiful, especially if you like the mountains and the ocean."

"I've heard it's just gorgeous," Barb gushes. "Is your family still up there?"

"My mom and my brother are. My stepdad passed away recently."

"Oh, sweetheart. I'm sorry," his mom says, concern clouding her expression.

"Thank you," I smile softly. "We're all doing a lot better now."

"That's good to hear. So, tell us a little about yourself, Briar. We would love to get to know you better."

"Oh gosh. Well, I work for Rossi Cheese as their senior director of sales and marketing," I begin.

"Do you like it?" his dad asks, taking a seat across from me in an armchair. Donna and Barb are both sitting on a loveseat to my left.

"I do. I love my job. I have a great team, and I find it chal-lenging."

"That's wonderful. It's a lucky thing when you love your work. And what about in your spare time? What do you enjoy doing?" his mom asks, pushing her dark brown hair behind her ear.

"Well, when I'm not working, I like to read. I also love interior design. I actually just rented a new apartment, so I was really looking forward to picking out furniture and décor, but—"

"Holden told us about the flood," his mom interjects. "How awful. But I think it's wonderful that it worked out having you move in with him for the time being. And it's so beautiful on Haven Harbor. You must be really enjoying it."

I place my hand on Holden's knee like a girlfriend would do. "It's beautiful. I'm going to miss living across the street from the ocean. I'll miss Holden making me tea every night before bed too."

Donna smiles, turning her attention to her son. The way she looks at him makes it clear how much she loves him. You can see how proud she is of him.

I wonder if she is noticing how quiet Holden has been since we arrived. He's avoiding eye contact, letting me do most of the talking. His mind just seems somewhere else entirely. If his mom does notice, she doesn't say anything to him about it.

"Oh! I'm being a terrible hostess. I was so excited to meet you, Briar, that I forgot all about the drinks. I made us all Barbie Breezers! I hope you're a drinker, honey," she says to me. "We like our cocktails in this house."

My fake boyfriend shakes his head and smiles as his mom leaves the room, returning a few minutes later with a tray full of bubble-gum pink drinks with lemon slices decorating the rims.

"I've never had a Barbie Breezer, but they look delicious," I say, leaning forward to take the cocktail from Donna. "Thank you."

The five of us sit in the living room and talk. His parents ask Holden about work, ask about his friends, about what he's been up to lately. The conversation between them all is easy and relaxed. I like seeing Holden in this setting, with the family who know him best.

Eventually we sit down for dinner, passing around platters filled with roasted chicken, glazed carrots and roasted potatoes. Holden's dad offers up a toast to welcome me, his son's new girlfriend, which I immediately feel guilty about. I already like his family so much, and I hate that I'm lying to them like this.

As we dig in, Donna gives Holden a play-by-play of their recent trip to New York. "I just love that city," she gushes. "The food, the people, the shows. There's just so much going on. Me and Barbie went to see *Wicked*. Holden, I think you would have loved it. Your dad didn't want to come see that one, but we did drag him up to the top of the Empire State Building."

Holden pauses, fork halfway to his mouth. "Wait... Dad went too?"

"Well, sure. I thought I told you he was coming with us? It was his first time to the Big Apple, can you believe that? The three of us had the best time."

"Great trip," David says, nodding in agreement. "It's a world away from Reed Point, that's for sure. I slept for 10 hours when we got back home, it was nonstop."

I stifle a grin, popping a bite of carrot in my mouth, then steal a sideways glance at Holden in time to see him shaking his head.

"Dinner is incredible," I say, rescuing him from having to hear any more details of his parents' getaway. "You need to tell me how you made this chicken, mine never turns out this good."

"I can do that, honey. Thank goodness Holden mentioned you don't eat pork. I was planning on making my mother's pork tenderloin recipe."

I turn to look at Holden. He remembered. Once again, he was looking out for me. I don't know if I'll ever get used to that. He clears his throat, knocking me from my thoughts before I get too emotional at the table.

"Well, I appreciate you going out of your way for me."

"I hope you saved room for cherry pie," Barb says. "Donna's secret recipe, you don't want to miss it."

"Wait until you taste it," Holden's dad adds. "Donna knows how to bake her way around a kitchen. You should have seen the elaborate cakes she would make for the kids' birthdays."

It's clear how much all three of them love Holden. I can't help but compare his relationship with his parents to mine. My mom and my stepdad have always accepted me and supported me, but I think when you have a parent who didn't love you enough to stick around, there's a part of you that always feels like you aren't enough. Don't get me wrong, I've ever let my dad disappearing from my life keep me up at night, but it's times like these that I can't help but feel a little out of place.

By the end of the evening, I'm feeling very full and very happy that I decided to accept the invite for dinner. It's been great meeting Holden's family, and after tonight I feel like I know him a little bit better.

As Holden says goodbye to his dad, Barb and Donna manage to corner me in the hallway. "We're so happy we got to meet you, Briar," Donna gushes sweetly. "It's obvious how much Holden cares about you."

"I care about him too," I say truthfully. "He is one of the sweetest people I've ever met."

"That's our Holden. When he was a little boy, he used to bake cookies with me, help me with the gardening. He was always wanting to help out. At school, anytime a kid was picking on one of the quieter ones, Holden would give them hell." Donna beams. "He's always had the biggest heart. To this day, he tells me he loves me before he hangs up the phone."

I listen intently, heart fluttering in my chest. Hearing this just confirms what I already know: Holden is the best kind of person.

As if on cue, he appears in the hallway, smiling when he finds me there with his mom and stepmom. He kisses the side of my face in a perfect display of affection.

"Ready to go?" he asks. He stretches his arms over his head, causing his shirt to rise just enough to show off a sliver of his toned stomach. Holden is breathtakingly gorgeous. I force myself to avert my eyes. As much as I'd like to soak him in, it will only make me want him more and that is dangerous for my heart.

I thank Donna and Barb for having me, say my goodbyes to them all and then head out to the truck with Holden holding my hand.

We drive back to the house in silence. I was looking forward to chatting about the evening with him, to telling him how much I loved meeting his family, but Holden is withdrawn again. The familiar frown is back. His eyes are straight ahead, his hands gripping the wheel tightly.

I look out the window, remembering just a couple of nights ago, when he asked me if it was okay that we fall asleep in one another's arms. Remembering how sweet he can be. Remembering what it felt like to curl up against him.

Letting myself fall for Holden isn't an option. I know how that would end: we would date for a little while until I decide I need something more serious, and then he would bail. I can't risk that after how badly Justin hurt me.

When Holden and I get home, he makes a right to go to his bedroom and I make a left to go to mine, where I get ready for bed and look forward to sleep.

It seems like it's the only time I stop thinking about him.

TWELVE

JUMPING THE GUN

Holden

I don't usually jerk off in the shower to thoughts of a woman when she's right across the hall, but I've been hiding out in my bedroom, and I need to release some sexual tension. It's not the first time I've come with my own hand thinking about Briar and I'm sure it won't be the last. For some reason I can't stop obsessing over her. There's something about her that makes me want more. I want to be around her all the time, I want her attention on me. When she looks at me with her emerald-green eyes, even from across the room, I can feel it like a heat across my skin.

I want her. That's exactly why I've stayed away from her. It hasn't been easy though. It's taken every ounce of my strength to not be near her. Not to kiss her senseless or pick her up and carry her to my bed and strip her bare and make her feel good. Briar deserves to feel good. She deserves to be worshipped, and I wish I was the guy who got to do that.

Fuck. I grip my aching cock in frustration. I need to get off. I need to take the edge off. I need more than a hallway separating Briar and me. I need a whole damn city between us.

I want to tell her that I've never thought about a woman more than I have thought about her. That I've never slept more peacefully than I did that week she slept in my bed. I want to tell her that I like making her tea and I look forward to getting up in the mornings knowing that I get to have breakfast with her.

Only I can't tell her any of those things because she doesn't see me the same way that I see her. So instead, I've kept a distance. It's better this way. It won't hurt as much when she moves out and I watch her walk away.

For the next couple of months, I'll try my best to avoid her even though that will be next to impossible considering we live together. But that's my own fault for sleeping with Briar. Sex with my roommate was a bad idea; it's a line I should have been smart enough not to cross.

My brain shuts off when my balls begin to ache. I feel like I've never needed a release so much in my life.

"Jesus." My cock throbs, blood rushing to my groin. I keep stroking as it hardens and lengthens while the hot spray of water from the shower flows down my back. I keep jerking my dick in my hand, feeling it plumping while I imagine Briar in those short shorts that she wears around the house. My dick throbs and the base of my spine tingles when visions of her tits fill my mind... the elegant column of her throat when I sucked on her neck and the curve of her hips that are almost as perfect as her ass.

My god, yes. Fuck, it feels good. I needed this.

Pleasure coils its way up my spine as I tighten my grip, increasing my pace. Pictures of Briar in my bed; her smile, the way her teeth nibble on her bottom lip when she's unsure or nervous, the way her stomach muscles flexed and relaxed when I was deep inside her.

My hand moves faster, my whole body beginning to tremble when my orgasm teases me, threatening to take me over the edge.

I feel guilty for a split second that I'm imagining Briar while I jerk my cock, but not enough to stop. I think about how tight and wet she felt when I was deep inside her, hand running over the length of me from root to tip before I focus on the head, twisting and tugging.

"Briar..." I grit out her name when my balls begin to draw up and my vision goes black and I see stars, my orgasm barreling into me at full speed as I shoot my load all over the tile wall.

I try to catch my breath, my forehead dropping to the tile. *Get your shit together, Holden*, I tell myself, turning around so the spray of water hits the front of me. I squirt some body wash into my hand to clean the jizz off my body then clean the tile wall before turning off the water and drying myself with a towel.

As good as the release felt, when I slip into bed a few minutes later, my mind is still on Briar. I hate that she's just across the hall from me, but I can't touch her. She's so close but so far away.

Dammit, I must be superhuman for not walking out of this room and down the hall to her bedroom and telling her everything she needs to hear before I strip her out of her clothes.

I groan. That would only ruin things between us. She doesn't want me the way I want her. Some idiot fucked her up so badly that she thinks all guys will hurt her. And maybe she's not wrong. I wish I could give her everything she wants, but we both know I'm just as messed up as her.

I've spent years building walls around my heart to keep everyone out... until Briar walked into my life with a sledge-hammer. Despite the intense need I feel to be close to her, I have to accept that I can't be the guy for her.

I'll have to settle for being her friend, and her fake boyfriend. But part of me knows that will never be enough.

I WALK ACROSS THE LAWN TO JAKE'S PLACE, RELIEVED FOR THE excuse to get out of the house. It's been five days since Briar and I had dinner with my parents. One week since we spent the night together. Things between us are as tense as ever.

So, when Jake texted to say that Everly was taking the kids to her parents' place and he was hosting a guys' night, I jumped at the invite. My alternate plan for the evening was to stay in my room and avoid Bee, so the text came at the perfect time.

She was reading one of her romance books at the break-fast bar in the kitchen when I left the house. She looked up as I walked by and smiled, and I did my usual head nod before heading out the front door. That seems to be the only way we communicate these days.

How long can we keep doing this? It's already uncom-fortable when our paths cross at the house, what will it feel like after another few weeks? Or at Amy's wedding, where we're supposed to be pretending to be a couple? What was I thinking having sex with the girl I'm sharing my home with? The knot in my chest tightens thinking about the space I've intentionally put between us. But there isn't another option. It's what I need to do.

Grayson and Tucker are already at Jake's, and I find the three of them sitting on the porch with beers in their hands.

"Hey, man." Jake stands and drags a chair from across the porch to where the guys are sitting. "Have a seat, I'll get you a beer."

I take a seat, nodding at Jake when he hands me a Miller Lite from the cooler. "Thanks, man."

"Welcome. How's it going?"

"All good," I reply. Okay, so that's a lie, but I don't want to talk about it. "How are the kids?"

"Great, man. West is walking all over the place and he said Dad the other day. His first word. Everly was pissed." He chuckles before taking a swig of his beer. "And Birdie is the best big sister. She's always on the floor playing with him, making him laugh. She's such a good kid."

Jake beams. Who knew Jake Matthews—serious, grumpy Jake Matthews— would be so damn happy being a dad? Turns out he's a natural. No matter what day of the week it is, you'll always catch him outside on the front lawn running soccer drills with Birdie. He even stepped up as the assistant coach on her soccer team. And when he's not busy with Birdie, he's playing with West or rocking him to sleep.

"How are things going over at your house?" Tucker asks, leaning back in his chair and crossing one ankle over his knee.

"They're fine."

Tucker doesn't even bother to hide the smirk on his face. "Briar told Daisy that things are kind of tense between you two. What's up?"

There's no point in hiding it. I don't even have the energy to keep up the pretense. Obviously, Briar has said something to Daisy. How much? I'm not sure. The thing is, I want to be able to talk to my buddies, and I know I can trust them. Anything I tell them on this porch will go no further than the four of us.

"We hooked up." Might was well rip the Band-Aid right off.

"Would you like us to act surprised?" Jake asks, as the other two laugh.

"It only happened once. The next morning, I was ready to see where things could go between us... and then she shut me down, and we haven't talked much since."

"You've been avoiding one another?" Tuck asks.

"Basically."

"And how's that been going, seeing as you're both living in the same small house?"

"Fucking terrible," I admit.

"Okay, so what were her reasons for shutting things down?"

"Fuck if I know. I guess she's not into me."

"But you're into her?"

I scrub a hand over the scruff on my jaw. "I am. Fuck, I wish I wasn't, but I'm definitely attracted to her. But it's complicated. I mean, we live together, she's Daisy's best friend, she's getting over her dickhead ex-boyfriend who messed her up pretty bad. Plus, I swore to myself I wouldn't hookup after things went south with Aubrey. I'm trying to work on shit, get my head straight. The last thing I need is a relationship. I think I've proven that I'm shit at those." I think about the fights, the making up, how I pushed Aubrey away and how awful it was when we broke up. I don't have it in me to go through that again. "I think Briar and I are both messed up from past relationships."

"And you're not willing to just try with her?"

"I thought about it."

"And?" Grayson asks.

"Honestly, I worry I'd just fuck it up. Besides, she wants to get married. She wants kids. I'm not interested in any of that and she knows it." My jaw flexes. "I've never seen myself with a family."

"That's what he said." Tucker flicks a thumb at Jake.

"I know." I exhale, leaning back in my chair. "I'm not saying I won't change my mind one day, but I can't guarantee it, so what's the point in giving Bee the runaround?"

"Beeeeee," Tucker drags it out. "How sweet... you already have cute nicknames for one another."

"Fuck off."

"Look, I know you say you can't imagine having kids, but I think you're jumping the gun, here, Holdey," Grayson says. "Maybe you just haven't met the right girl, one you *can* imagine having a family with. I know you're great with Sadie."

"I'm co-signing this. You are great with my kids," Jake adds.

"Maybe you're right. I don't know..." I take a long pull of my beer. The truth is I'm not sure what I want anymore. Do I want kids? I can't picture it, but I know I want *something* with Briar.

"Have you at least told her that you like her?" Jake asks.

I swallow. "No."

"Why not?"

"I didn't get a chance. She told me the next morning that nothing more could happen between us. There wasn't much for me to say after that."

"Maybe, but I still think it wouldn't hurt if you told her how you feel. Let her decide if you're worth getting to know better. I've seen the way that girl looks at you. Hell, I've seen the way you look at her too. There is definitely something there. Last weekend at Catch 21, you two weren't exactly subtle. You may as well have pushed aside the nachos and fucked right there on the table," Grayson says as Tucker chuckles.

"Not sure what's so funny."

"Gray is funny as hell," Tucker laughs.

I roll my eyes.

"Listen," Jake says. "I'm not trying to push you. We can stop talking about this. I just want to make sure that you know how natural you are with kids. My two love it when you come over. Birdie tells me you make her laugh the most."

Grayson's hands go up in the air. "What the f—"

"Shut up, Gray," Jake cuts him off.

"I'm definitely funnier than Holden," Grayson argues.

"Not to Birdie, you aren't."

Grayson clutches his chest as if his heart is broken.

"I'm not saying you need to have kids of your own, but I hope you've really put some thought to it." Jake's hand claps my shoulder.

It's so damn good to have friends that I can talk to. It's a bonus that they live right next door. Jake was the last guy I thought would ever settle down and have a family. But it was so easy for him to connect with Everly's daughter, Birdie, then fall seamlessly into the role of being a husband and a dad.

He has a point—I love spending time with Birdie and West. I love spending time with Sadie. I may not be an official uncle, but that's what they call me and that's what I feel like to them. What is it about me that doesn't know if I'm cut out to have kids of my own?

I had a great childhood with two parents who loved me. They even handled their divorce in a way that made my brother and me realize at the time that it was the best decision for the family. I have only good memories of growing up. So, why can't I picture having a family?

I look out at the ocean across the street. The weather will begin to change soon, and we won't be able to sit outside like this in the evenings. By that time, Briar will have moved out and who knows how often I'll see her then. I do know that I'm going to miss having her around. I should probably stop avoiding her and start enjoying the time we have left together.

"I know you, Holden, and if you're here opening up to us about Briar, then you're already in deep," Grayson says. "You were celibate for way too fucking long before Briar. I'm surprised you even remembered how to use it. You're a good guy. It's time to find someone who will be there for you after a long day. Someone to spend your nights with. You won't find anyone sweeter than Briar. You can't avoid the girl forever. Might as well face up to it."

I take a deep breath and then exhale it out again.

"There's one thing I haven't told you yet," I say. "I'm bringing Briar as my date to Amy's wedding. She's pretending to be my girlfriend. All her idea, for the record."

Tucker almost spits out his beer. "You're shitting us, right?"

"I'm not." Now that I'm saying this all out loud, I'm not even sure it makes sense. "I already brought her to my mom's house for dinner. She met my mom, Barb, and my dad."

"As your fake girlfriend?" Tucker asks.

"Yup."

"Oh boy." Tucker barks out a laugh. "You're not just in deep, you're fucking drowning."

"Are you okay? Have you gone temporarily insane?" Grayson asks. "I really need some clarity here."

"The short version is that Briar found the invite before I did. When I explained to her that I didn't want to go because Amy is my ex, she offered to be my date... my fake girlfriend or whatever. At first, I told her absolutely not, but... she can be very persuasive, and she made it sound like fun."

Tucker studies me. Having been my roommate for years, he knows me the best out of the guys. "You didn't think it through at all when you agreed, did you?"

"No, not really." I shake my head. "Apparently, I can't say no when it comes to Briar."

"You mean Beeeee," Tucker smirks.

I flip him off.

"Should make for an interesting night." Jake takes a sip of his beer and then burst into laughter. "This is the fucking cherry on the sundae of my day."

I know they're right—this is a crazy plan, especially considering the fact that Briar and I are barely speaking to one another at the moment. But if I'm being honest with myself, I'm actually looking forward to the date. Fake or not, the thought of spending an evening with her sends a spark of electricity deep in my belly. I don't give a fuck what anyone else thinks. I'll be proud to walk into the wedding with Briar on my arm.

I'm grateful to the guys for hearing me out, but I've had enough of talking about my fucked up life, so I steer the conversation to easier topics. We drink a couple more beers as darkness falls, until Everly comes home with the kids. West is sound asleep in his car seat, so she says a quick hello and then heads inside to put him to bed. Birdie, on the other hand, is only too happy to position herself in the middle of the porch and tell us every detail of her visit with her grandparents. Eventually, Jake tells her it's time for bed and the rest of us take that as our cue to head home.

I push open the front door, hoping to find Briar still awake, but I'm disappointed when she's nowhere to be found. I quietly walk to my room, glancing at her closed bedroom door. I can't help but wonder if she is regretting ever moving in here, even if it is just temporary. It's possible that she's gotten tired of having a roommate who barely talks to her. I wouldn't blame her.

I sit on the edge of my mattress, wishing I could get out of my head. Wishing I could stop thinking about Briar for just one night.

And if I can't do that, then what do I do next?

THIRTEEN

A LEVEL OF HOT I'M NOT USED TO

B riar
In the past three weeks, I've barely seen or talked to Holden. Not a single dinner together. Not a shared breakfast or even coffee in the morning. He's been quiet on a group chat we have with our friend group and when we do see each other in passing at the house, we say hello. But not much more than that.

Honestly, for the most part, Holden and I have felt like two ships passing in the night. He usually gets home late from work and leaves early for the gym in the morning.

I hear his alarm go off in the morning, but by the time I've showered and changed, he's long gone. If I cook dinner, I leave him a plate of food on the stove and in the morning, there is always a mug with a tea bag left out on the counter for me next to a warm kettle. And every single time I walk into the kitchen and my eyes land on the mug, I get a pang in my chest. Even with this tension between us, the energy that crackles in my veins every time I think about Holden is still there.

Holden might be confusing, but he's sweet and has a

gentle side, and no man alive has ever turned me on the way he does.

I miss his smile.

I miss being around him.

I miss being intimate with him.

Living in his house, hearing him shower, smelling the lingering scent of his aftershave—none of this is helping. It would be smart to put some real distance between us before I fall hard for Holden Banks, but I've spoken to my landlord about my apartment several times and it sounds like I won't be moving in any time soon.

Not that it's a hardship living at Holden's place. It's cozy and you can't beat the location. I've been trying to take advantage of the proximity to the beach by going for walks before bed. Sometimes you can hear the sounds of the waves from the living room window if it's quiet enough. But as much as I like living here, it would probably be easier on both of us if I moved out as soon as I can.

Thankfully, being back at work is providing a much-needed distraction from the mess that is my personal life. Not a lot changed in the year that I was away, so it's been fairly easy to get back into the swing of things. There are a few new faces at the office, and I've become friends with a couple of them—including a guy named Wyatt, who's around my age, single, and likes to flirt with me. I've toyed with the idea of going on a date with him, but every time I ask myself if I'm ready to date again, I can only see myself being with Holden.

I sigh, flopping back in my bed against the pillows that Holden bought for me. It always seems to come back to him. I miss him. Terribly. I feel like I've been on emotional over-load the past couple of weeks, and it's exhausting.

My phone lights up beside me with a call from Daisy, so I pick it up and swipe the screen to accept.

"Hey, Dais."

"Hey, you free?"

"I'm in bed with Bear and we were thinking about watching *Dateline*." I stroke Bear between her ears. "Isn't that right, my pretty, perfect baby? We're going to watch a show, just you and your momma. You'd like that wouldn't you?"

Daisy snorts. "You realize you're talking to a cat, right? It's weird. You definitely need to get out of the house."

Her comment only makes me sink further into the pillows. "I really don't. I'm too tired and I'm crampy and there's no way I'm getting out of my sweats. You can come over here, if you want."

"Come on, Briar. You need to leave the house. Let's find you a guy."

"No."

"How come?"

"I don't want to find a guy."

I want Holden.

"It's time. Let's go, it will be fun."

I know Daisy's heart is in the right place, but I really do not feel like going out tonight— I'm tired, I'm emotional, I'm pretty sure I'm on the verge of getting my period. I'd rather stay in bed with a slice of chocolate cake and a good book. But not a romance book, I've given those up. Right now, I want to read about a murder —the more murdery the better —because reading a swoony love story would just make me think about Holden even more.

"Okay, you win," Daisy relents. "I'm coming over."

Thirty minutes later, the two of us are sitting on Holden's couch with a Tupperware full of her to-die-for chocolate chip cookies and a bottle of wine. Daisy is filling me in on the drama between the doctor and one of the other receptionists, Hazel, at the clinic she works at.

"She realizes that it is highly unprofessional to be shoving her tongue down her boss' throat at work, right?" I ask through a bite of cookie.

Daisy sighs heavily. "I don't think she cares."

Daisy tops off her glass from the bottle, then holds it up to me. "You sure you're good with tea?"

"Yeah, I'm good," I say, legs criss-crossed on the couch with a hot mug of camomile in my hands, wishing I didn't feel so crampy. "So, Hazel had a little naughty time with Doctor Dick."

She rolls her eyes. "You sound like my husband."

I smirk. Daisy's boss is Doctor Scott Dickens and when Tucker found out Daisy went on one date with him ages ago, he came up with the nickname, Doctor Dick. Daisy hates it. To be fair, I've met Scott a couple of times and he seems like a nice enough guy. Unfortunately for him, the nickname has stuck.

"I bet Doctor Dick lives up to the nickname."

"Eww, Briar, that's gross."

The shock in Daisy's eyes makes me laugh. Daisy is truly one of the kindest, sweetest people in the world, but it's fun to push her buttons. "It's always the quiet ones who turn out to be a freak in the sheets. Maybe Hazel has a naughty side."

"Are you high?"

"I might be," I say, then stifle a yawn. "Sorry."

"Why are you so tired?"

"I'm not."

"The hell you're not. You haven't stopped yawning since I got here. Were you up late with Holden last night?"

"What? No."

I haven't even told Daisy about the night Holden and I spent together. Our incredible, unforgettable night. And then the next morning, when we woke up and everything changed. Sometimes I wonder if that night meant nothing to Holden, if I could have misread it that badly. But then I remind myself that he broke his year-long vow of celibacy, and he also came three times inside of me. I wasn't imaging that.

"What is going on with you two? Is he still acting weird?"

I've never been good at not being real with Daisy. We tell each other everything. For weeks I've kept this to myself, and I feel like I'm going to combust.

"I slept with Holden," I admit, squeezing my eyes shut, afraid of what she's going to say.

Her hand playfully nudges my shoulder. "'You *slept* with Holden?"

"I did. I know I shouldn't have. I had a moment of weakness. I clearly wasn't thinking straight."

She sets her wine glass on the table. "I need to know more. Tell me everything."

So, I do. I tell her how we shared a bed for a week while we waited for furniture to arrive for my bedroom. How he caged me in between his thighs in the kitchen before he took me to his room, where we had sex. Then, I tell her about the morning after when we agreed it couldn't happen again.

Daisy cocks her head at me. "From what you just told me, you and Holden did not agree that it couldn't happen again. *You* told him it couldn't happen again. There's a difference, Bri. It sounds like he didn't agree to anything."

Could Daisy be right? I mean, I thought at the time we both agreed, but now that I think about it, maybe that's not actually what happened. Is that why he won't talk to me?

He feels rejected. Like I only wanted him for one night of sex.

I fall back into the couch cushions. I feel bad, worried that I hurt him. "Oh god. You're right, maybe that's why he's avoiding me."

"But you like him?"

"Sorta."

"You like him," she teases. "So, how was the sex?"

"So good." The words fly out of my mouth before I have a chance to realize what I'm admitting to. My eyes go wide as Daisy laughs at me.

"Okay, so if you like him and the sex was good, then why can't it happen again?"

"We're at totally different places, Dais. Holden doesn't want a relationship, and I don't want to just sleep with a guy. I want to get serious with someone. I want a home, kids, all of it. Holden told me he doesn't want a family at all," I tell her.

"He told you he doesn't want to have children? Like, ever?" she asks, eyebrows raised.

I nod. "Holden is sweet and thoughtful and he's always thinking about me, doing nice things. Daisy, he makes me a cup of my favorite tea every morning and every night before I go to bed. He's funny and smart too, and he's nothing like... him. I trust him. But as much as I like him, we just want different things. And I am not looking to get into another relationship that goes nowhere."

She smiles sympathetically. "I'm going to be honest with you, like I always am. You did the right thing by telling him you couldn't sleep with him again. It was smart to end things before they began if you're not on the same page. I know it sucks, babe, but it's better this way before you get too attached."

She's right. There's no possibility of a future with Holden. We weren't meant to be.

"I'm sorry, Briar." She squeezes my thigh. "There's a great guy out there for you, I promise, but you're not going to find him on the couch, wearing that," she side-eyes my sweats, "and eating chocolate chip cookies with me."

I burst out laughing. "Okay, okay. Next time, we'll go out."

"I like that idea. You can wear your new fur coat with a sexy pair of heels. The guys won't know what's coming."

Daisy sticks around for another hour or so, and by the time I hug her goodbye and close the door behind her, I barely have the energy to wash my face or change into my pajamas before crashing into bed and falling asleep in seconds.

The first thing I do when I wake up in the morning is expel everything in my stomach, bent over the toilet bowl. I crawl back into bed and try to sleep it off. I'll be over it by lunch.

WHEN I WAKE UP A FEW HOURS LATER, I'M FEELING MUCH better, but I do feel a sense of guilt for sleeping away a beautiful, sunny morning. I plan on a walk along the beach to try to salvage what's left of the day.

I can hear Holden in the kitchen but decide to wait until I hear him leave the house before coming out of my bedroom. I groan in frustration when I see the mug with the tea bag on the counter. I had planned on talking to him today, to try to clear the air, but I wasn't feeling up to it. First, a bit of food and some fresh air. Then I can figure out what I want to say to him.

How can I fix this? How can I get us back to the way things were before we had sex?

It doesn't take me long to walk to White Harbor beach, and once I make it a little further down the boardwalk, I head straight to a food truck and order myself three tacos. Then I find a seat at a bench in the shade to eat my lunch.

The beach is busy with people, the air infused with salt and suntan lotion. It smells like the ocean. It smells like home.

After I inhale the tacos, I walk towards the grocery store to get a few things: chicken, asparagus, lettuce for a salad, bread for the morning. The strawberries look too good to pass up, so I throw a clamshell in my cart too. I wander through aisles, one by one, grabbing things from the shelves. When I pass the bakery, my eyes catch on an apple pie that I bet Holden would love, so I grab one of those and then a pint of vanilla ice cream to go with it.

By the time I get to the cashier, my cart is full. It's only after a woman with light mauve hair and a name tag that reads "Carla" bags my groceries that I remember I walked here and now I have to carry the six plastic bags home.

I consider booking an Uber to come pick me up but decide I can handle it. I head outside, juggling the heavy bags on both arms, the sun even brighter than when I got to the store.

I walk as far as the beach boardwalk when a wave of nausea rolls through my stomach. I set the bags down on a nearby bench, my skin erupting in a cold sweat. I feel awful. I thought I was better after that big sleep, but now I'm achy, exhausted, and sick to my stomach.

The smart thing to do would be to sit in the shade and rest for a few minutes, but all I want to do is get home and get into bed. So, I gather the bags back off the bench and start for home.

I just need to sleep. Charlotte at work had the flu last week, I must have caught it from her.

I'm walking as quickly as I can along the crowded boardwalk, which isn't quick at all, when I feel lightheaded and my vision blurs. The next thing I know, I feel someone knock my shoulder—hard—and one of the bags around my forearm slides to the pavement.

Oof. I crouch down to pick up a few of the groceries that have tumbled out of the bag. A woman kneels down to help me as my stomach turns and bile inches up my throat.

"You okay, honey?" she asks, handing me an orange.

"Thank you, I'm okay," I reply, reaching for a yellow pepper on the pavement. "I appreciate the help—"

"Briar?"

My heart stops beating in my chest because I know that voice. I hear it in my dreams at night.

"Briar," Holden repeats when I don't respond the first time. "What are you doing? Are you okay?"

He's kneeling down beside me, a hand on my arm. "Holden. It's fine. I'm okay." I struggle to slip the bags back onto my forearms.

I look at Holden for the first time, and it makes me even more lightheaded. He's shirtless, with a sheen of sweat over his tanned skin. His brown hair is damp with sweat and when his deep green eyes meet mine, I see the concern on his face.

He shakes his head. "I've got this, Briar."

"I can handle it."

"I didn't say you couldn't, but when I'm around, you don't have to."

He takes the bags from me as my stomach flips and flops. I'm not sure if it's from the flu or from Holden being commanding and protective over me. This version of him is a level of hot I'm not used to.

"What were you doing anyways? Why didn't you call me? I would have picked you up."

"I, um..." I swallow, feeling completely off-balance. I am hot and sticky and sick, and this is the first time I've talked to Holden in weeks. "I wasn't expecting on buying the whole store. I guess I got carried away. Sorry to ruin your run."

"You didn't ruin anything."

God. This is humiliating. All of it. My hair needs to be washed, I'm not wearing a stitch of makeup, I swear I must look green, and let's not forget that he found me picking up groceries off the ground in the middle of the busiest beach in Reed Point. I'm a gigantic mess.

The warm Reed Point breeze hits me almost as soon as we start walking home. I close my eyes hoping the nausea will pass but it only makes it worse. By the time we finally make it back to Haven Harbor, I'm feeling even worse.

I make it to the kitchen, where I immediately start to put away the groceries. I can feel Holden studying me. He must notice that I'm about three seconds from getting physically ill.

"Briar, you look pale. Are you feeling okay?" His expression and the tone of his voice has softened.

"Not really. I think I have the flu."

Before I even know what is happening, Holden is beside me, one hand on my forehead, the other on the back of my neck. "I think your temperature is okay, but you're getting into bed. You're sick, Bee. You need to rest."

"I'm okay."

"No, you're not." He wraps an arm around my shoulder and then guides me down the hall and up the few stairs to my bedroom. I stand beside the bed, shivering, as he pulls the duvet back and then gently motions me into bed and pulls the cover up over me.

"I'll be right back," he says, turning and leaving me in the room by myself.

When he returns in a few minutes, he has a wet cloth in his hand that he places on my forehead.

"Thank you. That actually feels good."

"You're welcome. What have you eaten today?"

"You don't have to—"

"I can feed you, Bee. It's not a hardship." He picks up a pillow from the other side of the bed and shoves it behind my back, making me extra comfortable. In a daze, I notice Bear has jumped up on the bed and nuzzled herself next to my feet.

"I had tacos at the beach. I'm not hungry, but thank you," I sigh. I have absolutely no energy left in me to banter with him, which disappoints me. "I need to just sleep off whatever virus I picked up."

"You need to at least drink something and stay hydrated. Fluids will help you feel better faster," he says before disappearing from the room again.

I close my eyes when the room goes quiet, wishing I wasn't feeling this way. I only open them when I feel a warm hand run softly over the apple of my cheek.

There's a beat of silence. For the first time in weeks, a smile tips the edges of his lips. He removes his hand from my cheek, and I want to ask him to put it back. Instead, he glances at something on the nightstand. "Here, I brought you orange juice, and ice water. I wasn't sure which one you'd prefer."

My heart flutters in my chest at the way he's looking at me— I can see the care and concern shining in his eyes.

"You should sleep."

"I'm not sure I can. I slept all morning."

He adjusts the towel on my forehead before he walks across the room to the dresser and grabs my laptop. He brings it over, fluffing the pillows against the headboard and then climbing on top of the duvet. The mattress dips with the weight of his 6-foot-one frame.

"What are you doing, Holden? I don't want you to get sick. Trust me, you don't want to feel like this."

"I appreciate that, but I'll be fine."

"What about Bear? You can't be in here."

"Briar, I'll be fine. I took an allergy pill a second ago." Holden's eyes flick to my cat. "Why did you call her Bear, anyway? It's kind of a weird name for a cat."

I laugh. "The day I got her, a friend came over to visit and brought her dog, which is big, a cross between a Lab and a Bernese Mountain Dog. I was trying to get Bear back in her carrier because I didn't want her to get scared, but she hid under the couch. A while later, me and my friend were having coffee at the kitchen table and the cat comes crawling out from under the couch, walks straight up to the dog and swats it on the nose with her paw. That's when I decided on Bear. She's cute, but she's tough—or at least she thinks she is."

Holden smiles, looking impressed. "Note to self: don't mess with Bear."

"Not if you value your life," I grin.

Holden opens the screen on the computer. "I'll watch a movie with you, then I'll make you some soup."

I glance over at him as he scrolls through Netflix looking for a movie. I can smell the scent of pine and man and everything that is Holden, and even though I know I'm fighting off something, I instantly feel so much better having him here next to me. It's feels nice to have him so close to me again.

"Holden, I mean this in the nicest way, but... you know how to make soup?"

"I wasn't going to make it from scratch, but I know how to open a can and heat it up."

A small smile tugs at my lips. "Canned soup is just fine by me."

He grins at me, and when it fades there's a resounding apology in his big green eyes, for everything that's happened between us over the last few weeks. Holden is a man of few words, and I've come to learn that he is very intentional with the way he looks at me. I want to offer him an explanation, and to ask him questions, but I don't have the energy today. He returns his attention to the computer on his lap, and I feel my heart beat a little faster in my chest. Holden is so good at not making me feel guilty for being taken care of. He never makes me feel like I am too much. I've been myself with him since the day I moved in, and he accepts me exactly the way I am. Even the crazy parts.

I watch him from the corner of my eye only to wonder how long this unspoken truce between us will last. Instead of worrying about what will happen tomorrow or whether we'll continue to be on good terms, I'm choosing to simply enjoy it while it's here.

He presses play on the movie then props the laptop on top of a pillow before stretching out beside me, his muscular arms propped behind his head.

The movie starts. He chose *Love Actually*. I swoon at the realization that he chose a romance for me.

I fight the urge to grin from being so damn happy. It also feels so good to have Holden in bed next to me again. I lean into the pillows to enjoy the movie with a hand on my stomach to settle the queasiness.

FOURTEEN

THIS CAN'T BE HAPPENING

Briar

I can't be. This can't be happening.

My legs begin to tremble, my heart is racing out of my chest. I clean up my mess and walk down the hall to my bedroom.

I need to be alone. I'm going to cry.

Shutting the door behind me, I collapse on the bed with my head in the pillows, feeling another wave of nausea roll through me.

"Oh god, how did this happen?" I whisper into the pillow, pulling my knees up to my chest in a fetal position. Of course, I know how this happened—I know how babies are made. But we used a condom. We were careful. What am I going to do?

I look at the two pink lines on the pregnancy test again, as if maybe I read the test wrong the first time. Tears leak from the corners of my eyes, blurring the little screen, but the two pink lines are still there.

I'm pregnant.

How am I going to tell Holden? How will he take it?

He doesn't want kids. He doesn't want a family. We're not even together. I can't even begin to imagine how he will react.

For three weeks, we barely spoke until last week when he found me on the boardwalk with a mess of groceries at my feet. After that night, we've had a few short conversations in passing, but we've both had a lot going on. Holden went away for two nights to his family's cabin while I stayed home to rest and try to kick what I thought was the flu. I bury my face in my hands, still in disbelief. How the hell is this happening?

Holden had taken care of me, assuming that I was sick with the flu. How could I be so stupid? Not once did it cross my mind that I could be pregnant. How didn't I know?

When he came home from the cabin, I had wanted to talk to him, to tell him that I missed him. That I missed our friendship, that before everything went off the rails I had more fun with him than I'd had in years. I was tired of giving him space and I hoped he'd come around to being my friend again, but the guy can be so stubborn. I guess I have been too.

Tears fall down my cheeks. Another wave of nausea passes through my belly.

Every day around dinnertime, the nausea and exhaustion return. All I seem able to do is lie in bed or read a book. I feel terrible.

And now I know why.

Dammit. What am I going to do?

One thing I know for sure: I'm going to have to sit down and talk to Holden. I have no other choice.

But how am I going to tell him?

I roll onto my back and stare up at the ceiling, the faint sound of the front door closing echoing off the walls. I sit up, wipe the tears from my eyes and try to gather the courage to go and talk to him. Delaying this conversation will only make it more difficult so I push off the bed and force myself out of my bedroom door and down the hall.

My stomach is in my throat, the air feels so warm and thick, it's hard to breathe. I'm not sure if it's the heatwave that continues to pummel Reed Point or just my fried nerves.

I find Holden sitting on an armchair in the living room, untying the laces on his runners. When he looks up and begins to talk, I realize he's not alone. Tucker is sitting on the couch across from him, taking a long drink from his water bottle. They must have been out at a baseball game. Holden and the guys play on a local beer league team.

"Oh, sorry... I didn't realize..." I stammer like an idiot. "Hey, Tucker... um, I'll just talk to you later, Holden." A heavy silence stretches between Holden and I as our eyes lock. It's like he knows I have something to say. But this is obviously not the right time. I jerk my thumb towards my bedroom. "I'm going to go—"

Holden holds up his hand. "Um, Tuck. I need to...uh..."

"Yeah, I need to get going. Daisy is waiting for me. See ya, Briar. I'll talk to you later, man." Tucker escapes out the front door, leaving Holden and I all alone.

My pulse hammers under my skin. The intensity of his deep-green eyes on mine unsettles me, and the contents of my stomach threaten to empty right here on the hardwood.

What do I do now? How do I tell him?

Holden stands up, a concerned expression on his face. Even though he's been distant for weeks, he cares. He knows something is wrong.

I haven't forgotten how beautiful he is, but it feels like

eons since I have been this close to him. *My god,* he is handsome. Way better looking than anyone has a right to be.

It feels like all the air is sucked from the room, and the silence between us stretches on until Holden finally breaks it.

"Is everything okay? You look like something is wrong."

I blink, completely unsure as to how I should start this. I stand in front of Holden on trembling legs feeling green and pale and scared to death, but I need to tell him. I take a deep breath, then look him in the eye.

"I'm pregnant."

FIFTEEN

WHAT DO I KNOW ABOUT HAVING A BABY?

Holden

She's pregnant.

The second she walked into the room I knew there was something wrong. Her arms were wrapped tightly around her body, her skin pale. I could tell by the way she was looking at me that she had something she needed to say. But never in my wildest dreams did I think she would announce that she's pregnant.

Fuck. Pregnant. Briar is pregnant.

I walk into the kitchen and reach above the fridge for the liquor cabinet, grabbing a bottle of whiskey.

Briar ran for the bathroom holding her stomach after she dropped the proverbial bomb on me. When I followed her down the hall to see if I could help her, she slammed the door in my face and told me she was fine. Then I heard the sounds of her vomiting into the toilet.

Rather than stand there and listen to her heave, I walked to the kitchen to give her some privacy, deciding I needed a drink. Or ten.

Dammit. How could she be pregnant? We used a

condom. We took precautions. We did what we were supposed to do.

Briar's confession is still ringing in my ears when I chug back the tumbler of alcohol and let it burn its way down the length of my throat. I finish every last drop before refilling the glass and throwing it back again.

What the fuck am I going to do? I have no clue, but what I do know is that the whiskey is going to numb this throbbing pain in my brain. But then I remember Briar is in my bathroom having to deal with this alone.

I might not want to be a dad, but I'm not an asshole and I'm not going to just leave her to shoulder this by herself.

So, I walk back to the bathroom door, feeling unsteady as I go. I'm not sure if it's from the whiskey or the fact that Briar is pregnant with my child.

Fuck. There's that word again. *That word.* Pregnant.

How long has she known? It's been around four weeks since that night together. I know this because I've counted the weeks off on my calendar like some lovesick idiot. Four weeks of trying to forget one of the best nights of my life.

Does she think about that night too? Does she lie awake every night trying to forget how good we were together like I do? How perfectly we fit, how good her skin felt against mine. The truth is there's no way I could ever forget. I hope she hasn't forgotten either.

But does she regret it now that she is having my baby? That's assuming she wants to have the baby. What would I do if she doesn't? What do I do if she does?

Fuck. Is this actually happening?

A baby.

What do I know about having a baby?

I don't even want kids. How am I going to be a dad?

I knock on the door.

"Holden, I'm fine. Go away."

I slowly nudge open the door anyway. Briar is wiping her face with a washcloth, so I take another from the cabinet, run it under the tap and wipe the back of her neck with it.

"I told you to go away." She squeezes her eyes shut as she's holding her stomach.

"I'm not going away, as much as you might like me to," I tell her, running the cool cloth over her shoulders. She leans into my touch.

Briar is resilient and strong, so it's hard to see her like this. Her green eyes are pleading, and I realize that what she needs right now is support, not a million questions.

"You don't need to do that but thank you. That feels good."

"I know I don't have to, but I want to," I say to her back before my eyes meet hers in the mirror.

"I haven't known for long," she says, as if reading my mind. "I just took the test."

I swallow down the lump in my throat. For the past few weeks, practically all I've thought about is wanting to be back in Briar's life. To be somebody to her. To mean something to the girl who walked into my life and changed me. But I never would have imagined that this would be the thing that would get us talking to each other again. Not a fucking chance.

"I haven't been with anyone but you," she says, and I nod my head knowing it's true. We live together. I know she's been here every night. Besides that, I trust her.

"I know. For what it's worth, neither have I."

I don't know why I just said that, but something in me wanted her to know so I hold Briar's gaze in the mirror silently telling her that it meant something to me. I need her to know that night was special.

But what happens next?

There is no way she is going through this alone. I'll be there for her in any way I can. She would want that, wouldn't she? Would she want more?

There is *something* there between us. I feel it every time I'm in the same room with her. She must feel it too. We have chemistry. It's palpable.

And now we're having a baby.

"I'd like to keep this between us... at least until we confirm it with a doctor." She looks down at the sink, her face going even paler.

"I guess that's probably smart. That's fine by me."

"Thank you," she murmurs. "I think I feel a bit better. I'm going to sit on the back porch and get some fresh air."

I nod, taking a step backwards so she can squeeze her way past me. Once she's down the hall, I lean forward on the bathroom counter.

Shit. What do I do now?

After taking a deep breath, I find my way to the kitchen, grab two water bottles from the fridge and crackers for Briar then I pour another glass of whiskey for me. After I've downed it, I bring the water and saltine crackers outside to Briar. She's sitting on a porch chair, her hair tied up in a messy bun on her head, her legs stretched out and propped up on the chair across from her.

"I got you water and crackers to help with the nausea." I lift her feet off the chair and sit down then put her feet in my lap. If she's uncomfortable at all with me touching her, she doesn't show it.

"Holden, I'm fine. Really. I don't need all this attention."

I rub the base of her ankle and notice the tears that are gathering in her eyes. My heart cracks in two. "I brought you water and a few crackers, Briar. It's hardly attention."

"Well, it's more attention than I've shown you in weeks."

"I haven't been any better," I admit, watching her lift a hand to wipe away a tear that slips from her dark eyelashes and down her cheek.

"Don't cry, Bee," I gently squeeze her ankle. "We'll figure it out."

I watch her bottom lip quiver as another tear falls, and it kills me. I move her legs off my lap then grab the arms of her chair and pull her closer to me so she's locked in between my parted thighs. I cup her face in my palms, my thumbs wiping away the wetness marking her pretty face.

"Please don't cry, Briar," I say to her. "You're not alone in this. I'm not going anywhere. I promise." I kiss her forehead. "I will support you, whatever you decide, I will be here for you."

Mentally I have no idea what *this* looks like, but right now my priority is making Briar feel safe. We can figure everything out later.

I move my hands to her thighs when her tears are dry.

"You're pregnant," I say, unsure if I say it out loud for her or myself.

"I'm not sure I've processed it yet," she sniffles.

"Me neither," I admit.

Briar is quiet for a moment, and I wish like hell I knew what she is thinking. Then her gaze drops to my hands on her thighs. "Holden we never should have stopped talking."

"I agree," I answer her.

"Let's not ever do that again."

I give her a sad smile as she sniffles again. "Okay."

We stare at each other for a long beat. She looks sad. Even worse, she looks scared. I wish I knew what I could say to her to make her feel better.

I tuck a few whisps of her hair that have come loose

behind her ear, just wanting to touch her. I'll take any excuse to feel the softness of her skin again. Being this close to her I can see the sparkling gold flecks in her green eyes, smell the scent of her shampoo. When my fingertips graze the shell of her ear, her eyes flick to mine.

"Holden, I didn't mean for this to happen."

"I know. I didn't either. I'm sorry."

"Me too," she murmurs.

I exhale a breath, then pull her onto my lap, my hand at the back of her head. She rests her cheek against my shoulder, and I hold her, never wanting to let her go. And as crazy as it sounds, I know it's going to be okay. I know we can get through this together. "Briar, tell me what you're thinking. Say anything."

She keeps her face against my shoulder. "I don't know what to say, but I know I want this baby. I won't abandon this baby like my dad did to me."

My heart aches for her. If I could have one wish, it would be that she never had to go through that. I've never seen a child in my future, I'm not even sure I can picture it now. I need time to get there, but what I do know is that I want whatever Briar wants and if she wants to have this baby, then I will get there and that's what we will do.

"I want this baby too... with you."

She lifts her head from my shoulder. "You do?"

"I do."

All the air rushes from her lungs as she leans against my chest again, burying her face in my neck. I wrap her in my arms, kiss the top of her head and rub her back. Three weeks ago, I would have been ecstatic to have her back in my arms, but I never would have thought it would be because she is pregnant with my baby.

"I'm nervous."

"We both are," I whisper. "But it's going to be okay."

It has to be okay; I'll make sure of it. I'll talk to my mom. She'll know what to do, she always does. I sure as fuck have no idea what happens next. So, I'll take Briar to the doctor, confirm the news, and then we'll talk to my mom. I feel the tightness in my chest start to ease now that I have a plan. At least for now.

"We'll take it one day at a time. First thing is to make an appointment with your doctor."

Briar sits up in my lap, shifts back to her chair. "I'll call today."

"I'd like to come with you if that's okay."

She untwists her hair out of the knot on her head then redoes it. She has a little more color in her face. I'm guessing that's the way it's going to be for the next nine months. Good days and hard days, but I'll be here to get her through it. She should probably give up her lease and stay here with me. It would be better if I was around to help her, but that doesn't need to be decided today. We have three or four weeks until her apartment will be ready for her to move into.

"That would be good," she nods.

I'm relieved that she chose not to argue with me about it like she tends to do about everything. Despite everything, I am happy we're talking, that we're getting along again. Things between us haven't been the same since we slept together. Do I have regrets that we had sex? Not for a second. Even if this is where we've ended up.

"Do you want to stay out here a little longer or can I take you for... oh, I guess I shouldn't take you for ice cream," I say, hoping to make her smile. When the corners of her mouth tip up, I consider it a win. "How about the bakery?"

"Sure," she says, taking a cracker from the plate.

I stand up, looking down at her. "Briar?"

She stands too, her eyes narrowing in concern. "Yeah?"

"Promise me you'll keep talking to me. Don't shut me out. You promise?"

"Holden," she pleads. "I hated that we stopped talking. I hated every minute of it."

"You didn't answer my question, Bee." I cup the back of her head, pulling her into my chest. Her arms snake around my waist. I kiss the top of her head. "Promise me you'll talk to me."

"I promise."

SIXTEEN

AN ATTITUDE LARGER THAN THE SIZE OF CANADA

Holden

I've known about today's appointment for a week but I'm still not sure I'm ready for the doctor to walk in. I'm pretty sure Briar feels the same way. She's sitting on the exam table, wringing her hands in her lap and staring at something invisible on the wall in front of her.

It feels surreal. The moment the doctor confirms what we already know, it will make this all real. We'll have a due date when we walk out of here.

God, this is really happening.

My chest feels tight like there's a 1,000-pound weight resting on it. Honestly, the thought of becoming a dad terrifies the fuck out of me. I don't have a clue what it takes to care for a baby. I'm man enough to admit that I've never been more scared of anything in my life. But when push comes to shove, I always figure my shit out, and I will step up and take care of both Briar and our baby. I would never want my child to question whether their dad loves them.

Briar's hesitant eyes land on mine, and she smiles at me shakily. The woman is so effortlessly pretty it makes me want to kiss that small smile right off her lips. Since I found out that she's pregnant, I feel so fucking possessive over her. I worry about making sure she's safe, making sure that nothing bad happens to her or the baby. I have this over-whelming feeling in my chest that makes me want to protect her.

"Say something, Holden. The waiting is driving me insane." Briar looks over at me from where she's sitting on the exam table.

"Did you know they say you can tell if it's a boy or a girl by the heartbeat? If it's high, it's a girl and if it's low it's a boy."

Briar's eyes widen. "Who's they? And how on God's green earth do you know that, Holden?"

I shrug a shoulder. "I was googling about pregnancy and babies on the internet. Oh, and I downloaded this cool app I wanted to show you."

I think her jaw actually hits the floor. "You were researching about parenting?" She says it like it's the most absurd thing she's ever heard.

"Is that surprising?"

"Well, yeah, a little. What else did you learn?"

"The baby is probably the size of a large bean right now."

Briar's eyes turn glassy right before she looks down at her stomach and places a hand on it. Her lower lip trembles. Fuck, I wish I could ease her mind. I wish I knew what to say. I hate that we're about to meet the doctor who will bring our baby into the world, and I am nothing but... Briar's friend? Fake boyfriend? Both feel all wrong. What I really want is for Briar to be mine.

Her cautious eyes meet mine. "I know this a lot for you, Holden. It feels the same way for me too. But thank you for being here with me. I know this would be a lot scarier if I was doing it alone"

Well, damn. There's a sincerity in her voice that calms my racing pulse. She wants me here with her. Even though I am still trying to wrap my mind around being a father, I'm grateful she is giving me this chance to be involved.

"I wouldn't miss this. Not for anything. Thank you for allowing me to be here."

"This is just as much your baby as it is mine, Holden."

I nod right as the doctor walks in, a woman who looks like she's in her forties and introduces herself to us as Dr. St. Claire. She extends a hand for Briar to shake before turning her attention to me. I wipe my clammy hands on my jeans.

"You must be Dad?"

Dad. That's the first time anyone has referred to me as that. I'm left momentarily speechless before I gather my thoughts, shake her hand and nod.

I pride myself on being cool even in the most chaotic circumstances, but right now I am a bundle of nerves. For God's sake, get it together, Holden.

"I understand you took a positive home pregnancy test," the doctor says, taking a seat at the end of the exam table with a comforting expression on her face. "How are you feeling, Briar?"

Briar relaxes slightly. "Very nauseous but I've only vomited a few times in the last couple of weeks. Other than that, just a little tired."

"All very normal." Dr. St. Claire smiles before standing and removing a blood pressure cuff from where it is kept on the wall. "I'm going to do a few tests then we'll have a look at the baby."

Briar slips off the light sweater she's wearing and hands it to me before Dr. St. Clair takes her blood pressure, then her temperature. She asks Briar a few questions and then asks her to lie back on the exam bed. Briar's eyes flick to the ceiling when she tells her she is going to need to insert a wand inside of her to see the baby.

"Is this your first baby?" she asks, slipping on a pair of latex gloves.

"Yes, for both of us," Briar answers, turning her head so she's looking at me, fear and anticipation swimming in her eyes. "If we both seem a little nervous, that's probably why."

"Also perfectly normal. Most first-time parents *are* a little nervous. I'm happy to answer any question you have." The doctor has a wand in one hand and a bottle of gel in the other. "This might be a little uncomfortable." She squeezes a clear gel on the wand before slipping it inside of Briar. After pressing a few buttons on her keyboard, a fuzzy gray image fills the screen. The doctor explains what she is looking for, but my attention shifts to Briar as she reaches for my hand. I lace my hand in hers before looking at the fuzzy image with a dark circle. Within the image is a small, bean-shaped baby.

"There is your baby." The doctor points to the screen. "And that flicker right there is your baby's heartbeat." Briar exhales a long sigh of relief, her eyes glued to the screen. I lean closer to Briar so I can get a better view of our baby— the baby I made with Bee. That's our tiny miracle. The internet was right. It looks like a little bean, but it is *our* little bean, and it has a heartbeat. Briar gasps, covering her mouth with her hand. This is good news. She is just as relieved as I am. I notice the tears welling in the corners of her eyes. It's surreal, such a gift to see a life growing inside her.

"Let's see if we can hear the heartbeat. Sometimes it's too early," the doctor says before a click of a few buttons. Within seconds there's a steady whooshing sound that fills the quiet room.

"Your baby's heart rate is 150 beats per minute," she says after a moment. "Completely normal."

It's a boy. From what I read online, 150 is on the lower side and that means the chances are higher that it's a boy. I look down at Briar, who is still smiling at the image of our baby on the screen.

"You're measuring eight weeks along, and baby looks great," the doctor confirms. "It's too early to tell if it's a boy or a girl. If you want to, you can find that out at your mid-pregnancy ultrasound around 20 weeks or a blood test around 11 weeks. Until then, I'd like to see you once a month to monitor the baby. I'll ask you to come in more frequently at around 31 weeks. Now, let's find out when your baby is due." A few seconds later, she gives us the due date: May 9th.

She clicks a few buttons on her computer then removes the wand. She prints off a few photos before asking us if we have any questions before we leave.

"Is there anything that Briar shouldn't do? Anything that isn't safe for our baby?" I ask, feeling a little awkward.

"No raw fish or unpasteurized foods and limit your caffeine. Take your prenatal vitamins, eat a balanced diet, stay active. Most dads appreciate being reassured that having regular sex is fine. In fact, it is great for relieving stress. Near the end it can also help induce labor. Briar, you may also find that you have an increased sex drive, so have all the sex you want."

I file that information away as Dr. St. Claire shakes both of our hands and leaves the room. Briar and I exit the clinic a few minutes later.

"Do you think it's a boy or a girl?" she asks.

"It's a boy, I know it."

"Why do you think that?"

"You heard the heart rate. It was low and from everything I've read, that means it's a boy."

She shakes her head. "Well, I think it's a girl."

I laugh, not surprised in the least. Briar can't resist an opportunity to challenge me. She's cute as hell.

Since she moved in with me, I haven't been able to stop thinking about her. I can't imagine anyone else having this effect on me. Just the thought of any other guy touching her —especially with *my* baby inside of her—has me losing my mind. Now that she's having our baby, I feel this strong sense of possession. I groan inwardly when I think about how badly I want to touch her, how it's getting harder and harder to keep my hands to myself when I'm around her. My dick twitches in my pants. Fantastic. Now I'm going to be sitting next to her in my truck with a hard-on.

When I reach for the door handle on the passenger side of my truck, I can't resist dipping my head into her neck until my lips are millimetres from the lobe of her ear. "You're carrying my little slugger, Bee. I'd bet the damn house on it."

Briar shivers, then covers up her response with a laugh. "So cocky for a guy with only a 50/50 chance of being right."

I have her caged in against the door of my truck. When she turns around to face me, her cheeks are flushed. She looks happy. She's beautiful. I could spend forever just looking at her.

It blows my mind. This woman walked into my life and turned it upside down, overwhelming me in the best way with her joy for life and spontaneity. Not to mention a mouth on her that drives me absolutely crazy. Every time she sasses me, I have to clench my jaw to stop myself from grabbing her by the neck and kissing her senseless. Stubborn, uninhibited and carefree. She has an attitude larger than the size of Canada. She has wrecked me in all the best ways.

But as good as we've been getting along lately, there's a chance that's as far as our relationship will go. I would be smart to remember that.

But I want her.

I want more.

My hand moves to the small of her back to help her into the cab of my truck.

"You realize I'm not as big as a house yet, right?" she asks. "I can get into your truck without your help."

"This again?"

She rolls her eyes and shakes her head.

"Get in the truck. I'm taking you somewhere." I reach for a loose strand of her hair, tugging on the tendril.

"Where are you taking me, Holden Banks?"

"You'll see." I round the truck and hop into the driver's seat, then pull out of the parking lot. I steal a look at Briar, who has rolled her window halfway down and has her eyes closed as the warm breeze blows a few loose strands of hair around her face. She looks the most relaxed I've seen her in days.

She catches me staring and smiles, making my pulse beat a little faster, and I have to remind myself to keep my eyes on the road and not on her.

"How are you feeling?" I ask.

"Right now? Good. Ask me in an hour and it might be different," she says.

"The doctor said it's normal."

"Doesn't mean it's any fun."

Her phone buzzes and she looks at the screen then sighs before dropping it back into her lap.

"Everything okay?"

"Yeah, it's just my mom asking how my week has been. I feel guilty for not telling her." She drops her face into her hands. "I'm worried how she's going to take the news."

I reach across the console, my hand sliding across the nape of her neck. Her muscles tense beneath my touch then begin to loosen as I rub the column of her neck with my thumb, back and forth, over and over.

"Are you worried she's going to be upset?"

"No, that's not it…. I'm just nervous. What if I disappointed her?"

"I doubt you could ever disappoint her, Briar. If you're worried, we can FaceTime her and tell her together."

She immediately shakes her head. "Thanks, Holden, it's sweet of you to offer, but I think this is one conversation I need to have myself. I'm sure she is going to ask to meet you though."

"Then I'll meet her. I told you, Bee. Whatever you need, I'm here."

She nods and we drive the rest of the way in silence until we arrive at a small Italian restaurant away from the bustle of the beach and Main Street. I know we can have dinner here without running into anyone we know.

Afterwards, we decide to go for a drive, neither of us ready to go back to Haven Harbor. Living in this little bubble we've been in all day, just the two of us, not having to deal with the outside world has felt good. I sense that she feels that way too. Just her and I… happy. Afraid, but definitely happy. Briar and I are in a good place; we're getting along, and we both seem to have accepted the fact that we're having a baby together. I'm not ready to have anyone burst our happy bubble.

"ARE YOU BLIND? THAT IS A PLANE, NOT A SHOOTING STAR, Holden!" Briar smacks my thigh with the back of her hand where she's lying next to me in the bed of my pick-up truck. "And you don't make wishes on an airplane."

"It's definitely a shooting star. I don't care what you say, Bee."

She drapes her arm over her eyes, shaking her head. The sun set an hour ago, and the moon is high above us, casting a silvery glow over her face. A million stars light up the sky overhead.

After dinner, we drove north along the highway—stopping at a gas station so Briar could pee and we could load up on candy and chips—until we got to Lookout Point. Luckily, I had a blanket in the back of my truck and now Briar and I are lying side-by-side gazing at the stars. And possibly an airplane, but I'm not about to admit she's right.

"You are ridiculous," she says, lowering her arm to stare up at the sky again.

"Or maybe it's a sign."

She's silent for a moment as her hand flattens over her belly. I'm pretty sure it's a subconscious movement. "Yeah, I like that. Maybe it's a sign. Let's go with that, Holden."

We both turn to look at one another. Her eyes, bright green oceans, are wide as they stare back at me. There's a thick tension in the air between us, and the way her lips part as my eyes dip down to her mouth makes it harder and harder not to seal my lips to hers.

There's nothing I want more than to kiss her. I want to roll her onto my chest, kiss the life out of her and make her fucking mine. Baby or not, that has nothing to do with it. My pulse races under my skin at the thought of being inside her again.

I bite the inside of my cheek to stop myself from pulling

her to me; crossing that line will only make things more confusing. We just found out we're having a baby together, we share a friend group, our lives are intertwined. Right now, things are good, we don't need another reason to avoid each other. But still...

"Briar..." I say softly, hearing the frustration in my tone. "I want to kiss you right now more than I want air to breathe, but..."

"Holden..." she nods, scraping her teeth over her bottom lip. "I know. I just think we need to be careful. It's not just us we have to think about now."

I know that she's right. The stakes are too high to risk messing this up. We're finally talking again, we're connecting. That will have to be enough. For now.

I reach across the bed of the truck and squeeze her hand. "Whatever you want, Bee."

"It's not what I want."

"It isn't?"

Wordless, she turns her head to look at me, leaving her hand in mine.

"Let's take our time," I say. "Get to know each other. For Slugger."

Her gaze turns back to the sky, but my eyes never leave her. There are so many questions that I'm dying to know the answers to. The most important being ... does she want more from me than just being her baby daddy?

All that will have to wait. For now, I stay lost in Briar Moore, on top of a bluff, in the back of my truck, until she's asleep next to me, pressed into my side.

SEVENTEEN

KEEPING SECRETS

Briar

"Are you almost ready?" Holden hollers at me from the living room. "Not trying to rush you, but we need to get going."

I'm in my bedroom, reapplying my lip gloss for the tenth time telling myself it's going to be fine. In other words, I'm stalling. Tonight, we are going next door for dinner. It will be Jake and Ev, Grayson and Sierra, Tucker and Daisy, and Holden and me, and all of the kids. As excited as I am to be hanging out with friends, I'm worried that one of them will figure out that I am pregnant.

I don't look pregnant; my body hasn't changed a bit. But I'm nervous that I'll have to explain why I'm not drinking, or why I'm yawning at 8:30 p.m. I've never been any good at keeping secrets.

I realize that it's foolish to think we'll be able to keep the pregnancy news from our friends for much longer, but I'm not ready just yet. Besides, Holden and I made a promise to one another that we would tell our parents before we tell anyone else. We've been dragging our feet on having that conversation knowing that once we do, life as we know it will never be the same.

"I'm ready," I holler as I give Bear a scratch between her ears. "Mommy will be back soon, my beautiful girl, then we can cuddle all night long."

I grab my purse and take one last look in the full-length mirror. The jeans that I squeezed into are tight, purposefully showing off my hips and ass for Holden. I paired the light denim with a spaghetti strap body suit that I'm also hoping he will like. I'm relieved to see that my skin looks a little less green now that the nausea that tormented me all day has passed. A bit of blush works wonders.

Holden is sitting on the couch watching a hockey game, looking entirely too handsome wearing a pair of perfectly faded jeans and a short-sleeved black T-shirt. His hair is tousled in a way that looks effortless even though I saw him running pomade through it in the bathroom. How any man can look this good in 10 minutes is a mystery to me.

Also a mystery: how I was able to keep my hands off him given the fact he was wearing nothing but a towel. My mouth literally watered seeing his sculpted abs and defined pecs, not to mention the soft trail of hair that disappeared into the towel at the V of his pelvis. I deserve a medal for keeping my hands to myself.

"You look hot as fuck," he says, our eyes locking. I give him a small smile but inwardly I'm kicking my feet.

Holden is always telling me how beautiful I look and sometimes I'm not sure how to take it. I'm not used to getting compliments, especially from the men in my life. At first it made me feel weird, but I admit I'm starting to enjoy it.

Things have definitely changed between Holden and

me. We're walking a thin line between just friends and lust. I'm pretty sure he wants me just as much as I want him.

I sit down next to him to put on my shoes, my stomach in knots not from the nausea but because I'm a nervous wreck. Holden seems calm and cool—the exact opposite of how I feel.

"Tonight is going to be okay, Bee," he says, reading my mind. "Stop worrying."

"I know." I shake my head, trying to ward off the anxiety. "I'm just the world's worst liar. I'm worried someone will catch on to us. Specifically, I'm worried about Daisy. She knows me better than I know myself sometimes."

"I can't believe you haven't told her."

I blink. "Have you told the guys?"

"Well, no, but it's killing me."

"I guess one of us needs to be the courageous one. It's definitely not going to be me."

He slants his head to the side, glancing at me. "Do you really think our friends won't be happy for us?"

"It's not that. I know they will be once they're over the shock. It's just... the news is going to come out of left field, Holden. We aren't even together."

Holden looks upset, and it's actually quite cute. This gorgeous, 6-foot-1, self-proclaimed bachelor looks flustered that... what? That he's not in a relationship with his baby momma?

"No, we're not together. Unless..." Holden looks at me like he has something up his sleeve.

"I thought we were getting to know each other?"

"I'm trying really fucking hard here," he says. "It doesn't help when you wear outfits like this."

His words make my breath hitch. There he goes again, making my heart soar.

"I guess it's a good thing that we're late for dinner then. No time to tempt you. We should probably get moving."

He groans and leans closer to me until I can feel his breath against my neck, making goosebumps erupt over my skin. "Or I can pick you up and carry you over to the kitchen counter and make you come on my face instead."

Oh my effing god.

Holden is a confident dirty talker, and I admit it turns me on.

"Getting to know each other, remember?" My lips tip up in a teasing smile as I stand up from the couch. He stands up too.

"For Slugger." He presses a kiss to my forehead and my world feels like it shifts on its axis. I haven't allowed myself to think too much about what it will be like to share a baby with Holden. Up until now, the thought has been terrifying, but he has been doing and saying all the right things. He's interested in our baby, the pregnancy, and making sure I'm feeling good. He seems to be too good to be true. "I'm doing this the right way for little Slugger." I feel the sting of tears welling in the corners of my eyes. I'm blaming it on the hormones.

The truth is, I'm falling for Holden—falling so hard, even though I know I shouldn't. My life is complicated enough, the last thing I need to do is fall in love with a man who wants none of the same things in life that I do... no matter how sweet and sexy he is. When it comes down to it, there is still a chance Holden will leave.

I try to block it all out as we cut across the lawn to Jake and Everly's place. Jake greets us at the door with baby West on his hip, the sounds of laughter and the scent of barbecue hitting us as we walk through the door.

"Uncle Holdey!" Birdie's face lights up when she spots

him. She makes a beeline for the door in her polka-dot dress and sparkly, cat-eared headband. Holden catches her when she launches herself into his arms.

My skin erupts in goosebumps as I watch Holden's face light up to match Birdie's. Her tiny arms wrap tightly around his neck, and it makes my heart feel like it may soar right out of my chest. He looks so natural with a child; it makes me wonder how I could ever have doubted it.

Holden tickles Birdie under her chin before setting her down and straightening her headband. "How's my favorite girl today?"

"Ready to play soccer with you." She holds out her tiny hand to Holden. "Dad bought me a Manchester United soccer ball. I can't wait to show you."

"He did, did he?" Then he's pulled away by the sweetest little girl, glancing over his shoulder at me as they go. He winks. I wave. Then I need to inhale a deep breath to even out my erratic heartbeat. That... that was something. Heat warms my core and my thighs press together. *Get a hold of yourself, Briar.*

I manage to pull it together when Daisy finds me, squeezing me to her in a tight hug. I spend the next 30 minutes pretending to sip from the glass of wine that Everly hands me while making small talk in the kitchen with the girls. From my seat at the kitchen table I have a clear view through the patio doors of Holden, who is outside with Jake, Grayson, and Tucker. Our eyes seem to find one another's every few minutes and every time they do, my stomach gets that fluttery feeling.

Holden is nothing like I thought. He's sweet and thoughtful. Ever since I told him about the baby, he's been by my side. At this point, I'm not sure I can control myself around him any longer; my need for him is growing much too strong to deny myself.

"Can you take West for a second?" Everly asks, interrupting my thoughts. "I need to get his dinner ready."

She hands me the cutest little guy on the planet, who settles happily into my arms. He giggles as Daisy and Sierra take turns tickling him, and the sound of it melts me.

Loved. This little boy is loved beyond measure.

Love is something my little girl—or boy, if you ask Holden—will have in abundance. I may not know much about being a parent, but I know that for sure. This baby will be loved by Holden and me, by grandparents, aunts and uncles, and this circle of friends. Our chosen family.

Tears threaten to fall at the realization that Holden and I aren't going to be doing this alone.

As Everly slices strawberries, I look at West, his tiny nose, bright eyes and little grin showing off all four of his teeth.

It won't be long before I'm holding my own little one. Will our baby's hair be dark like Holden's or blonde like mine? Will he have his dad's emerald eyes or my lighter green ones? I inhale West's sweet baby scent, imagining holding my own little one in less than eight months.

I look up when I hear the patio door slide open, and see Holden standing in the doorway, a small smile on his face as he watches me. Chills tingle up my spine when he comes to stand next to me and then leans down to whisper against my ear, "Suits you, Bee. You look even more beautiful with a baby in your hands."

Holden's hand rests on the small of my back, his chest so close to my shoulder I can feel the warmth of his skin seeping through his T-shirt into my skin.

"Behave," I warn in a whisper, glancing around the

room. "They're going to think there's something going on between us."

"Well, isn't there?"

I tilt my head to the side, one eyebrow raised. *My god. This man.* I'm pretty sure I just whimpered. I bite down on my bottom lip to try to ease the lust simmering under my skin.

A smug smile raises the corners of his lips. He kisses the top of West's little head and walks back outside, leaving me wishing I could kiss that smirk off his face.

I'm not sure what just happened, but I'm pretty sure today changed everything.

HOLDEN DRIVES WITH ONE HAND ON THE STEERING WHEEL, the other resting out the open window. He's wearing a pair of black Ray-Bans and a backwards baseball hat, the entire look making me ache between my thighs. He's confident and laid back and has a natural sex appeal that I am so attracted to.

We're driving home from the veterinarian's office with Bear in the back seat in her condo—aka her pet carrier. She has been sick and lethargic for the last couple of days and when she wasn't getting any better, I decided to make an appointment. Holden offered to come with me, knowing I'm a bit of a mess. Turns out she ate one of my hair elastics that needed to be brought back up. The procedure took an hour. She's already looking more like herself.

I'm so glad Holden was there. For a guy who hates cats (and is deathly allergic to them), he stepped in and took charge. Carried Bear's crate, talked to the vet, asked all the right questions, and held my hand in the waiting room. It meant a lot to me.

My phone rings in my lap, distracting me from my thoughts. It's a FaceTime call from my mom.

"It's my mom," I tell Holden.

"I think you should answer it, Bee. We need to start telling people before you start to show."

He's right. I've put this off for far too long.

His eyes hold mine, urging me on to answer the call. Another moment passes with my heart in my throat until I decide I need to have this conversation. I scrub a hand over my face, muttering a curse word to myself before finally hitting accept on the screen.

"Hi Mom."

Holden gives me a nod of encouragement, then he reaches his hand across the console, placing it on my thigh.

"What's wrong?" she asks.

"Mom." I shake my head. "I'm fine."

Not even a second into the phone call and she can already tell I'm not myself. That's my mom. She has always had a strong intuition with her kids, apparently even through a screen from 10,000 miles away.

"I haven't talked to you in two weeks. I wanted to see your face. You look beautiful as always, but a little pale. Are you feeling okay?"

Holden pulls into his driveway and turns off the engine. We both get out of the car, but I motion to him that I'm going to walk across the street to the beach. I draw in a deep breath, inhaling the ocean air saturated with salt and seaweed. My favorite smell.

I sigh, sitting down in the sand. "I've been a little under the weather, Mom, but not for reasons that you probably think... I'm pregnant."

There. I said it. I wait, my heart in my throat.

Mom's jaw drops. "Oh my god."

"Yeah, I know. That's how I felt when I found out too."

"How far along?"

"Ten weeks. The baby is Holden's and before you ask... no, we're not together but he wants to be in both of our lives."

"Well, that's a good thing," she nods. "Have you been to the doctor?"

I tell her about the appointment as well as my upcoming ultrasound where we're going to find out if the baby is a boy or a girl. I watch my mom's eyes fill with tears.

'Mom, you're crying." My chest aches.

"Of course I am." She pats the tears from her cheeks. "My baby is having a baby. I'm going to be a grandma. It's a wonderful thing."

I feel an overwhelming sense of relief. My mom and I have always been close. I've never wanted to disappoint her. I was nervous to tell her, but I feel so grateful that she's embracing the news. I should have known she would. She's always been supportive and accepting of me.

"You're the first person we've told. We're going to tell Holden's moms and dad this week."

"Holden's moms?"

I nod. "His mom and dad are divorced, and his mom remarried a woman. They are all so nice. You would really like them."

Her eyes well again. "I hope they take good care of you, sweetheart. I wish I was there to help. It takes a village to raise a child. It breaks my heart that I'm so far away."

"I wish you were here too, Mom. You know you're my best friend."

She swallows hard, wiping her eyes again with her fingertips. "I love you, baby."

"I love you too."

"Can I tell Grandma and Grandpa and your brother?"

"Yeah, you can. Do you think Grandpa will be disappointed?" I ask nervously, looking out at the ocean.

"Never, honey. A baby is a blessing. He's going to be happy for you! We are all going to want to meet Holden, though. Maybe we could arrange a time to FaceTime?"

"Yeah, he wants to meet you too."

After ending the call with my mom, I walk back home feeling like a weight has been lifted from my shoulders. Holden is waiting for me on the porch with Bear in his hands. He looks so good in a navy T-shirt, his ball cap turned around so that I can see the nervous look in his piercing green eyes.

"Holden, you are going to itch all night if you don't put her back in her condo," I say, sitting down next to him.

"I can handle it. What I couldn't handle was listening to her cry in there. Poor thing had a rough day." He massages the white patch of fur between her ears before looking at me again. "You okay?"

I sigh. "I'm good."

"Did you tell her about the baby?"

"I did. She cried... happy tears."

A smile tugs at his mouth, which I want to kiss. Without thought, without worry, and with every fiber of my being.

He slips a big, strong arm around me pulling me into his side. "It's all going to be okay." He grins, his eyes sparkling as the sun sets over the beach, and nothing has ever felt this good or this right.

I just wish he would hurry up and make a move on me.

EIGHTEEN

CAT AND MOUSE

Holden

I've asked Briar every single day for weeks if we can tell our friends about the baby. So far, it's been a hard no. She's nervous how our friends will take the news, and I get it, but if they react anything like both of our families did, then it will be hugs and high-fives all around.

My mom was ecstatic when I told her the news. Definitely surprised, but mostly overjoyed. Ever since, she has become sort of a mother hen to Briar. The two of them, along with Barb, have been talking on the phone and texting each other regularly. My dad even got emotional when I told him he was going to be a grandpa.

It makes me happy that we have my family's full support. Happy that Briar can feel like she's part of our tribe.

Even though I did not have "get my roommate pregnant" on my bingo card for this year, it happened, and I don't regret where we are today. In just a few months, I've fallen for Briar. And I've fully wrapped my brain around the fact that I'm going to be a father.

I'm flipping eggs in a pan when Briar walks into the

kitchen wearing a pair of low-slung sweatpants and a T-shirt. She glides straight to the counter next to me and picks up the mug of peppermint tea that I left for her. She takes a sip, and I watch her sigh, her eyes fluttering closed, the happy sound she makes going straight to my cock.

When her eyes open, she catches me staring. She cocks her head to the side, and I smirk in response. She knows by now I can't get enough of her. The two of us have been playing a game of cat and mouse for way too long.

The moment is broken when I glance down at the swell of her belly, and she exhales.

"Briar," I say with enthusiasm. "You've popped."

Her hands fly to her belly, which only yesterday looked flat. It seems to have grown overnight. She looks down with an absentminded smile, staring at the bump. Her fingertips trace tiny circles over the cotton of her T-shirt, and my own hands are absolutely itching to be splayed over her little round bump too.

My emotions are all over the place these days. I'm excited to meet my little Slugger, which seems bizarre. It wasn't long ago that I didn't think I wanted kids at all, and now becoming a father is practically all I can think about.

"My clothes are all too tight. The little muffin has made an appearance." Briar lifts her shirt a few inches and looks down at the smooth curve of her stomach.

"Can I?" I ask quietly nodding at her stomach.

"You want to feel my baby bump?"

My brow crinkles. "Is that okay? If it makes you uncomfortable, you can say no. I won't be upset. I'm just excited."

I haven't touched Briar in a meaningful way since the night we conceived Slugger. She lifts her shirt so my hand can cover the curve of her tummy.

"Sometimes I think I can feel the baby move, but I'm not sure. It feels like little flutters."

"It won't be long according to the app," I tell her as my palm moves slowly in circles over her tight skin. "Will you let me feel it when it does?"

"I'll tell you. I promise."

"Thank you." I exhale, removing my hand from the place where Briar is growing our baby. A month ago, Briar's pregnancy would have been a mystery to me. Thanks to the app I read every night before bed, I know my slugger is the size of a bell pepper and growing fast. There's no way Briar is going to be able to keep the baby a secret for much longer.

"You look good. The perfect little baby bump," I assure her.

She gives me a long look then her cheeks flush pink. She's been blushing like that around me for a while now; admittedly, I know what makes her cheeks rosy, and I try my best to make it happen often.

For the last few weeks, Briar and I have been spending all our free time together at home. We binge episodes of *New Girl*, play board games, cook together. Ever since she passed her first trimester, Briar has had more energy and her nausea has faded. She's back to her firecracker self, funny and giving me shit at every opportunity. She hasn't, however, been seeing her friends. I'd like to think she just really loves my company, but I'm pretty sure she's been hiding out at home because she's not ready to tell everyone that she's pregnant. At this point, I'm just hoping she's ready to tell them before she gives birth.

Briar needs her friends, and although the time we've been spending together has been important in getting to know each other, I have a feeling that a part of her is lonely.

To be honest, I've liked having her all to myself, but I know how much her friends mean to her.

I've let her set the pace, I've given her time, but eventually that time is going to run out.

After breakfast, a meal that Briar miraculously now enjoys ever since she passed the 12-week mark with Slugger, I tell her to relax on the couch with one of her books while I tackle the kitchen cleanup. When I walk into the living room to find her, her head is tilted back against a cushion, her feet propped on the coffee table.

"I have something for you," I say, dropping onto the couch next to her.

I hand her an envelope and wait as she hesitantly opens it and pulls out the gift card I got her for a spa here in Reed Point. She spent weeks feeling sick to her stomach and tired, working long days through it all, and then coming home and making dinner—even though I insisted she didn't have to. I bought her the gift card because I thought she'd appreciate being pampered.

And I want her to know that I appreciate her.

"What is this?"

"I thought you could spend a few hours at the spa. Get your feet rubbed, or a massage. Anything you want, Briar."

"Holden, this is so thoughtful of you. I don't know what to say."

"I give terrible massages, and I know how much you like them. You deserve to relax. You're cooking our baby."

Tears instantly spring to her eyes, which I should be used to by now. Briar cries at everything these days: commercials, her books, cats on the internet, every time I talk about Slugger. But a swirl of emotion barrels through me anyways seeing her cry.

"I'm sorry," she sniffles, wiping her eyes. "I don't know

why I'm crying. This little bean seems to have turned me into a crier. Thank you, Holden. I can't wait to use this."

"Just make sure the masseuse is a woman, Bee."

Her eyes narrow. "Why does it matter?"

"If another man touches you, it will be a problem."

Her mouth falls open, jaw practically hitting the floor. "Why? You're jealous of another man touching me?"

"Is that even a question? It's just a matter of time before I make you officially mine."

My back stiffens, bracing for the impact of my admission. I'm not sure exactly what we are. More than friends, but beyond that I don't know. I have the sense that if I asked her to be my girlfriend, she'd say yes. Jesus. That sounds archaic. Do adults in their late 20s even ask each other out anymore?

I'm pleasantly surprised when she says, "I don't blame you, Holden. I wouldn't like anyone's hands on you either."

"It's that simple," I respond, when what I really should do is lift her up onto this counter and make a meal out of her. "I don't like others touching what is mine."

Her lips part but no words come out. Her eyes find mine, and I meet her stare. Silence stretches between us for a moment before she finally looks away.

"Well, thanks again, really," Briar says hoarsely, picking up the envelope and then hurrying out of the kitchen, her blonde ponytail swaying. I'm used to this by now with her. I seem to gain an inch before I'm stopped in my tracks. Luckily, I've never been one to give up on something that I want.

My intense need to have Briar again has been building over the last few months. Now all that is left of my resolve is rubble.

Following Briar through the door of Buttercup Bakery, I spot Sierra behind the counter as soon as we walk inside. She waves at us as we take a seat at a corner table, her attention on a little girl at the counter who is choosing from the selection of colorful, frosted cupcakes.

Briar tugs the hem of her shirt down. "This feels risky."

I scooch my chair closer to hers. "What does?" I ask, lowering my voice to a whisper. "Do you think the cupcakes are laced with something?"

She swats my arm, narrowing her eyes at me. "Sierra is here, and she might notice the bump."

"And?"

She huffs. "And... then she'll know that I'm pregnant."

"Ah, right. My Slugger is fairly well hidden behind the table. I think you'll be fine." I wink at her.

She rolls her eyes, but grins. "I promise we'll tell our friends soon, Holden. I know keeping Slugger a secret is eating you alive."

"Yes, it is, but I'm trying to be patient."

She looks at me like "patient" is a stretch, but I truly have been. I haven't said a word, even though there's nothing I want more on this earth than to share our news with the most important people in my life. They won't believe it. Six months ago, I wouldn't have believed it myself. People change; I am proof of that. And I'm so fucking happy.

A few minutes later, Sierra appears at our table carrying two cupcakes with purple and blue frosting.

"For you," she says, setting the plates on the table with a warm smile. "These are from me. What can I get you two to drink?"

"Thanks, Sierra. A coffee for me, please," I say before looking at Briar. "Tea for you?"

"Peppermint, please."

Fork in hand, I scoop the icing from the top, putting the sugary topping to the side before stabbing off a chunk of the vanilla cupcake. I like sweets, but the cake is enough for me. It's a perfect bite. Not surprising, since Sierra is *the* best baker. So good, she opened Buttercup Bakery a few years ago with the encouragement of Grayson. The guys and I spent a few months helping with construction.

"You're not eating the best part," Briar says flatly.

"Says who?"

"Says me." She flashes me a sassy grin before scooping the icing off my plate and onto hers. Her mouth forms an O as she sucks the frosting from the fork.

I take a sip of the cup of coffee that Sierra brought to the table, my cock plumping in my shorts from the expression on Briar's face. I haven't forgotten how good her mouth felt wrapped around my cock. It is on the long list of things I like about her— her magic mouth and the incomparable way she uses it.

I'm snapped out of my fantasy when the bell on the door chimes and I look up to see... my ex. Amy walks in, and her curious eyes bounce from me to Briar and back to me again.

"Holden, I thought that was you. Hi!"

I lift my hand in a wave at Amy, who walks across the bakery to our table in workout gear, a yoga mat in her arm. "Hi, Amy. It's good to see you."

Reed Point isn't big, so I've run into Amy from time to time over the years. Seeing her is no big deal. I've been over her for a long time. Besides, there isn't anyone on the planet who could tear my attention away from Briar.

"This is my girlfriend, Briar." I gesture towards Briar, who looks back at me like I've grown a third eyeball.

Amy's mom is still best friends with my mom, so I'm sure by now she's heard all about the girl who is the "plus one" on my RSVP to her wedding. But it feels wrong calling Briar my girlfriend under false pretenses. If it was up to me, Briar would be mine for real.

"It's nice to meet you." Amy sticks a hand across the table and Briar stands in order to reach it. When she does, Amy's eyes drift immediately to her belly. "Oh! I didn't realize you're expecting. Congratulations!"

My stomach drops and I swivel to see Briar's eyes wide with panic. She chews her bottom lip, working herself up while I brace for her reaction.

"Umm, thank you," she squeaks out. "I'm not... well... we haven't told many people yet."

"How are the wedding plans, Amy?" I interject, trying to put Briar out of her misery.

"They're pretty much done. I mean, they better be, I'm getting married in three weeks."

"We're looking forward to it."

"I'm glad you'll be there."

I shoot Amy an easy smile before we say our goodbyes and as she turns to walk towards the counter, I notice Sierra's eyes on Briar and me. *Shit.* I don't know for sure, but there is a very good chance she overheard the entire conversation.

I try to play it cool until Sierra gets drawn into a discussion with a customer.

"I think we may have a problem," I tell Briar. "Sierra might have just heard all of that."

Briar grimaces like she's in pain.

Sliding my hand along her thigh under the table, my palm settles on her knee. "We're going to tell our friends tonight, babe," I warn her. "It's time."

She sighs but doesn't argue. "Okay. How do you want to do it?"

"We're going to invite everyone over for pizza then we're going to tell them our news. Sound good?"

Her eyes meet mine and she nods, then places a hand on top of mine under the table.

I lace my fingers through hers, and despite everything else that is happening right now, all I can think is: I want her.

God, do I want her.

And I am done waiting.

I JUMPED INTO ACTION ON THE WAY HOME FROM THE BAKERY. We made a quick stop at the grocery store to pick up a few things then I texted the group to invite them over for a last-minute hangout at my place. Fortunately, everyone can make it. Briar seems nervous, but also excited. I've reassured her time and time again that our friends are going to be happy for us. I think she's starting to believe it.

Jake, Everly and the kids are the first to arrive, followed by Tucker and Jake, Grayson and finally Sierra with baby Sadie. I had pulled Sierra aside before leaving the bakery to ask her to please keep anything she may have heard to herself for just a little longer. She gave me an innocent look as she claimed not to have any idea what I was talking about. But now, when I give her a quick hug hello, she whispers, *I am so excited for this* into my ear.

One by one, our friends make it out to the backyard to enjoy the warm fall night. Birdie is on the grass playing with a backpack full of dolls she brought along, while baby West is in Jake's arms looking happy as a clam. Briar takes a seat beside me. The off-the-shoulder sweater she's wearing is barely covering her bump and she's absolutely glowing. It's a mystery how someone hasn't caught on at this point.

"Give him to me." I hold my hands out to West, then transfer him from his dad's arms into mine. He instantly giggles as I bounce him up and down on my knee.

Everly smiles. "He loves his uncle Holdey."

I blow a raspberry into his neck. "His uncle Holdey loves him too."

Little by little, Briar relaxes next to me, sipping from a glass of iced tea. Every now and then her eyes slide to meet mine and I try my best to reassure her without words. Sitting next to Briar, surrounded by our friends, feels good. An incredible sense of pride that she's *my* baby momma blooms in my chest.

The bubble bursts when Grayson takes advantage of a lull in the group's conversation to ask, "So, is there a reason for the last-minute soiree, Holden?"

"It was our turn to host," I reply innocently.

I feel Briar sit up a little straighter beside me, and I am sure her heart is pounding just as hard as mine. We were going to wait until after we ate, but it doesn't look like that's happening now. I turn my head to look at Briar, who already has her eyes on me. She nods, giving me the okay to tell them.

"Briar and I have news."

Tucker rolls his eyes. "I might be slow sometimes to figure shit out, but I think we all know what you're about to tell us."

Daisy looks from me to Briar then back to me. "Please tell me you two are finally together. Make my whole life. Please."

Briar laughs next to me, and that gives me all the encouragement I need to share our news. My core warms from the inside out at the sound of her happiness. I plan on keeping her laughing like that for a very long time.

"Or maybe that's too obvious, Dais," Tucker nudges his wife with his shoulder. "Here's another guess: Briar put a glass on the coffee table without a coaster and Holden has called us all here to stage an intervention."

"Please just spit it out," Everly groans, leaning closer, propping her forearms on the table. "You're killing me."

"First, Tuck, you're an idiot. And no, we're not together. Yet." I look at Briar. "While I have every intention of making Briar fall in love with me, we brought you all here to tell you... we're having a baby. Briar's pregnant."

We wait in suspended silence as they all stare at us with wide eyes, before the backyard erupts.

"Oh my gosh, this is the best news ever!" Sierra exclaims while Daisy rushes over to us, eyes already filling with tears. The guys high-five me across the table.

"Holy shit, that is not what I was expecting," Jake laughs, clapping me on my back. "Are you serious?"

Briar nods. "He's serious." All eyes fly to Briar, who covers her face with her hands. "I'm 18 weeks along."

"But... you're not together?" Grayson asks.

"Grayson, that's not the point right now." Sierra shakes her head, elbowing her husband in the ribs. "Where are your manners?"

"It's fine." I glance at Briar and smirk. "We're not officially together, but there's no other woman on the planet for me and I'm going to prove that to her."

Briar's mouth lifts into a slight smile when our eyes connect, and my insides turn to mush. A second later she turns her attention to Daisy, who is pulling Briar into her arms. "Oh my god, girl, I am so happy for you."

"Okay, I need details, you two. When did you find out? Does your mom know? How are you feeling?"

"Better now. It was a rough first trimester."

Daisy nods, squeezing Briar's hand., "Why didn't you tell me sooner?"

"We didn't tell anyone. I was in shock. We both were. I just needed time to process the whole thing. It finally now feels like it's all real."

I curl my hand around Briar's thigh.

"You could have told me," Daisy continues. "I could have been there for you both."

Briar nods. "I know, and I'm sorry. Are you mad?"

Daisy's palm flies to the space over her heart. "What? Of course not, but now it all makes sense. You were spending less and less time with me. I thought either you were falling for Holden, or you were going through something that you didn't want to tell me about."

"Who would have thought I was hiding a pregnancy from you?" Briar snorts, her laugh mixed with a cry.

"Not in a million years," Daisy replies with a chuckle.

I squeeze Briar's knee at the same time West releases a wail, arching his chubby baby back in my arms.

"You hear that, my sweet little baby muffin?" Everly coos, taking West from my arms. "You're going to have a friend to play with. Uncle Holden and Auntie Briar are having a baby."

I slump back into my chair, a wave of relief washing over me. I turn to Briar, pressing my lips against her temple before pulling her into me. Everyone we really care about now knows about the baby. It feels like coming up for a breath of air after being held for too long under water.

Now there is only one more thing I need to do. I want Briar. I want Briar to myself.

I've taken things slow. I've had to, because I know the stakes are high. I have so much to lose. The last thing I want is for our child to be caught in between us if things didn't work. I don't ever want Briar or our child to be hurt.

But I know I want her. I want her and our baby and our little house on Haven Harbor.

A family.

And after tonight, I am done waiting for what I want.

NINETEEN

CAN YOU BE A GOOD GIRL?

Briar

"What do you think? I think that went pretty well."

Our friends headed out about half an hour ago, but not before the girls planned a gender reveal party for us. And a shower. And started tossing around baby names. There was no stopping them once the shock of our news had worn off. When I hugged them goodbye at the door they were brainstorming where to source a cannon that shoots pink or blue confetti in the sky. Slightly over the top, but I have to admit that it felt good. For the first time since I found out I was pregnant, tonight we really and truly celebrated the news.

"I think it went great," I agree as I start the dishwasher. It was a wonderful night, but I'm happy the house is quiet again. Just me and Holden. "Although I think I hurt Daisy's feelings by keeping her in the dark."

"She'll get over it," Holden assures me as he tosses the last of the empties into the recycling bin. "She loves you. She's happy for you. You two just need to talk. I'm sure she has questions."

"I'm sure she does." I look up at the ceiling, exhaling a

breath. "Holden, what do I tell her when she asks me why we're not together?"

As soon as the words leave my lips, he's crossing the kitchen towards me. The air is charged all around us, there's a shift in our energy. My breath hitches in my throat from adrenaline that is suddenly coursing through me.

"Briar..."

Holden's fingertips brush over my cheek then behind my ear, pushing away a few loose strands of hair. My skin pebbles under his touch, a shiver rolling down my spine. Holden smirks, knowing exactly what he's doing to me.

"What? I'm cold."

"Un-huh. Sure."

His fingers dust a path down my neck before he's walking me backwards, pinning me against the countertop. His chest presses to mine, and I swear I can feel the pounding of his heart. "We're done pretending, Bee."

"Done." I glide my hands over his pecs.

"You're going to tell Daisy, and your mom, and anyone else who asks, that we're together."

I smile and he kisses the smile from my lips. I'm a mess for this man. The love I have for him is limitless. Holden has been by my side every step of my pregnancy even though just months ago he never saw himself being a father. He's taken care of me. He's planning for our future. He has spent the last few months learning everything he can about a baby he's never met.

"Is that really what you want?" My voice comes out ragged, breathy.

"I've always wanted you. I just didn't realize I could have you," he whispers. "All I want is to make you happy."

"You do make me happy."

"I want you to trust that I am here for you and Slugger."

He cups my face in his palms. "Now that I have you, Bee, I'm never letting you go. I'm not going anywhere."

Oh god. I love it when he talks to me like this.

I've never been spoken to in such a beautiful, vulnerable way. I nod, realizing how badly I needed to hear him say that. I've been mistreated and thrown away in the past, but this feels different. I wasn't sure I would ever be able to really trust a man again, but Holden has changed that.

"I trust you."

And I'm falling so hard for you.

He reaches for me, his strong hand capturing the nape of my neck, holding me in place. It takes me by surprise but when he pulls me to him, my body goes willingly. We collide together, my chest pressed against his, his mouth colliding with mine.

I swallow his moan as he kisses me. Holden is kissing me, and I finally give in and let him take control. The kiss is demanding, as if he's making up for not kissing me all these weeks. His fingers grip the back of my hair, and mine snake around the back of his neck, urging him on, needing him to kiss me with everything he has. I've waited so long for this, for him. I hold him as close to me as our bodies will allow, breathing him in, kissing him harder until his tongue sweeps along the seam of my lips begging for entry.

I taste him, my tongue sliding against his, desire and lust winding through my body. What was I thinking waiting this long to kiss him again?

He sweeps my hair over my shoulder to kiss along my jaw then down my throat. "I've missed you."

"You could have had me whenever you wanted," I murmur, my toes curling against the hardwood floor as he presses open-mouthed kisses over my skin.

"You weren't ready."

"Oh, I was." I feel my cheeks heat.

"You were always going to be worth the wait."

A grin creeps over my face and when he smiles back, I am not okay.

Holden knows how to turn my entire body into liquid. He can turn me on with just a look.

"Mine, Bee. You are mine, and I won't ever pretend again that what we have isn't real because it is." He pulls away to look at me, intensity in his eyes. "We're real. You are the only thing that I want. You and our baby. Fuck." He rakes his hand through his hair. "This is the last thing I ever expected to happen, but you and Slugger mean everything to me. I don't care about anything else. All I know is I want you and our family."

Tears blur my vision as his hands cup my face in his hands. "Don't cry, Bee. It kills me."

"They're happy tears, I promise. Blame it on the hormones."

"Whatever you need to tell yourself." He cocks his head with that smirk that buckles my knees. Then his mouth crashes into mine in a frenzied need. My body hums with anticipation as his tongue sweeps over every corner of my mouth.

Holden is a passionate lover, and I finally know what it feels like to be in the arms of a real man. My hands fist his shirt when he begins to trail slow, wet kisses down my neck.

"God, you are fucking beautiful. You have no idea what you do to me. All I want to do is make you happy." I whimper when he nips my shoulder with his teeth, marking me, claiming me, his need matching my own. I melt into him, letting out a quiet mewl, knowing there will be a mark on my skin tomorrow. Just the thought sends a bolt of heat to my core.

Holden Banks is irresistibly sexy. I've never stood a chance with him.

I'm breathless, heart pounding, as he kisses a path along my jaw. His hands wrap around me, gripping my ass and pulling me closer, tugging my pelvis into the hard ridge of his erection.

We both moan at the friction. In reply, Holden presses the bulge in his pants firmly against my clit and his name rolls off my tongue in a desperate cry. I've never felt like this before. The attraction I feel for him is beyond anything I've known. It's more than physical. Holden is my calm in the midst of a storm. A touchdown in the last five seconds of a game. A breeze on a hot, sticky afternoon. Sinking into a hot bath at the end of a long day. He makes me feel safe, seen, loved. He makes me want a future... with him.

Holden's mouth covers mine as his fingers slip under the hem of my sweater. His warm hands skim the sides of my ribs. "Holden," I pant.

His hands explore the lace of my bralette, moving over the swell of my breasts as our pelvises rut against one another's. Dear god. The foreplay is killing me, and all we've done is kiss.

My chest heaves as his nose brushes over the column of my neck until we're staring at one another.

"I'm going strip you out of your clothes." His voice is a raspy threat. "I'm going to make you come so hard your soul leaves your body. If that isn't what you want, you need to tell me right now because once I get started, I won't be able to stop."

"Please don't stop."

He wraps me in his arms, lifting me off my feet like I weigh nothing and sets me on the counter. Slowly, he slips my sweater up my body and over my head, dropping the fabric onto the floor. "I've dreamt about this body, pretty girl. I've been dying to have it back in my arms."

I've dreamt about this too. Far too many times to count.

I grip strands of his hair, pulling gently as he lowers his head to my chest. He tugs down the lace of my bra, exposing my breast. My nipple tingles and hardens as I arch into his touch. My body shudders and my head tips back in a moan when his warm mouth covers my nipple, sucking the stiff peak and kneading my other breast in his palm.

"Holden... your mouth... so good," I breathe. I want him to move lower to where I've been aching for him for so long, but he's taking his time, laving and sucking, swirling and licking. My body is on fire, my panties already soaked.

I scoot forward to the edge of the counter, widening my thighs, whimpering, until my pelvis connects with the hard ridge behind his zipper. A needy desire explodes in my body when Holden's cock moves against my center.

I break the kiss, unwillingly, when my back arches into Holden's hard-as-stone body. Chest heaving, my hands tangled in his hair, my eyes lock with his.

"Hands around my neck, legs around my waist, Bee," he demands. I do as he tells me, then he sweeps me off the counter and carries me to his bedroom, kissing me the entire way.

The room is dark when he lies me down on the bed, hovering over me as he sucks my bottom lip into his mouth. "Don't move."

Like I would go anywhere. Doesn't he know by now that I want him as badly as I need air?

He walks to the nightstand and flicks on the lamp, then moves to stand before me at the side of his bed. His hair is a tousled mess from my hands weaving through it. He's wearing a simple gray T-shirt that's stretched over the hard surfaces of his torso. He is the sexiest man I have ever laid eyes on.

And then it gets better when Holden pulls the shirt over his head. He slips his hand in his pants, adjusting his noticeable erection that's pressing against the zipper of his jeans. When he's more comfortable, he dips his head down to kiss me before knocking me off kilter with a mischievous smirk.

"So hot." My hands press against the smooth muscle of his back as he kisses me breathless. I run my fingers down over his perfect ass, up his 8-pack abs, finally landing between us at his belt buckle. Fumbling, he helps me until we're a mess of tangled limbs and discarded clothes, both naked in the center of the bed.

"Can I?" His eyes flick to mine. He's asking for permission with his hand hovering over my belly. I nod, touched by the awe in his expression. He has seen my growing belly from afar, but he's only ever touched it once. I hold my breath as his hand gently stretches across my navel. His lips follow, pressing a soft kiss to the taut skin. His tenderness and devotion to our baby has my heart in my throat.

Then Holden is crawling down the bed until he's positioned between my spread thighs. "Lie back while I make you come," he instructs me. "I'm going to fuck you, but before I do, I want you wet and aching for my cock. Can you be a good girl and come for me while I lick you?"

Oh my flipping god. This man and his filthy mouth driving me crazy.

I suck in a breath when he spreads my legs wide, nodding wordlessly, knowing exactly what Holden can do with his mouth.

"I haven't forgotten how good you taste, Bee. I plan on having my face between your legs for a while so get comfortable."

My muscles tense and I clutch the sheets when his tongue licks a path from my opening to my clit. "Oh god," I moan when his mouth closes around the swollen bundle of nerves, sucking hard. So hard, my body shakes. His tongue swirls and flutters as a cry escapes my mouth.

I am dripping wet, and it feels so good. Closing my eyes, I widen my legs even further as he continues to lick and suck, adding one finger before adding a second a minute later.

"Feel good, baby?"

"So good." I writhe. I could lie here for an eternity if I didn't want Holden's cock inside of me so badly. The noises that are coming from me are proof I'm drowning. It's an overwhelming torture. I groan again at the sheer pleasure of his mouth.

"Holden, do you—"

"Like eating you as much as you like it when I lick you?" I nod, my bottom lip trapped under my teeth, unable to speak when his tongue enthusiastically licks the length of me. "If I told you I could spend hours between your thighs with my face buried in your pussy and never be full, would that answer your question?"

He grins. A jaw-dropping, naughty smirk before going back down on me. My god, this man.

Holden doesn't stop in his relentless pursuit and when his fingers hook inside me, fluttering against my inner wall, I see bright white, earth-shattering stars. I rock against his face, panting, silently begging him for more but unsure of just how much more I can take.

I hold off my orgasm for as long as I can until my back is arching and my hands grip the strands of his thick, dark hair. More pleasure than I've ever known wracks my body until I'm spent and boneless, lifeless and blissed-out. Moaning and crying.

When I finally catch my breath, I open my eyes to see Holden on his knees, wiping my arousal from his mouth, his cock jutted between us. He fists his thick shaft, leaning forward to suck on my tongue.

"I want you bare. Do I need a condom?"

Holden waits for my answer.

"I've been tested and I'm good."

"I'm good too."

He sighs. "You look so fucking beautiful sprawled naked on my bed with my baby in your belly, Bee. Do you have any idea how hot you look?"

"I'm getting bigger by the minute." I smile, absentmindedly running my palm over my tummy.

"I've never seen anything sexier."

He has no idea what his words do to me. None. I've always been confident in my body but when your boyfriend is built like a professional athlete and your body is changing by the second, it's hard not to be a little self-conscious.

"You're beautiful and I want you," he murmurs, stroking my hair.

"I want you too." My eyes drift down to his cock, which is rock hard and weeping at the tip.

Holden positions himself at my entrance, his eyes seared to mine. I haven't forgotten how my body had to stretch to accommodate him, how I felt him for days between my thighs. Holden is large.

"You ready for my cock, pretty girl?"

"I'm ready."

The look in his eyes steals my breath. Intense, like I'm the only thing that matters to him in this world. His eyes are heavy-lidded with desire, and it leaves goosebumps over my skin. He notches his erection into my opening and slowly sinks inside of me, inch by inch, stretching me. Pleasure mixed with pain. "Relax for me, Bee. Let me in."

He covers my lips with his own, kissing me deeply until he's buried all the way to the hilt, and I can feel the smattering of groomed, dark hair brushing against my clit. "Holden."

"You feel unbelievable." He rolls his hips, pinches my nipple, pulling out to the tip and thrusting back in. I am so full, addicted to the way Holden feels buried inside of me.

"Better than incredible." I reach for his nape, drawing his mouth down to mine, our mouths fusing together in a desperate, needy kiss.

He doesn't hold back, the muscles in his arms and torso tensing as he grinds into me. Needing to feel him, my fingers dust over the hard planes of his taut muscles until they tighten even more.

He groans a desperate sound. "Don't stop touching me."

I love it when he tells me what he wants. When he's unhinged for me. My fingers continue exploring the grooves and valleys of his torso, digging into his sides.

"Such a good girl for me, Bee."

Holden lets out a possessive growl, thrusting into me, and I gasp when he hits me at just the right spot. "I'm so close. Oh god, Holden."

"Come for me, baby. I want you to drench my cock so I can fill you to the brim."

He reaches between us, circling my clit with his middle finger. My legs start to shake, and the base of my spine begins to tingle.

"Holden... baby.... Oh god, right there... I'm going to come."

Holden thrusts into me and I vibrate, coming with an

intensity that I've never felt before. Wild shocks of pleasure wrack my body, every nerve ending exploding.

My walls clench around him. My eyes squeeze shut in ecstasy. "Holden," I cry. The sounds of sex fill the room as he flexes his hips into my center.

"Mine, Bee. Do you understand me? You are mine. I want you to say it."

His hand fastens around the nape of my neck as he drags me closer. "Say it, Bee. Tell me that I belong to you. Tell me that I am the only man who gets to fuck this perfect pussy."

"Yours, Holden. Only yours. You were meant for me."

"Mine, baby," he cries, grinding against me one final time before pouring inside of me, unravelling before my eyes.

I run my hands down his spine when he falls over me, his still-hard cock pulsing inside my walls.

"Briar." He rolls to his back taking me with him. "I can't squish the baby."

Giggling, I reach for his dark hair, pushing it from his forehead, the concerned look on his face filling my chest. "Don't worry, the baby is fine. But we made a mess of your bedsheets. I think you're going to have to change them before you sleep."

He lifts his brow. "Were you going to make me sleep here all by myself?"

"Don't pout," I coo. "I was about to get to that."

He scoops me from the bed into his arms and carries me to the hall. "I hated sleeping without you. I don't plan on sleeping without you ever again. You better get used to me, Bee. I'm not going anywhere."

TWENTY

I WILL RUIN ANY MAN

Holden

A knock on my door hauls me from sleep. The light filtering in through the window tells me we must have slept in.

Briar's back is nestled against my chest, my leg slung over her hip.

Last night I learnt that Briar is a cuddler. She fell asleep next to me, but not before nuzzling her ass into my groin and pulling my arm around her. I didn't think I'd be able to fall asleep in that position, but it's morning, and it appears that I slept like a baby.

I reluctantly peel myself from her warm skin, trying not to wake her. But when I shift the blinds to see who's at my door, she stirs.

"Holden. Is someone here?"

"I'm not sure, baby, but go back to bed. I'll take care of it."

Tugging on a pair of athletic shorts, I pad down the hall, dragging my hands through my hair.

I glance at my watch. 10:10 a.m. It must be Birdie wanting to kick a soccer ball around. That kid is obsessed.

Another knock raps against the door. When I look out the large living room window, there's an SUV I don't recognize in my driveway. That's weird. Haven Harbor is a private street. The only reason you would be here is if you live here or if you know someone who does.

I open the door to a guy I've never met. He's tall, about two inches taller than my 6'1" frame. He's wearing a polo shirt, jeans and a pair of Nike Blazers. He glances behind my right shoulder before looking at me.

"Can I help you?"

"Who are you?" he gruffly commands.

What in the fuck?

"This is my house. How about you telling me who *you* are."

"I'm looking for Briar Moore," he says. "Where is she?"

The hairs on the back of my neck stand on end, my jaw muscles instantly tightening. I have no idea who this guy is but there's no way I'm letting him anywhere near Briar.

"Briar doesn't live here. Sorry, I can't help you."

"Well, do you know where I can find her? It's important, I need to see her."

I fold my arms across my chest, shaking my head. "Sorry man, not a clue."

Anger radiates off him, his eyes bouncing around the room, looking, I assume, for *my* girlfriend.

Before he can say anything more, I shut the door and lock it, then turn to find Briar stepping out from the hallway. She's pulled on one of my T-shirts, the hem tucked into a pair of shorts. She looks beautiful—she always does—but the expression on her face stops me in my tracks.

"What was he doing here?" she asks, wrapping her arms around her middle.

"Looking for you." I swallow hard. "Briar, who was that guy?"

Her chin lowers, and she takes two steps towards me, grabbing my hand and pulling me to the couch. I sit and pull her down into my lap. "Are you alright?"

She nods. "I'm fine."

She doesn't seem fine.

"That was Justin... my ex. I had no idea he was even in Reed Point. I'm sorry he showed up at your house."

"Well, I'm sorry you had to date him. That guy is a total asshole."

"I know," she sighs. "He's terrible. I hate that he knows where I'm staying."

"How does he know that you're staying with me? Who would have told him? Does he talk to Daisy or your mom?"

"No, never. I honestly don't know. I don't get it. It doesn't make—" Briar stops mid-sentence, her eyes suddenly going wide. She jumps up from my lap, walking towards her bedroom. When she returns, she has her phone in her hand. "He tracked me. I am so stupid."

She drops down onto the couch beside me and I can see that she's shaken.

"He was *tracking* you?"

She nods. "When we were together, he set up a location label for me without telling me so he could track me. I found out he did it when he accused me of cheating on him. He wanted to know why I was out at one of our favorite places for dinner one night, and who I was with. When I asked him how he knew I was there, he didn't have an answer for me until he finally admitted he had tracked me. The ironic part is I was just out with a girlfriend that night

—but I found out later that *he* was cheating on me. Stupid ass."

She places her phone on the coffee table with a sigh. "I can't believe I didn't think to delete it and now he knows where to find me."

"So, he essentially stalked you, then he accused you of cheating, then he slept with someone else?" I seethe. "Asshole is an understatement."

There's a pause before she speaks again. "It gets worse. He didn't just cheat on me. He broke my trust in the worst way, Holden."

"What did he do?" My jaw clenches.

"He humiliated me," she says, her voice shaky. "He shared personal photos I sent him with his friends. In a group chat. One of the guys knew it was shitty and sent me a screen shot."

"I will kill him," I growl, shooting up off my chair, pacing the floor like a caged animal. I doubt I've ever been so angry in my entire life. What kind of a guy betrays a woman's trust like that?

"Holden, come here. Sit down. Please. Being angry isn't going to change things. I've moved on. I won't give him that kind of power over me and neither should you."

I reluctantly sink back into the couch beside her—I'd much rather jump in my truck and go find the guy, but I don't want to make the situation even more stressful for Briar.

She turns to me, hugging the throw pillow to her chest.

"Justin isn't a nice guy. I don't know why I didn't see it sooner, but eventually it became clear. He made me feel small. He controlled me. He liked feeling powerful. I accepted his shitty behaviour because I wanted to see the good in him, and I know it sounds silly, but I thought he would change. I always made excuses for him—he was just stressed out, or tired, or he had a hard week at work. I wanted to believe that deep down he was a good guy and that he loved me, but I learnt the hard way that I was wrong. He's selfish and mean and I'm still mad at myself for accepting the way he treated me. Honestly, I think that's why he wanted me. He knew I always try to see the good in people and he took advantage of that. He thought I would stay forever, that I would just keep forgiving him. But he was wrong. I left. And when I moved back to Reed Point, I promised myself I would never allow another person to treat me the way he did."

I knew she was doubtful of men and relationships when she moved back here, and now that I know the reason why, I don't blame her. Anyone in her shoes would feel the same way. Hearing this, I'm glad we decided to go slow. She needed time to believe that she could trust me.

"You know I would never hurt you, right? Tell me you know that."

"I know that, Holden. You have always been good to me. You accept me for who I am. You build me up instead of tearing me down. You make me feel good. I think I've spent the last few months letting myself believe that I deserve this. That I deserve you. I'm making myself whole again, making myself better."

She leans into me, and my heart does a flip inside my chest. "Thanks for listening. But can we please forget about all of this? I'm done talking about him."

I wrap my hand around the end of her ponytail and pull. Her face tips up to mine. "Let's talk about something else."

I kiss her. She smiles.

"Should we talk about how turned on it made me to see you get so protective over me?"

"I will ruin any man who tries to hurt you."

She wraps her hands around my nape and straddles my thighs. I kiss the underside of her jaw, earning a giggle. "You are sweet, Holden Banks."

"I'm lucky."

"You are?"

"I am. I have you. Him not seeing how good he had it is my gain."

Her gaze holds mine, fingers playing with the strands of hair at the base of my neck.

"Holden, you need to stop saying the most perfect things while I'm pregnant," she says, smiling softly. "All you're going to do is make me cry."

Curling my arms around her waist, I kiss her, showing her that I'm here for her, and that I always will be no matter what.

TWENTY-ONE

WHAT IF IT ISN'T A BOY?

Briar

Holden sings the lyrics to a Riley Green song with one hand gripping the steering wheel of his truck, the other holding mine in my lap. Golden hour oranges and reds stream through the windshield, highlighting the vivid green of his eyes. I ask myself for the hundredth time how I got so lucky.

I take my time admiring my boyfriend while my heart flip flops in my chest. I silently tell myself not to cry when I feel tears prick my eyes yet again. My life feels like a dream. I've been like this for two days, my heart in my throat, since leaving my 20-week ultrasound with Holden.

I lost it when the ultrasound tech showed us our baby on the screen. A little head, arms and legs. *Our baby*. Holden and I were both in complete awe as the wand slid over my stomach. When she was done taking the measurements, she printed off a photo with the baby's sex and sealed it in an envelope. We drove it straight to Daisy's so she could get ready for the gender reveal party she was co-hosting with

Sierra and Everly—the party Holden and I are on our way to now.

"What if it isn't a boy?" I ask him.

"What?"

"The baby. If it's a girl, will you be okay?"

Holden laughs. "Are you really worrying about that, Bee? Of course I will be okay. I'll be more than okay. It doesn't matter to me if it's a boy or a girl. But I happen to know it's a boy."

I groan. "How are you so sure?"

He shrugs with that damn smirk. "I just am."

I shake my head. "You're impossible."

I look down to where my hand is resting on my belly, which has gotten so much bigger over the last two weeks. As have my boobs. Most of my clothes are too tight, my pants now held together with a hair elastic looped through the buttonhole and then around the button.

It's still wild to me that I'm growing a baby inside my body. I've never been happier in my life.

Holden and I have settled into an easy routine. We spend every minute we can together when we're not working. Dinners at night. Showers in the morning. Beach walks. Coffees shops. And sex. So much sex. But my favorite moments are the quieter ones, like when Holden and I are on his couch reading. Me with a romance book in my hand, Holden reading a copy of *What To Expect When You're Expecting*. He borrowed it from Everly. My heart exploded into a million pieces when I caught him reading it for the first time one night in bed. I am falling so hard for this man.

I haven't seen or heard from Justin since the morning he stopped by the house. I'm relieved, but part of me is surprised that he would fly all the way here from Vancouver and not try harder to actually find me. Then again, it's just like him. He never tried hard at anything with me. He never cared enough.

My gaze wanders to Holden again. When he stops at a red light, he rakes his eyes over me. "Give me your mouth, pretty girl."

Leaning over the console, I press my mouth to his, kissing him with intention. Showing him that I care. That I'm here for him no matter what happens around us.

"Mmm. I like your mouth," I say to Holden after we break the kiss.

"I like *you*." He lifts our joined hands to his mouth, pressing his lips to my knuckles.

After circling Buttercup Bakery a couple of times, we finally find a parking spot a few blocks away. Holden helps me down from the truck, because according to him, anything I do can possibly cause harm to the baby. His eyes rake down the length of me as I run my hands over the flowy fabric of my dress. "I know, I shouldn't have worn this one. It clings to me in all the wrong places."

"Briar." He grips my shoulders, speaking so reverently I hang on to his every word. "You had me speechless the moment I saw you in this dress. If you hadn't spent an hour in the bathroom doing your hair, and I wasn't so worried you'd kill me if I made a mess of it, we would have been late for the party. You had my cock hard by just looking at you." His hands slide down my arms to the top of my belly. "If I was attracted to you before you got pregnant, I'm even more so now. You knock me off my feet by just walking into a room."

"Holden."

"I'm warning you, baby. I won't give a shit about messing up your hair when I get you home tonight."

I laugh at his bluntness, but my panties are now damp.

Damn this man and his mouth for making me go to my own party this way.

"Ready?" he asks, slipping my palm in his.

"I guess I am." I lean into him. "This is a big day, Holden. I can't believe we're about to find out if we're having a boy or a girl."

"A boy. Remember I told you so."

He winks.

I melt.

This man is too much for my heart.

We walk down the street hand in hand in silence, the excitement and nerves we both feel growing stronger as we approach the party.

Laughter and cheers greet us when we walk through the doors of the bakery. "Oh my god, what did our friends do?" I squeal, looking around the space, which has been transformed. Everything is covered in pink and blue. There's a giant balloon arch, cupcakes on stands of different heights, jars of candy, and the most beautiful vases of fresh flowers that are no doubt from Bloom, my favorite flower shop.

"Daisy doesn't know how to do anything simple," Holden smiles, kissing my cheek before my best friend is rushing across the room towards me. Holden veers towards the guys as I let Daisy pull me to where Sierra and Ev are waiting.

"Happy gender reveal day! I know I said I would try to keep it simple, but you know me... I couldn't," Daisy gushes, shrugging.

"I do know you and I love you for doing all of this for us."

"You're here and you look adorable," Sierra says. "Also, I know what you're having." She places a hand on the curve of my stomach. "I told Daisy there was no way there would be confetti cannons going off in my bakery. I'm not cleaning that shit up for days. So, we settled on a layer cake for the reveal. She had no other option but to spill the beans. I spent all morning icing it."

"Do you know too?" I ask Everly, who has baby West on her hip.

"Nope. I had nothing to do with this. I can't wait to find out what it is. I think it's a boy."

"You really think that, or you've heard Holden say it so often that you've been influenced?" I ask, my gaze drifting to Holden, who is talking to his parents with a glass of champagne in his hand.

"Just a hunch."

"You better go say hi to your in-laws," Daisy says with a smirk, following my gaze. "They just about talked my ear off about how excited they are to become grandparents. It was cute. I'm going to grab you a glass of sparkling apple juice."

I leave the girls and join Holden, his mom and dad and Barb. Donna and Barb pull me into a hug so tight I can barely breathe. Holden's dad, David, embraces me too, and I'm surprised to find it makes me a little weepy. It has been a long time since I've been hugged by my stepdad; being with Holden's dad makes me miss him.

"We have a bet going, Briar. It's three against one. I'm the only one who thinks it's a girl," David says with a big smile. "We've got 50 bucks at stake."

"Well, I'm not sure I can help you out too much with that, but we'll find out soon," I laugh. "I'm surprised Holden hasn't gotten in on that bet."

"There's still time." He winks at me as he pulls his wallet from his back pocket. "How much am I in for?"

Before I can finish rolling my eyes, I'm pulled away again

by Sierra, who apologetically explains that she needs me for a photo with the rest of the girls by the balloon arch.

I spend the next hour or so catching up with friends and Holden's family, and answering the same questions over and over again: *How are you feeling? What do you think you're having? Are you ready for the baby to get here?* But I don't mind. Looking around the room, all I can think about is the fact that our baby is already so loved.

Standing by the bakery counter, Daisy taps a fork against her champagne glass and the room slowly quiets.

"I want to thank everyone for being here. I know we are all so excited to celebrate our friends Holden and Briar," Daisy says, emotion in her voice. She pauses for a moment before continuing. "But it's now time to find out if they are having a boy or a girl!"

Our friends holler and cheer as Daisy points to the beautiful cake that Sierra has made for the occasion. It's heart-shaped, with three tiers, smooth buttercream frosting decorated with pink and blue alphabet blocks.

"Can I get you two over here to cut the cake?" Daisy calls.

I look around for Holden, who is on the opposite side of the room next to Tucker and Jake. When his eyes find mine, his lips tip up in a knowing smile. I take a deep breath.

We cross the room to join Daisy and as soon as I'm next to him, Holden pulls me close to his side. When he presses a kiss to the top of my head, I don't need a mirror to know that I'm blushing.

I take a quick moment to survey the room with appreciation in my heart. We are surrounded by people here to celebrate our baby. The only thing missing is my family.

"One sec," I say. "I need to FaceTime my mom and my brother." I quickly grab my phone from my purse before dialing her number. My heart lurches in my chest when their faces appear on the screen. It's times like these that my heart hurts being so far away. I'd do anything to have them here with me sharing in my happiness. "Hey, you two. We are going to do the reveal now. Are you ready?"

"We're ready, baby. It's so good to see you. Hi Holden. I can see you're taking good care of my girl. She looks like she's glowing."

"Mom, everyone is listening." I giggle. "I'm going to prop up the phone so you can see, okay?"

"Here, honey, let me hold the phone so they have a better view," Holden's mom offers, stepping forward to take the phone from my hands.

"Hi, I'm Donna, Holden's mom," she says to the screen as everyone listens on. "It's so nice to finally meet you. We need to make plans to meet in person. We would love to host you! My wife, Barb, and Holden's dad, David, both can't wait to meet you guys too. We'll have to exchange numbers—"

"Mom," Holden laughs. "Maybe you can work out the details later? We're kind of in the middle of something here. The wait is killing me."

The room erupts in laughter.

"Cut the cake!" Daisy burst out. "I am dying for you to cut that cake!"

"Would you like to do the honors?" I ask Holden, picking up the knife. "I don't think I should be holding a sharp object. My hands are shaking."

"I've got this, babe." Holden takes the knife from my hand, his other hand still wrapped tightly around my waist. I smile up at him, green eyes with flecks of gold staring back at me. "You ready?"

"I'm ready," I whisper.

I watch the blade of the knife sink through the cake. Holden repeats the motion until he's carved a perfect slice.

Heart in my throat, I get a glimpse of the bright icing between the layers of cake.

It's blue.

It's a boy.

"Briar," Holden shouts. "We're having a boy!"

"Oh my god," I cry next to him, my hands covering my mouth before he takes me in his arms, lifting me off my feet. I'm engulfed in his scent and comfort as he embraces me as fiercely as he can without squishing our little boy between us.

"You were right," I whisper into his ear as my hands wrap around his neck.

"I knew it," he spins me around. "I felt it deep in my bones. Holy shit, we're a having a boy."

When he puts me down, his parents are by our sides with tears streaming down their faces.

"Congratulations, you two," his mom says with her hand on her heart. She gives me a quick hug and then hands me my phone. "Here's your mom, honey."

"Hi guys," I say, looking at my mom and my brother on the screen through tears in my eyes. "Did you see it all?"

"We did, sweetheart. Thank you for including us. We would have been devastated to miss that." My mom beams, dabbing tears from her eyes with a tissue. "I couldn't be happier. Why don't we talk tomorrow so you can get back to your friends?"

"Okay, Mom. I love you."

"I love you too."

It's not the same as having her here with me, but I'm happy my mom could share such a big, life-changing moment with me. I was so young when my dad left, but my mom is front and center in every childhood memory I have. She was there for us in every way that she could be, and she always made sure we knew we were loved. I hope I can be half the mother to my little boy that my mom was to me.

Daisy throws her arms around me, bringing me back to the present moment. "You two are going to have the cutest little boy."

"I just hope I can do this. It's scary to think I'll be responsible for a tiny human being in just a few months."

"Of course you can," she says, running her hand up and down my arm. "There isn't a doubt in my mind that you will make the best mom, and Holden seems to be really excited."

"He is, Daisy," I sigh. "He's been amazing. He won't let me do anything on my own because he thinks I'm going to hurt myself or the baby and I'm pretty positive he knows more about what's going on with my body than I do thanks to all the research he's done."

"He's sweet, Briar. I've always known that about him. He watched re-runs of the *Gilmore Girls* with me, for Pete's sake. I couldn't even get *you* to do that."

I laugh. I'm not sure I realized how lonely I was until Holden came into my life. The thought of being without him every day makes my chest tighten. I can't imagine not seeing his shoes and his gym bag by the door when I come home. I can't imagine not seeing his truck next to my car in his driveway. I can't imagine not sharing every dinner with him. But my apartment will be ready soon and he hasn't once asked me to stay. A few more weeks, maybe less, and I'll be moving out.

As if on cue, Holden is at my side, slipping his arm around my waist. He smiles down at me, but behind that smile I can see the desire to take me home.

He pulls me into his chest. "You must be tired. You've been on your feet for hours. How about we take off?"

For the first time in my life, I'm ready to leave a party if it means I get to be home alone with him.

"Only if you rub my feet when we get there," I smirk. It's a running joke, knowing how he feels about feet.

He arches one brow. "Or I could run you a bath?"

"A foot massage would be ideal." I give him my most innocent, wide-eyed look, one hand moving back and forth across my bump.

He laughs, shaking his head. "You don't play fair. I will massage your feet. Then I will massage—"

"Holden, don't you dare. Your parents are right over there."

"Can you believe it?" he asks. "Slugger's a boy."

"I can't." I lean my head against his shoulder. "I guess we need to talk about a name."

"I've got ideas."

"Why does that make me nervous?"

"What's wrong with Slugger?" he asks with one delicious brow raised.

"Absolutely not." I shake my head. "But it makes the perfect nickname, I'll give you that."

"We are so agreeable."

"Let's go home, Holden. You look tired too." I brush the back of my knuckles down his cheek.

"Maybe if you weren't so pretty, I would have slept last night."

My lips tip, my pulse already racing.

Oh my.

His hand catches mine and he nips my knuckle with his teeth before mouthing the words, *let's go home, baby,* and my heart trips knowing what's in store for me when we get there.

TWENTY-TWO

TOUCH ME THE WAY I LIKE IT

B riar

"What were you like as a kid?" I ask. Now that we know we're having a son, I keep imagining a little boy who takes after Holden.

He shrugs one shoulder. "I think that depends on who you ask."

"What do you mean?"

"I mean if you ask my brother, he'll tell you I was an arrogant jock who thought he knew it all but if you ask my gramma, she'd say I could do no wrong."

"Okay, but what about your mom? What would she say?"

His big hands dig into the arch of my foot, and the pressure of his fingers remind me that before Holden, I was rarely touched like this. With care and concern, with no ulterior motives. I've always been the one to look after other people. The way that Holden goes out of his way to take care of me is new to me.

"You need to relax." He rolls my ankle from side to side. "Your muscles are tense. Loosen up."

I adjust my neck against the pillow I have propped up on the couch behind me. "I'm relaxed as I can get."

Holden laughs and continues to rub the arch of my foot. "Which is not relaxed at all."

"I have a baby doing cartwheels inside of me right now, so excuse me if I can't get comfortable."

It's Friday night. Holden spent the evening mountain biking and then having a beer with the guys while I went over to Everly's with the girls. Now, we're both back at home, lounging on the couch, my feet in his lap. He's decided my feet aren't so bad and I've decided I like receiving massages as much as giving them.

"You didn't answer my question, by the way." I side-eye him before I freeze, and my body goes bone straight.

"Holden!"

He drops my foot in his lap, sitting up like I've scared the life out of him. "Bee, are you okay? What happened? Is it the baby?"

"No, I'm sorry, it's not the baby. Well, it is the baby, but I'm fine. I think I just felt him move."

"Are you serious?" he grins, his eyes wide with excitement, and that's when I know that I'm in love with him.

I smile, tracing my fingertips over the place where I felt the movement. "I'm pretty sure I felt a kick."

"Do you think he'll do it again?"

"I don't know."

Two weeks ago, I started feeling the baby move, and at first it felt like tiny gas bubbles. Since then, they've gotten stronger, but I've been waiting until I can feel them on the outside and tonight, I finally think I can.

Suddenly, I feel what surely must be a karate chop to my side and my eyes widen. Holden is off the couch, crouching next to me.

"Did he kick you again?" His eyes are glued on my belly as I nod.

"He's making himself known. He really is our little Slugger."

"Can you hear me?" Holden says gently to my belly, running his fingertips over my stomach as I lightly shudder.

We sit together in silence, Holden's palm stretched out on top of my belly hoping for another kick. Just when I think he's settled inside of me for the night, I feel the sharpest, quickest movement.

"Did you feel that?" I ask.

"I did!" Holden stares at my belly, his long, masculine fingers curled over the bump of my stomach. "Jesus, he's got quite the kick."

"He can feel your hand," I whisper. "He wants to say hi to his daddy."

"Hey, little guy," he says softly as his thumb brushes back and forth over my skin. A wave of emotion rocks through me. Until now, only I had been experiencing the physical part of growing our baby inside of me. Having Holden—my boyfriend and the father of our baby—feel it too is surreal. I place my hand on top of his.

"There really is a baby in there," he says with astonishment in his sparkling green eyes.

I laugh. "Yeah, there is. It's wild, isn't it?"

He leaves his hand where it is, right under mine, and leans down to kiss me. I ruffle his hair with my free hand. Holden's lips brush over mine, and his eyes turn darker. It's the look he gives me when he needs me. In this moment, I need him too.

I kiss him faintly, my lips lingering on his as I sit up. My thighs widen and Holden moves to his knees between them as he takes my face in his hands, eyes searing into mine.

Our gazes hold in a potent, deep moment making my heart expand and soar. I'm falling harder and deeper for Holden Banks, and I'm praying that he feels the same way for me too.

"Need you, pretty girl."

My fingers ball his T-shirt into a tight grasp. "Need you too."

Then he is on me, and I'm on him. We collide, his hands in my hair, his lips fastened to mine. His tongue delves into my mouth, sweeping inside, kissing me hard, brutally, as I cling to his shirt.

He's all hard muscle, so perfect against my soft curves that I never want to let him go. Adrenaline streams through my veins. Needing to feel his skin against mine, I shove his shirt up, dragging my fingertips down his spine. He growls against my mouth and ruts his hard cock into my core.

"Briar." He sucks on my bottom lip, nipping at the flesh with his teeth before he goes back to ravishing my mouth.

My tank top is pulled over my head, and his mouth is sucking a nipple into his mouth. He grabs and flicks, licks and swirls his tongue until I'm a writhing mess, begging him to give me more. He groans against my nipple, like just the taste of my flesh is getting him off.

I arch into his mouth, giving him more of what he wants as my hands tug on the strands of his hair. "Baby, I need you. You're going to give it to me, aren't you?"

He nods. "What do you want, pretty girl? Be a good girl for me and use your words and tell me exactly where you want me."

His jaw is in my hands, and I pull his mouth to mine, again wedging his cock into the apex of my thighs. I groan as he hits my clit through the fabric of my shorts.

"There, Holden. I need you there, baby," I pant before

the rest of my clothes are shed and he pulls his shirt up over his head. I ache everywhere at the thought of having him inside of me. I'm desperate and on edge. One of the side effects of my pregnancy is that I'm never satiated. I'm always wanting more.

Or maybe it's just what Holden does to me. I doubt this need for him will ever fade.

My heart races when his thumbs hook inside the waistband of his joggers. And when he slips them over his hips and his cock juts out for me, I am crazed.

"Wrap your hand around my cock, Bee, and touch me the way I like."

I reach down between our bodies, taking his smooth, velvety erection in my hand. Holden Banks is beautiful beyond belief when he's naked and hard for me. It's a sight that I will never get tired of.

Holden's fingers graze over the curve of my belly, and I widen my legs, making it easier for him to touch me. I groan when his fingers slide along my soaking wet slit and then push inside of me. Pumping two fingers in and out of me to make room for his astonishing length, the sound of my arousal is the only thing I hear.

"How are you this wet when I only began to touch you, pretty girl?"

"Holden," I moan, my hips riding his fingers, already so close to coming in under a minute. "You, baby, it's you."

How does he turn me on so quickly? I'm on the verge, needy and helpless as he gives me what I need.

"I know, baby." He curls his fingers against my inner wall, hitting my G-spot. "My pretty girl. Perfect tits and so damn wet for me. You're such a good girl. Now, I want you to come for me so I can give you my cock."

He uses his other hand to play with my clit, quick

circular motions until my inner muscles clench around his fingers and I'm crying out his name.

"Oh god," I groan. "You don't know what you do to me."

Laughing to himself, he stands and sits down on the couch next to me, legs wide, cock hard as steel lying flat against his abdomen, the tip touching the dip of his belly button.

"Sit on it, pretty girl," he grips the base of his erection that's glistening from his arousal, offering it to me. "I want you to ride me."

My hands latch onto his shoulders, and I swing my leg over his thighs. I groan, lips parted, eyes squeezed shut as he prods my entrance with just the head.

In no mood to tease either of us, I sink down onto his steely hard cock in one motion, until I'm seated on the patch of dark hair above his erection. His eyes hold mine, his width stretching me as I rock back and forth.

"You're so damn tight but I love the way you take me." He sucks a nipple into his mouth. My back arches and my head tips back.

"Let me feel all of you, Bee. I need you. Do it now."

Holden's hands grip my waist, lifting me until just the tip of him is left inside me before slamming me back down his length. Over and over, I ride him, his hips thrusting up into me in smooth, careful strokes. I roll my hips, and his fingers dig into my ass, spreading me wide as my arousal slicks his length and covers his full balls.

"You feel so good," he grits out. "How does it feel? Does it feel good to you too?"

I hold onto his shoulders, his strong hands on my hips as I ride him, drawing out my pleasure. Holden is the best sex of my life. I've never felt this desired by anyone, like I'm needed on such an emotional, heartfelt level. "Stop talking and give me your mouth."

He licks at my mouth, his tongue clashing with mine. He rocks into me, pumping his hips in long, even strokes. I claw at his shoulders, his back, his thighs, keeping him close to me, whimpering as my inner walls clench around his shaft.

"I love watching your tits bounce when you ride me like this." He groans, and there's no holding back. The pressure is too much. He's rutting too deeply and perfectly, hitting me in just the right place, for me to last another second.

My nails dig into his shoulders, and I see stars. One final thrust and Holden is coming on a groan, filling me up, coating my inner walls. His rigid, muscular body goes lax once he rides out his orgasm.

"Briar." His lets his head fall back against the couch, looking sated and spent. "Your body was meant for me. I'm addicted."

I twist my long hair with one hand and lift it from my neck, smiling down at him. "You say the sweetest things."

He holds my belly in his hands as I erase the gap between our bodies, collapsing onto his chest. "They're true," he says, running his hands down the length of my spine. "I'm going to need you riding my cock more often."

I laugh into his neck. "We'll see."

I want it again too, and soon, but it's fun to rile him up.

TWENTY-THREE

I HAVEN'T GOTTEN ENOUGH OF YOU

H olden

What a wild start to the day.

I toss my iPhone on my bed, trying to process what I was just told.

My landlord, the owner of the house I've been living in for the past four years, has decided to put the place up for sale. She's giving me four months before I need to either move out or make her an offer—an offer I'm dying to make but one I'm not sure I'll be able to afford.

Living anywhere in Reed Point is expensive, let alone an oceanfront property on a secluded street in Haven Harbor. Home values have increased significantly over the last few years which is probably why my landlord is looking to cash in.

This couldn't have happened at a worse time. Briar and I should be living here together getting ready for the arrival of Slugger. I've pictured us bringing our baby home here in a few months. As far as I'm concerned, Briar never needs to even see her restored apartment, but what if I can't afford the mortgage? Then what? Briar has also made no mention of staying with me. Now, with my looming eviction, I'm not sure how I can even ask her to stay when everything feels like it's up in the air. I'm not even sure where I'll be living at this point. I hate that everything is so out of my control. My landlord could sell, Briar could choose to move into her new apartment, and I would have to watch her walk out the door.

If I keep thinking about it, I'll just end up spiralling, so I resolve to wipe the thought from my mind. I'll have more time to think about it tomorrow. Today is Amy's wedding day.

Briar is in her room getting dressed for the wedding. The ceremony starts in an hour, so I do my hair, change into my suit and spray myself with Briar's favorite cologne. I grab my cell phone from the bed and walk to her room, trying to shake the negative thoughts from my head.

On the bright side, at least Briar and I don't have to follow through with our plan to fake a relationship. We're together now. There's no need to pretend.

I gently push open the bedroom door and find Briar standing in front of the full-length mirror in her bedroom putting on a pair of earrings. I stop in my tracks at the sight of her in a long, emerald-green dress that dusts the floor. Her blonde hair is pinned back in a mess of curls at the nape of her neck. The dress is fitted around her tits, which have grown larger throughout the pregnancy, and the swell of her belly is on display. My pulse bolts as I take in her delicious curves. She is breathtaking.

When she sees my reflection in the mirror, the look of concentration on her face shifts to a smile; a full-on beaming smile that is meant just for me.

I stand behind her, gripping her hips before sliding my hands around her body to rest on her bump. She arches her neck to the side, giving me access. She knows it's one of my favorite parts of her body.

"I'm going to be walking around the damn reception trying to hide an erection thanks to you in that dress."

I run my nose along her jaw, inhaling her scent. The smell of Briar is like a fucking addiction to me, and so is her body. I constantly crave her. My eyes meet hers in the mirror. We look good together. Her golden blonde hair in contrast to my light brown. Her sea-green eyes are a few shades lighter than my own. My hand drifts up the olive skin of her arm until it reaches her shoulder. My mouth sucks on her neck.

"Holden, you're going to leave a mark."

I watch in the mirror as her lips part, enjoying the feel of my mouth on her skin. She mewls the sweetest sound that goes straight to my cock.

"Good. Then you'll remember how badly I want you every time you look at yourself in the mirror. Everyone at the wedding will know just how much I want to take you home and get you out of this dress." I gently nip at her neck with my teeth.

"Is that so?" She turns in my arms, hands tightening around my biceps.

"You're beautiful. You know that, right?"

"You're not too bad yourself, Mr. Banks."

Her ankle-length gown swishes against her legs as we stride out to the car, the high slit up one leg making me weak in the knees. I take her hand in my own and kiss her knuckles, knowing if I kiss her mouth, I'll ruin the crimson color she's wearing on her lips. I imagine it will look equally good on my cock.

"You're gorgeous, Briar."

She grins. "You've told me already."

"I'm going to tell you every hour," I say. "I don't know how I got so lucky to be yours."

"Mine."

I kiss her knuckles one more time. I might not want to be going to my ex's wedding tonight, but at least I'm doing it with the most beautiful girl in the world on my arm.

LATER, AFTER WE MET MY PARENTS AND BARB AT THE CHURCH, after we watched Amy marry Preston in a nice enough but also boring ceremony where Briar sniffled softly next to me and blamed it on the hormones, after I snuck kisses and my hand up her dress in a quiet hallway while we waited for Amy and Preston to take photos, after we took our seats in the ballroom of a golf course, after toasts and dinner and avoiding talking to anyone who wasn't sitting at our table, it's finally time for speeches and dessert and then I can finally whisk Briar out of here and have my way with her.

All eyes are on Preston as he steps up to the microphone in his tux, a glass of champagne in his hand. He begins his speech, sharing how he met Amy on a blind date and knew instantly that she was the one. He tells his guests of their ups and downs, how she nursed him back to health when he broke his ankle and how they've compromised on three kids; Amy wanted four and he wanted two. His gaze shifts to Amy, who is crying into a napkin when Preston promises to love her all of her life. Sickness and health, richer or poorer. As the words roll off his tongue, I look at Briar next to me, her hand tangled in mine under the table, her damp eyes locked on *me*.

She leans in and kisses my cheek then rests her head against my shoulder.

The speeches end with a toast to Preston and Amy. The music starts and soon the dance floor is full. I manage to sneak in one dance with Briar before my mom and Barb sweep her away to introduce her to a table full of their friends.

I slip out of the ballroom, needing some fresh air and a few minutes to clear my mind. I was a bit nervous about today—going to an ex's wedding seems potentially awkward. But it turns out I didn't need to be. Everything has been fine, and it's actually been fun to have an excuse to get dressed up and spend the evening with Briar and my family. I haven't been able to enjoy it entirely, though, because as much as I've tried not to think about it, the call with my landlord hasn't been far from my mind.

My life is changing soon, for the better. But I need to figure out where I'm going to live, where Briar is going to live, and I need to do it soon before the baby is here. She hasn't made any mention of wanting to stay with me. In fact, just the other day she was beaming about moving into her apartment. But there's no way that is happening. I won't let it. I want her and the baby with me, which means I need to find a way to buy the house.

"Are you hiding out here? Had enough of your ex's wedding?"

I look up to see Briar walking towards me, a sexy sway to her hips. Hot as fuck with her contagious smile. And I can breathe again.

"I have, but I haven't gotten enough of you."

"I will never get enough of you."

I lean back against the bench, offering her my lap, and she sits down, the fabric of her green dress billowing around us.

"What's made this line right here?" She softly traces the

line between my brows before intertwining her fingers with mine.

"I have something on my mind, I guess."

"Something you'd like to share?"

I cup both sides of her jaw in my hands. "I love you, Briar Moore."

She nods. "I love you too."

I exhale a deep breath before I kiss her. A careful, lingering kiss. "I've loved you for weeks."

"I've loved you for weeks too." She smiles back at me. "I was too afraid to tell you."

"I was too afraid too. I should have told you."

"I wish we said it sooner, but I'm glad we said it now, because I want you to know how I feel about you."

"I wasn't ready when you moved in. I had made promises to myself that I wanted to keep. I was tired of pushing relationships away." I seal my eyes closed for a second. "But then you happened, Bee, and I didn't stand a chance. I think I fell in love with you the day you redecorated my house and there wasn't a chance that I wasn't able to stop falling. You've owned my heart since then. It's yours, pretty girl. Please don't break it."

She collapses into my neck, her palm firmly on my jaw. My hand strokes the back of her hair, holding her close to me. We sit this way, hugging, holding each other, being together in the most vulnerable way.

"Please say it again, Bee," I whisper into her hair. "I need to hear you say it."

Her pretty lips press a kiss to my Adam's apple before she raises her head. "I love you, Holden Banks."

I run my thumb over the apple of her cheek. "I love you, pretty girl. And I don't just say that to anyone."

"I know. I know it's a big deal for you."

"Briar, just so we're clear. The way I feel about you is bone deep. I love the little life we are creating together. I love coming home to you. I love your chaos and spontaneity, your smile and all the vulnerable moments you save just for me," I tell her, watching her smile spread across her mouth and her cheeks flush. She's gorgeous. My beautiful girl. "I want this family we've created. I want to be the reason you smile. I want you and I forever. I have never loved anyone as much as I love you. You are the only woman I want, the only woman I will ever want, and I will marry you one day, baby. I want the three of us to have the same last name."

"I want that too," she whispers. "He's ours."

"Ours. I love my little Slugger and his mom. You're mine. Both of you, understand?"

"We are." She slips her hand through the sides of my hair to my nape, pulling me into her.

She rises to her feet then reaches out her hands to pull me up with her. My arms close around her, holding her tight against my chest. I press my lips into her hair, inhaling her sweet, intoxicating scent, and exhale my relief.

I have everything I'll ever need right here in my arms. Now I just want this wedding to end so I can take her home and show her just how much I love her.

TWENTY-FOUR

A BOYFRIEND ISN'T NECESSARILY FOREVER

Briar

Holden loves me, and it's the best feeling in the world. But for some reason, I'm still not able to ease the tightness in my chest.

This is what I've been hoping for, what I've wanted. To hear him say that he loves me, that he wants the three of us to be a family, making him mine for forever.

I throw a T-shirt on over my sports bra, feeling anxiety rise inside of me. I left a message for my landlord to call me with an update on my apartment and ever since I hung up the phone, I haven't been able to steady my breathing. When I arrived back in Reed Point, I'd been so excited to move into the cutest apartment in the best location, but ever since living with Holden, I can't imagine living anywhere but here... with him. The only problem is that Holden hasn't asked me to stay or even brought it up at all.

After the wedding, when he told me he loved me, I thought he might tell me that he wants me to move in. For good, this time. But he didn't. It kills me to think that I'll be moving out soon. I wish my almost renovated apartment would go up in flames.

This is exactly why it was dangerous to fall in love with Holden. I have zero control over where we go from here. He's my boyfriend, yes, but a boyfriend isn't necessarily forever. People change their minds; it happens all the time. They're in love until they lose interest, and they don't always stick around. I could lose him. This little house isn't my home. I'm a visitor, a temporary guest. Everything has moved so fast with us—first living together, then finding out that we're having a baby together. I guess it would make sense that Holden wants me to move out so we can take a step back and properly date. And if that's what he wants, then I have no other choice.

Everything feels completely out of my control.

I twist my hair into a knot and throw my belt bag across my body. I can sit in this house and make myself crazy with worry, or I can head to the maternity store and buy myself a new pair of work pants that actually fit. I'm not sure there's a hair elastic on this planet big enough to fasten my waistband together. I walk down the hall to tell Holden I'm leaving.

"I'm running to the maternity store, babe. I'll be about an hour."

I grab my car keys and my purse, then sit down on the bench beside the door to put on my shoes.

"Bee?" I hear him call from the kitchen, as I'm lacing up my runners. "Wait five minutes and I'll go with you. I wanted to stop at the bubble tea place. I have a craving for mango."

"When did you all of a sudden like bubble tea?" I chuckle.

"When Birdie told me it was her favorite and that I needed to try it."

That sweet girl could get him to try chocolate-covered grasshoppers if she asked him to. She has him wrapped around her little finger.

"I would never want to come in between you and a mango bubble tea," I tell him.

"You wouldn't be able to live with yourself if you did," he says, joining me in the entryway.

He flips the baseball hat he's wearing so that it's backwards, grabs his Nikes and slips them on. I roll my lips together. My heart does this boisterous flip in my chest. Holden in a suit is gorgeous but looking like this—in sweats and a ballcap—he puts all other men to shame.

"Did you see my wallet?" he asks, looking at the console table by the door where he usually leaves it.

"And you call me the disorganized one? Check the dresser. I'll meet you outside," I say as I head out the door.

There's a sharp chill in the air, but it's a sunny, blue-sky day; it's the kind of day that reminds you that spring will be here soon. I wrap my oversized cardigan around me as I look across to the beach, putting a hand over my head to shield my eyes from the sun.

I suddenly startle at the sound of my name.

"Briar." The voice is like sandpaper. A hand snakes around my elbow.

I try to tug my arm free as I look up to find my ex-boyfriend staring down at me.

Justin's grip on my arm tightens. "Briar, we need to talk. I've been trying to get a hold of you. I flew all the way here just to see you."

I'm momentarily speechless, too shocked to form a coherent sentence. What is he doing back here? It's been months since I've talked to him, but it feels like a lifetime seeing how much he has changed since then. He looks different somehow—bigger, like he's been spending hours at the gym. Or maybe he looks different because my feelings for him have changed. He no longer looks like the man I thought I loved, with the boyish good looks and charming smile. Now, all I see is all the time I wasted on him, and all the ways he let me down.

"Justin... why... what are you doing here?"

"What else was I supposed to do? You aren't taking my calls. I'm here to talk to you, Briar. I'm going to take you home with me where you belong."

Is he out of his mind? I look around, worried that someone will see us. I don't want to have to explain this to our friends. I also don't want to have to explain this to Holden, if he walks out and sees Justin with his hands on me.

"Justin, let go of me."

He rolls his eyes. "Do you really think I would hurt you? Jesus, baby, it's me. I've been going crazy trying to find you. Your mom wouldn't tell me where you're living, and your friends won't answer my calls."

"Then you should have taken that as a hint that I didn't want to be found." I tug on my arm, trying to loosen his grip on me. "Please, can you just let go of me?"

"Baby," he rasps out, sounding desperate. "We just need to talk, and work this out."

"Work what out? The fact that you have a problem keeping your dick in your pants and you can't be trusted? We could definitely agree on that."

"It was one time." He shakes his head, acting as if it's not that big of a deal. "Why can't you just get over it? I love you. I always have."

This has to stop. He needs to leave. I know Justin would never physically hurt me. For all his faults, he isn't an aggressive guy, but I'm uncomfortable and I've had enough. "Justin, please let me go."

"You heard her." I whip my head around to see Holden stalking down the steps. "If you don't get your fucking hands off my girlfriend right this second, I will break every bone in your goddamn body. Do you understand me?"

Justin's grip on my arm immediately loosens enough that I can move away from him and over to Holden's side. I feel his lips press against the top of my head as his arm slips around my waist. "You okay, baby?" He smooths his hand in a line down my arm.

"I'm fine. I just don't want to talk to him."

Holden turns to Justin.

"You can leave know. Briar has nothing to say to you. You proved to her what kind of a guy you are and now she's with me. End of story. You can go book your flight home."

Justin's gaze shifts to where Holden's hand is holding me tightly against him. Then I watch his gaze drift to the curve of my stomach.

"Are you *pregnant*?" His eyes widen. "You've got to be kidding me. We've been broken up for what... six months, and you're already having a baby with some other guy?"

"I'm pregnant and I'm happy and I've moved on," I tell him. "Now you need to move on too. This is over. To be honest, it was over the day I found you on my couch with that girl."

"I can't believe it." Justin drags a hand through his dirty-blond hair. "I thought you just needed to cool down. I know I fucked up, but you always come around."

Justin stares at me with wide, glassy eyes, and if I wasn't still so hurt about how he treated me, I might feel sorry for him. "I don't know what world you live in to think I would ever get back together with you after what you did to me... and you know what you did, I don't think I need to remind you."

I feel Holden's entire body stiffen next to me, as if he's prepared to swing at Justin. He knows that I'm referring to the pictures Justin shared of me that I had sent him in confidence.

"Briar, that was—"

"Finish that sentence and see what happens," Holden seethes. "I'm not sure how I've put up with this for as long as I have. You are an asshole who doesn't deserve Briar. You never did. You mistreated her. You humiliated her. You are a shit excuse for a man, because a real man would never do what you did to her. You hurt her so badly that she got on a plane and moved here to get away from *you*. She is mine now and she will be until I take my last breath. So, you can go now, and don't ever come back. We are done here. Get the fuck off my property."

Justin stares at me for a second, but I don't have anything else to say to him. I am just as done with this as Holden is. He finally turns and walks down the driveway.

Holden pulls me into his chest, and I melt against him. "Thank you, Holden."

"You don't need to thank me. It's my job." He runs his hand in long strokes up and down my back. "I will always protect you. I will never allow anyone to hurt you again."

I exhale a heavy sigh, pushing the unsettling feeling of seeing Justin again out of my mind. Holden dips down, brushing his mouth over mine. When he draws back, he looks at me closely.

"I promise, Briar."

I nod.

And I know that it's true.

I CAN HEAR HOLDEN IN THE SHOWER, SO I TAKE MY BREAKFAST —scrambled eggs and toast, the only thing I feel like eating these days—to the couch. Picking up my phone, I see that I missed another call from my landlord. Sighing, I dial him back. I've been avoiding him for the past few days, but I know I can't put it off forever.

"Hi Mitch," I say when he answers on the second ring. "It's Briar Moore, sorry I missed your call."

"No problem. Just calling to let you know I have an update on the condo."

"Okay," I say nervously, realizing I'm not sure what I want him to tell me. On one hand, I've been waiting for months for the renovations on the place to be done. On the other, if they are done, that means I will be moving out of Holden's place.

"The painters will be finishing up over the next few days and then I'll have the contractor go in and install the new appliances. You should be good to move in at the end of next week. I'm sorry it's taken a little longer than we expected."

"That's okay, Mitch. Thanks for the update, I appreciate it."

"I thought you'd be happy to hear. If you'd like to come and take a look at it, I'll be there tomorrow. Happy to show you around, otherwise I'll call you next week with a move-in date."

"I wouldn't mind seeing it. I'll stop by tomorrow." With a tightness in my chest, I thank him and end the call. This should be good news.

I can move in.

The realization hits me like a ton of bricks.

I don't want to leave.

I hate the thought of leaving this house. I hate the idea of being that far away from Holden, especially now that I am pregnant. I like knowing he'll be walking in the door 10 minutes after me on weekdays. I like falling asleep in his bed wrapped up in his arms. I like his company, and the attention he shows me. I like the way he makes me feel happy and appreciated.

I know that Holden likes having me here, but I can't ignore the fact that he still hasn't asked me to stay. He lived on his own for a while, maybe he just wants to have his home back to himself. Maybe he's not ready to embrace the chaos that surely comes with having a baby in the house— bouncy chairs and play mats and swings, bottles and bibs cluttering the kitchen counter. Holden has really stepped up to embrace this pregnancy and he's clearly excited to become a dad, but it's a big change, and I know he can be set in his ways.

As I toss my phone on the couch beside me, I realize Holden is behind me. He's normally gone to work by now, but he skipped his early morning workout after keeping me up all night. It was incredible. You'd think I'd be exhausted after he gave me the greatest orgasm of my life last night. I woke up feeling euphoric. But the phone call I just had served to bring me back down to earth.

"Was that your landlord? What did he have to say?"

Forcing a smile, I tell him, "That was him. My place is going to be ready for me to move into next week. He said I could pop by tomorrow if I wanted to see it. Do you want to come with me?"

I stare at Holden, trying to get a read on what he's thinking, but his expression is impossible to decipher. I want him to tell me to stay. God, the thought of living apart kills me. I wait, holding my breath, hoping he'll tell me to cancel my lease.

Instead, he says, "That's great, Briar. If you want me to come with you, you know I will."

My heart drops. The somber realization that he isn't going to ask me to stay makes me feel sick.

"I'm late for work. We'll figure out the details tonight." He kisses my forehead, but the gesture is lacking real emotion. His brows are furrowed, his eyes are blank and hard. It feels nothing like Holden.

"Okay."

Before he walks away, I catch his hand, bringing it to my mouth to kiss the inside of his wrist. My eyes plead for him to ask me to stay. "I've got to go, Bee. I'm going to be late."

Reluctantly, I let his hand go. "Have a good day, babe."

He walks to the front door and then he's gone.

Now that I have Holden, I don't want to let him go. I might only be moving out, but it feels a lot like I'm losing him.

TWENTY-FIVE

YOU'RE GORGEOUS WHEN YOU COME

H olden
Briar looks happy.

Before today, she's only ever seen the apartment online. When her flight touched down in Reed Point, the place was already under two inches of water.

Now, it's a brand-new apartment with fresh paint, gleaming hardwood floors, and white kitchen cabinets. There's not a scratch or a speck of dirt. It's beautiful.

My hand intertwined with hers, she leads me down the hall to the bedroom, pointing out the reasons that she fell in love with the place from the listing.

"The bedroom has a little balcony, and there's a view of the park across the street. I thought I could do yoga out here." She pulls open the sliding glass door and steps onto the balcony, an enthusiastic grin on her face.

"I didn't know you like yoga."

"I don't, but you can picture it, right?" She beams, her eyes sparkling.

"Absolutely."

I *can* picture it. The place is perfect for her. A spacious living room, new appliances, one and half bathrooms and a small den for Slugger. The walls are white, but she would add her pillows and plants to make it colorful. Just like she did at my house.

I want to hate it. I want it to be too small or poorly finished, anything so that she wouldn't be this fucking impressed. But if this is what she wants, I can't stop her. If she wants to prove to herself that she can do this on her own, then I have to let her. I never want to be the person who stands in her way.

"Come look at the ensuite! Maybe it will have a shower big enough for the both of us when you visit."

When I visit.

I've never hated three words more.

"Do you think it's too small?" she asks, a crease forming between her eyebrows.

"No, I didn't say that. Why? Do you?"

"No, you just looked... I don't know... like you don't like the bathroom."

I bring her hand to my mouth, kissing her knuckles, trying harder to be happy for my girlfriend. "I think it's perfect." I kiss the tip of her thumb. "Look at the cabinet. It's big enough for all 200 of your hair products."

She bends forward to look inside the cupboard. "You'll appreciate having your bathroom back the way you like it. No more of my mess. You won't do that eye twitch thing you do every time you walk past it and see my things."

"I'm going to have to hire you a cleaner."

She shakes her head, grinning. "Very funny, Holden Banks. And anyways, a cleaner would be pointless. I'd just mess it up 20 minutes after they left."

"My favorite hurricane," I tease, but I'm not feeling it. I

don't have the energy or mental capacity to fake it. How the hell am I supposed to be happy that she's leaving?

I have to suck it up. If this is what she wants, then there's nothing I can do about it. Besides, how can I demand that she gives up her dream apartment when I don't even know where I'll be living?

"Hey," Briar says, interrupting my thought spiral. "I'm hungry, should we go?"

"We should," I reply, not able to get out of here fast enough. "What is my Slugger craving today?"

"Eggs and toast." She wrinkles her nose. "Everything else is gross. Let's go to The Dockside."

I press a kiss to her shoulder, trying to turn my mood around. "Sounds good. Lead the way," I say, motioning to the bedroom door.

I smile as she passes me, but no part of me feels calm or collected. All I can think about is what will happen to us when she moves out.

Will she like living alone better than living with me?

Will she push me away?

Will she forget about me?

Does she want to be with me at all?

The questions consume me, overtaking any and all logic. I love Briar. But I have to let her go and pray that this isn't the beginning of the end.

THE MINUTE WE WALK THROUGH THE DOOR AFTER DINNER, I'M on her. My hands slide through her hair, my mouth sealed to hers. It feels like a dam inside of me broke with the way I'm wildly kissing her. There's nothing sweet or soft about it. The way my mouth slants over hers or how my teeth scrape over her bottom lip. My tongue licks all four corners of her mouth, and it feels like I can breathe again. The relief is palpable when we break apart and she's looking at me through hooded eyes with her hands fisted in my shirt.

I kick the door shut then walk her backwards until the back of her thighs hit the console table. She perches on the edge, widening her thighs so I can push my hips in between them. It feels so fucking good, my cock screaming for more; all I want is more.

My fingers grip into her thighs, a crazed feeling rushing through my veins, overwhelming me. Today it felt like things between us are changing—*everything* about her moving into her own apartment feels wrong.

Briar means everything to me. She's who I want to wake up to every morning and fall asleep to every night. We were so close to having that, and now it feels like it's all slipping away.

"Holden," she breathes into my neck and the way my name sounds falling off her lips feels like an answered prayer inside my head.

"Yes, pretty girl." I suck on her neck, pushing my cock between her legs. "What do you need? I'll give you anything you want."

"You, baby. I need you." She digs her nails into my back as I rut against her clit with the ridge of my erection.

"I'm here, Bee."

I wish these damn layers of clothing between us were gone. Frustrated, I slide my hands up her heated thighs to the hem of her skirt, taking a journey along her skin. She's wearing a dress that falls to the middle of her thighs and gathers at her tits with a ribbon tied in a bow. It's not fancy, but fuck, I get hard every time I see her in the damn thing.

She rakes her fingers through my hair as I cage her in

with my body, her belly wedged between us. Her eyes are glassy. She needs sleep. But after following her around her new apartment like a lost puppy I need her too badly to wait.

She leans forward, searching for my mouth as my fingers hook into the waistband of the pale pink lace. I remove her underwear, tossing it to the floor before taking her mouth with mine, needing her like a drought needs rain.

My Briar.

How am I going to watch her pack her things and go? Just thinking about her leaving makes my heart thump a dull ache in my chest.

"Lean back." I push the pile of mail off the table and onto the floor. She stares back at me with a desperate look in her eyes and my cock throbs. She's so fucking beautiful with her hair a mess from my hands and her lips pink and swollen from my kisses. I sweep my tongue over the seem of her lips and she opens for me, letting me in. I moan into her mouth, the kiss slow and deliberate.

"Mmm," she whimpers against my mouth as her hands slip under my T-shirt and up my spine. I love it when her hands are on me. Needy and impatient for her, I grip my shirt by the neck and pull it over my head, tossing it on the floor.

"I want to worship you, Briar. I want to kiss you everywhere until you're lifeless and spent from coming so hard." I tug the bow on her dress and pull it loose until I can see her tits tip over the fabric. I lick my lips and adjust my cock in my jeans, so it's pointed up and tucked under the waistband of my pants. "Jesus, these tits."

I pinch a nipple with my thumb and forefinger, earning me the softest groan before I dip my head down to suck the stiff bead into my mouth.

My body tingles. Every drop of blood in my body rushes to my groin then I'm on my knees in seconds pressing a kiss to her slick core.

"Baby," she murmurs. "More. I need more."

"I've got you, baby girl. I'll spend all night with my face buried between your thighs. I'll never stop until you can't take it anymore."

I spread her thighs wider with my palms on her inner thighs licking and sucking her as she rides my face. I bury my nose in her folds, inhaling her scent and I lick her and suck on her clit until she's a writhing mess.

"I'm so close, Holden," she pants. "Right there, don't stop."

Like I could. I could never stop.

I'll eat this woman until the day I die.

Briar is the sexiest woman I have ever laid eyes on. She tastes sweet, like heaven. She's beautiful with her soft curves and smooth, olive skin. She takes what she needs and tells me what she likes, and she makes me harder than I've ever been with anyone else. I am constantly distracted with thoughts of fucking her. Some days I'm not even sure how I've driven home.

My tongue thrusts deep inside her. Her hands curl in my hair, tugging my face closer. She's shaking and moaning when my mouth latches onto her clit with a hard suction, and I spread her wider.

She comes on my tongue, her orgasm long and lasting. I lap at her until she's boneless and limp.

"You're gorgeous when you come." I stand and lick my tongue into her mouth. "I've never tasted anything better."

Briar's hand slips between us into my jeans, wrapping around my thick erection. "My turn to make you come. My handsome man needs to feel good too."

"Fuck, baby, I'm hard as stone for you." I pick her up off the table and carry her to the bedroom.

She unbuttons my jeans. I lower my zipper. She takes me out. I push my pants to the floor.

I relax against the mattress as Briar settles between my legs. She's still in her dress but it's falling over one shoulder exposing her perfect tits with her small, blush-coloured nipples.

"You taste good when I kiss you here," she says pressing her mouth to the base of my shaft. "And here," at my tip.

I'm trembling beneath her as her tongue caresses the head as if she's savoring every inch of me, my balls aching and my cock throbbing.

Briar continues to travel my cock with her mouth until she wraps her mouth around the head and takes me to the back of her throat. When she gets halfway down my length, she looks up at me under long lashes and hooded eyes, and I nearly arch myself off the bed.

She does it again and again. My fingers winding their way through her blonde hair while my heels dig into the mattress to ground me. I'm going out of my mind, humming with pleasure, with the feel of Briar's warm mouth wrapped around my cock.

"Baby. God, Bee. I need to be inside you. How do you want me?"

I've never needed this connection with her more. So fucking much. I can feel the space between us growing and she's still here in my bed with me.

"I know what you want," she answers simply, sitting up, and I turn on my side so she can nuzzle her ass into my groin.

She knows I love taking her from behind with my arm wrapped around her body. This time, I kiss the back of her neck, rubbing my cock along the crease of her ass until I'm notching the head of my cock at her entrance and pushing inside.

We both groan in unison when I'm fully inside, my hand gripping her breast, her ass pushed against my groin. My head spins and my skin is on fire when I start to rock back and forth inside her, and all I want is more.

More.

Right now, I'm a battle lost, and I feel out of control with the thoughts slicing through my mind. *I don't want you to go. I can't live here without you. I can't sleep in this bed if you're not in it. You need to stay. Don't leave me.*

Briar is my home.

My balls draw up so high I know I'm not going to last. I fuck her harder, saying her name as I pump my hips against her ass. And five strokes later, I'm coming hard inside her, room spinning and lights flashing behind my eyelids.

"Dammit, baby. You feel so good."

With my cock still buried inside her, I hold her close, kissing the salty skin of her neck. We couldn't be any closer, but it still isn't close enough. When she tries to move, I tighten my hold on her, wanting to stay this way forever.

"We're not leaving this room tonight," I warn.

"I know."

"I love you, Briar."

"Love you too, baby."

I hold her close. Soon our breaths even out as I nestle her to my chest.

I feel zero control over her leaving, but right now, she's here. For the next half hour, I listen to the soft sounds of her breathing against my chest as she falls asleep in my arms then without waking her, I climb out of bed. I can't sleep. My heart is racing against my ribs. This isn't happiness, though.

This is a wave of panic slamming into me at what I'm about to face.

I have a lot to think about, and I can't do that in my current state of mind. My chest hurts. My stomach is in knots. I look out the living room window to the beach in the distance and I know in my core that I want to stay in this house. I know what I need to do. In the morning I have an appointment with the bank. I'll figure out Briar after that.

TELL ME TO STAY

Briar
I trace the rim of my water glass, staring at the untouched sandwich on the table. My new apartment is beautiful—anyone would think so. A top-floor unit with huge windows, gleaming floors, and a kitchen that will get a lot of use. But with all that said, it's just another place that isn't *his*.

I think back to when we walked through my apartment together. I wanted him to care. Wanted him to smile at the bright-white kitchen, joke about how I'd fill the empty bookshelves with romance books with naked dudes on the cover, but most of all pull me close and say, *The place is nice, but you're not moving in here. You belong at home with me.*

But he hadn't.

I take a sip of water, ignoring the sting in my throat. This feeling is familiar. It was there when my dad left without looking back. It was there when I found Justin with someone else, as if I had been nothing more than a place-holder. And now, here it is again—this aching certainty that I'm not someone people choose to keep.

I set my glass down with a thud, the weight of it settling deep in my chest.

I hoped Holden would be the one to prove me wrong.

And once again, I'm still hoping.

Earlier that day he barely spoke to me before he left for work in the morning. I thought maybe I was just being hypersensitive, but that night he was quiet; he seemed to barely register the fact that I was there.

I thought things were better last night when he could barely get me through the door without mauling me, but today the silence returned. When I asked him if there was a day he preferred to help me move out, he said, *as soon as you want.* I haven't seen or spoken to him since.

All the signs are there. Holden has been distant. I would be a fool to ignore that. It wasn't that long ago that he told me he didn't see a family in his future. Maybe now that the baby news has really sunk in, his initial excitement is fading. I know Holden will be a good dad to our child, but I also know there are no guarantees that mean he and I will be together.

Maybe it's for the best. When I arrived back in Reed Point, I was fresh off my break-up with Justin, and then my relationship with Holden moved so quickly. It might be good for me to be on my own, to stand on my own two feet. If we put a little distance between us, we can date like a couple would normally do. It doesn't have to be a breakup, even though it feels a lot like one.

It might even make our relationship stronger. A newborn can put a lot of stress on a relationship, so it's probably best for us to have some space.

It will be a good thing. It has to be.

And if Holden has decided he wants to put distance

between us, I will still have little Slugger and my cute new apartment.

And a broken heart.

I have 10 minutes left on my lunch break, so I send Holden a text. I need something from him. Anything that tells me we're going to be okay.

> Briar: How does spaghetti carbonara sound for dinner tonight? Thought I'd stop at the store and pick up what I need on my way home.

I wait for a response from him, but when none comes, I toss my garbage into the bin with a heavy sigh and walk back to my desk.

When my phone buzzes 20 minutes later, I knock over my glass of water in my rush to pick it up. I swipe the screen to life as I sop up the spill with a napkin.

> Holden: Sounds good, but I have to stop at my mom's to help her with her garage door. I'm not sure how long I'll be.

Tossing the device onto my desk, I stare up at the ceiling in frustration. I'm disappointed that I may not see him tonight since things feel so tense between us, but I know Holden well enough to know that if someone he cares about needs him, he'll be there for them as soon as he can. That's one of the things I love about him.

There are just so many things I want to say to Holden. I wish I knew how he is feeling. I wish I had the guts to ask him. But I'm too afraid of what his answer will be to have that conversation.

A few minutes later, after I've composed myself, I pick up my phone and reply.

> Briar: Say hi to your moms for me. I'll save you some pasta. Have a good night.

I stare at my phone, willing him to answer.

Say something.

Say anything.

Tell me you love me.

Tell me to stay.

He doesn't reply, and my heart hurtles to the ground.

I'm trying not to spiral, but the overwhelming feeling that he's shutting me out eats at me. If I was braver, I would tell him that moving in with him on Haven Harbor is the best thing to ever happen to me. I would tell him that I never want to leave, that my home is wherever he is.

But I can't.

The fear of being rejected is too overwhelming.

So instead of calling Holden, I chew on my bottom lip while my heart continues to ache, missing him. I know deep down that it's irrational, but that's the way insecurities work.

THE SOUND OF BIRDIE'S LAUGHTER FLOATS ACROSS THE LAWN as I cross the road from the beach.

She and Jake are kicking a soccer ball around, something they do most nights after dinner. Slipping my sunglasses onto my head, a smile tips my lips. The evening sun is shining down on Birdie even though it's chilly, but it pales in comparison to the smile on her face when she sees me.

"Auntie Bee," she hollers, running to the edge of the lawn and throwing her arms around my thighs before her little hand drifts to my belly. "Have you named the baby, yet? I have a few good ideas if you want to hear them."

"Of course I do. I want to hear them all," I tell her, smoothing her hair and placing my hand next to hers over my shirt. I'm wearing one of Holden's old baseball T-shirts under my puffer jacket, my belly stretching the thin cotton. It's still warm enough to wear my jacket unzipped, but in a few hours when the sun sets, there will be a deep chill.

"Walking by yourself?" Jake asks, lightly kicking the soccer ball in Birdie's direction. "Did you lose Holden?"

"He's at his mom's," I answer, looking down at my shoes. "It's feeling like my after-dinner walks will be coming to an end soon, so I'm enjoying them while I can, with or without him."

"Getting tired?"

"I'm definitely slowing down." Between work and the baby stealing my energy, I have very little left in my tank these days. Most nights after dinner and my evening walk, I've been curling up on the couch to watch a show. Most of the time, I fall asleep halfway through.

"Why don't you join us? We were just going to the backyard to sit around the fire table. Birdie wants to roast marshmallows and Everly is going to meet us out there after she's done putting West down."

"I don't want to impose."

"Come on, Auntie Bee. Please." Birdie picks up her soccer ball and tosses it to her dad while I melt a little at hearing her call me Auntie Bee.

"Okay, one marshmallow, then I better head home."

"Yay!" she hollers, then she takes off for the back yard. When she's out of sight, Jake's eyes lock on mine.

"I haven't heard from Holden in a few days. Tell him if

he doesn't start returning my calls, I'm going to come knock down his door."

I shouldn't be happy that he hasn't heard from Holden either, but it gives me a glimmer of hope. Maybe it isn't just me that he's pushing away. Maybe there's something else that's weighing on his mind. I wish I knew what is really going on with him so that I can stop second-guessing everything.

"Are you okay?" Jake frowns "You seem quiet."

"I'm good, just a lot going on. My apartment is ready. I'm moving in next week."

"Sorry, what?" Jake asks, a curious look in his eyes. "Is Holden moving with you?"

"No, just me."

I feel awkward talking about this with Holden's best friend. And considering the fact that I'm terrible at concealing my emotions right now and likely to burst into tears at any moment, I should probably stop talking and head home.

"Oh... okay." He scratches his head. "I just... well, it really doesn't matter. If you need help with the move, just let me know."

"Thanks, Jake. I appreciate it."

We walk together to the backyard to find Birdie already has a marshmallow hovering over the fire under Everly's watchful supervision. The first couple burn and drop into the fire, but the third one turns out just right.

We spend the next 10 minutes or so chatting, the fire casting a magical glow around the small yard. Birdie talks Jake into letting her have one extra marshmallow—he doesn't stand a chance against her, she's way too cute—before Everly takes her into the house to wash her sticky fingers and get ready for bed. I say goodbye and make my exit, heading back to the house next door.

Holden's not home when I step inside, and the house feels lonely and eerily quiet. Everything feels off. Bear must sense it too when she struts to the end of the bed, leisurely swishing her tail side-to side, with her beryl-green eyes focused on me. She purrs affectionately, rubbing her head against my thigh as I absentmindedly stroke the soft fur between her ears.

I change out of my clothes and into the oversized T-shirt of Holden's that doubles as my pajamas these days, then climb into bed without him for the first time in months. The sun has slipped below the horizon and there's a chill in the air outside, but I leave the window open just enough to hear the rushing echo of the waves against the beach.

I miss him. The bed feels far too big and empty without Holden next to me. I prop a few pillows behind my back and reach for my laptop. I have an email to look over and a rental agreement to sign. In six more days, I'll be living in my new apartment, pregnant and all alone.

I sigh, running my hand over my belly as I make a mental to-do list. This little boy is going to need a nursery: a crib, change table, maybe a cute little mobile and some artwork for the walls. I'd love a rocking chair if I can find one. I'm also going to need to choose a paint color for the walls. Maybe a pale blue?

I have so much to do, but I'm too tired to think about it. Instead, I lie here with Bear keeping me company and try to focus on the contract on my screen.

TWENTY-SEVEN

ADMIT THAT YOU'RE BEING A TOTAL
JACKASS

Holden

As I walk through the doors of the bank, I feel a headache coming on. I just met with a bank representative who told me I'd need a minimum of five percent down, which is a lot, and a number that I'm still not sure I can come up with. On the bright side, she said that based on my credit score, if I could come up with the down payment things looked pretty good. Now I just need to figure out how to come up with the money and then wait for the pre-approval, which will likely take 2 to 3 days.

I'm in my truck about to turn the ignition when I get a text from Jake wanting to meet up for a drink. It's been a long day, and I'd rather just head home and see Briar, but I know Jake is impatient to talk. This is the second message he's sent me today, and for him I think that might be a record. He's probably annoyed that I've been out of touch lately, but I've been busy trying to figure out how I'm going to buy the house, on top of dealing with the fact that Briar is moving out in a matter of days.

I heave a sigh, worry snaking its way through my body.

I've known this day was coming, but I think I just haven't wanted to accept it. I rub my forehead, trying to alleviate the pain throbbing behind my eyes. I message Jake back to say I can meet him for a quick beer and then drive the 10 minutes to the pub. An hour, tops, and then I'll go home to Briar.

When I walk into the bar, I quickly find Jake sitting at a table near the back of the room. I sink into the booth next to him, nodding a hello.

"I thought you were dead," he mutters after a pull of his beer.

"I feel like it." I dig out the two pain killers I stuffed in my pocket before getting out of my car.

"Headache?"

"A killer one."

"Well, I guess I shouldn't give you too much shit for ignoring my messages then." Jake slides a glass of water across the table to me.

"Thanks," I reply, popping the pills in my mouth.

"So, what the hell is going on with you?"

I sigh. "My landlord is selling the house. I've got four months before I need to move out."

Jake looks shocked. "Shit. You can't move. You love that house. It's always been you, me, and Gray on Haven Harbor. What are you going to do?"

I shrug. "I'm trying to get a mortgage so I can buy the house. I just left the bank. I'll know in a couple of days if I qualify or not."

"Wow. You've got that kinda money for a deposit?"

"No, but I'm figuring it out," I answer as a waitress reaches our table. She hands me a beer before taking our order.

Jake takes a swig of his beer then wipes his mouth with a napkin. "Where's Briar in all this?"

He knows. I can tell by the look on Jake's face that he already knows she's moving out.

"Her apartment is ready at the end of the week. She's moving out."

"I know. I talked to her."

"You talked to her about this? When?"

"I ran into her. She was coming home from a walk after dinner. It was the third time this week I saw her coming home from a walk alone."

I open my mouth to try and explain what's been going on, but he beats me to it. "Are you breaking up with her?"

"Fuck, no." I shove my fingers through my hair. "That's not what I'm doing. I would never break up with her. I could never—"

"Then why is she moving out?"

"Because she wants to. Her place is ready, and she loves it. You should have seen her face when she did the walk through. Staying with me was a temporary solution, she never planned to stay forever."

He huffs out what sounds like a laugh. "I don't care how nice the place is. There's no way on this earth that she'd rather live there alone than with you. Did you have a conversation with her? Did you bother to ask her if she'd like to stay?"

I don't answer right away, instead distracting myself by peeling the corner of the label on my beer bottle.

His head blows back like I've physically hit him. "You didn't ask her."

"No." That is the only answer I've got for him. I feel like a fucking idiot. "I didn't think she—"

"Don't say it isn't what she wanted," Jake cuts me off. "You have no idea what she wanted because you didn't fucking ask her. She shouldn't have to ask you to let her stay.

It's your house and if you want her to live with you then you need to ask her. That's on you, Holdey."

"Stay where? I don't even know where *I'm* going to live if I can't get this loan."

"If I was betting man, I'd say she'd rather weather the storm with you and figure it out together than live on her own with a new baby. *Your* baby."

"I haven't told her."

"That you've been given notice to move?"

"Yeah."

Jake winces. "As someone who knows a lot about keeping secrets, I think you're making a huge mistake. You need to be honest with her. Explain to her what's going on with your landlord. Tell her you've had a meeting with the bank. Admit that you're being a total jackass."

I heave out a breath. "Appreciate that."

He raises one brow. "From what I've seen, you are. Before last week, there wasn't a second you weren't together. Now suddenly, you're not around and you're encouraging her to move out of your house. If this is how you show her you love her, you're failing miserably."

I lean my elbows on the table, pressing my fingers into my temples. Jake is right. I fucked up. I should have asked her to stay.

I was so focused on figuring out a way to stay on Haven Harbor and so busy feeling sorry for myself that I was going to lose Briar when she moved out that I'd pushed her away without realizing it.

Briar is upset, and rightfully so.

If I made her feel like she wasn't wanted, that couldn't be further from the truth. Briar is my forever and losing her is not an option.

A little while later, we've paid our bill, and Jake takes his last swig of beer. He stares at me for a long time before he asks me, "Do you want her to stay?"

I nod. "Of course I do."

"Then you need to choose her. You need to go home and tell her." He pushes back from his chair and stands. "I need to get home to Ev, but I'm glad we talked."

I check the time on my phone, and shit, it's later than I realized. Jake gave me a lot to think about. I feel like I'm seeing things more clearly now. I know I made a gigantic mistake, but if Briar is willing to stay with me then we can figure out the rest together because without her, I have nothing.

I make it home 15 minutes later, eager to see her and get everything out on the table. I walk through the front door, listening for any sound of her. I go to the living room, hoping to find her curled up on the couch with one of her romance books. The room is empty, but my heart twists when I see the mess of colorful throw pillows, the throw blanket and collection of fruit-scented candles scattered around the room. I hated all of it when Briar first brought this stuff home, but now I couldn't imagine this place without it. Without Briar, this house isn't a home. It's just four walls. I was fooling myself to think I could ever just let her walk out of here.

The kitchen is dark, so I check my bedroom first and then quietly push open the door to her room, only to find both are empty.

Where would she be on a Monday night?

Feeling panic rising, I sit down at the kitchen counter and send her a text.

> Holden: Home and wondering where you
> are. Checking to make sure you're okay.
> Message me.

I pace the floor, worried about her and the baby. My mind is spiraling, and the knot in my chest only increases in size as the minutes tick by. By the time I'm ready to start calling every one of her friends, I get a notification on my phone. Thank god, it's from Briar.

> Briar: I'm fine. I'm at Daisy's, but I'm tired
> and I'm going to crash here tonight. Tucker
> has an away game.

Right. I remember Tucker saying something about a road trip with the Outlaws this week, and Briar often stops by to keep Daisy company when she's on her own. If my head wasn't so wrapped up in my own problems, I would have thought of that.

I slam my fist onto the kitchen counter, then drag my hands through my hair. I feel desperate. I need to see her. It wasn't that long ago that I liked my alone time. My space. That was before Briar. Now I understand it's because I was never with the right person. I've never loved someone as much as I love her.

> Holden: Do you need me to bring you
> anything? Pajamas? A toothbrush?

> Briar: No, I brought some things in case I
> decided to stay.

Hearing that she was planning on spending the night is like a punch to the gut. She's probably over there questioning whether I want her or not, and fuck, that makes me feel like an asshole.

I pushed her away. I made her feel like she's not the most important thing in my life. I have to take responsibility for that because I know I hurt her.

I slide my phone across the counter, holding myself back from texting her again. She deserves an apology from me in person so she can see the truth in my eyes. It's too late now to stalk over to Daisy's and win her back, so instead I start brainstorming ways to show her I want her to stay.

Ten minutes later, I'm firing up my laptop, knowing exactly how I can make it up to her

TWENTY-EIGHT

I'M GOING TO BE BRAVE

Briar

What am I doing here?

I woke up next to Daisy this morning, and as much as I love her, she isn't Holden.

When he didn't come home for dinner last night, I messaged Daisy to see if I could come over because I knew I wouldn't survive another evening alone in his house. Sierra and Everly also stopped by with ice cream for me and a bottle of wine for them, and we watched *The Bachelor*. It was nice to be with the girls, but it was also a reminder that I am the only one not in a solid relationship. I held it together until Everly and Sierra left, but when it was just Daisy and I in our pajamas in her bed, I broke down. I told her everything—about the apartment, about wanting to stay with Holden, about him not asking me to stay.

Daisy held my hand as I fell apart. My sweet, supportive friend listened to me vent until I was too tired to talk anymore. Then this morning she got up early and made me breakfast.

I've been on the verge of tears all morning, too emotionally exhausted to talk about the situation with Holden. I need to go home, get changed and get to the office. My plan is to bury myself in work today until I forget about all of this, at least for a few hours. Hiking my duffle bag on to my shoulder, I give Daisy a hug goodbye. "Thanks for everything, Dais."

"It's going to be okay, Briar. But you need to talk to him."

I press my lips together, unsure of what to say to Holden now, and nervous about how he'll respond.

She nods her head, folding her arms over her chest. "He would have said yes."

"If I asked him if I could stay?"

"Holden is so far gone for you. Think about it, Briar. There must be a misunderstanding somewhere."

"Maybe you're right." I shrug one shoulder. "Thanks for last night. I love you."

"Anything for you." She smiles.

I drag myself to my car. Thinking over Daisy's advice, I am starting to realize how badly Holden and I messed things up. I let my insecurities get the best of me. I should have swallowed my fears and talked to him. We both failed miserably at communicating.

I flip the visor down to look at myself in the mirror. There is no hiding the dark circles under my eyes. I barely slept, but it doesn't matter. I can't wait another second to talk to Holden.

By the time I pull my car into Holden's driveway, tears are starting to roll down my cheeks. But this time they aren't tears of a girl who hasn't been chosen. They're tears of hope. I'm going to be brave and ask Holden for what I want. If he wants something different, then at least I'll know.

I'm getting my duffle out of the backseat when I hear the front door slam. I look up and my heart slams against my ribs when I see him striding towards me.

It's Holden. He jogs down the few stairs and comes to meet me, determination in his eyes. And I know before he says a single word: He wants me. I feel it in my bones that he wants me to stay.

"Briar, baby..."

"Holden."

Dropping my bag to the ground, I wrap my arms around his neck as he lifts me into his strong arms. I'm home. His face is in my neck. The hold he has on me is so tight I'm breathless.

"I was on my way to see you," he whispers against my ear.

"I was coming to see *you*."

"Briar, I don't want you to leave."

"I'm not going anywhere. I'm staying."

He drops me down to my toes, gripping my face in his hands. His mouth seals to mine in a searing kiss, his tongue forcing his way into my mouth. He breaks the kiss before I'm ready, locking his eyes with mine. "You'll really stay?"

"Yes, baby. I never wanted to leave. I thought you didn't—"

He cuts me off with another quick kiss. "I know. I should have told you what I wanted. I should have asked you to stay. I never wanted you to leave, but I thought... it doesn't matter what I thought anymore. What matters is you're staying, Bee."

"I'm staying."

Holden smiles at me with a promise in his green eyes before pulling me back into his chest. "There are things we need to talk about, but we can do that later. I have half an hour with you before we both need to get to work. I need you, Bee. I need you so bad." Then he's dragging me into the house with him, tears still swimming in my eyes.

"I've gone too long without you, Briar, and I'm fucking starved."

"I know, baby."

"Do you realize how long I've had to go without kissing you?"

"I know, baby."

"Never again, Bee. Never." He runs the back of his knuckles along my cheek.

"We're us again."

I squeal when he picks me up, carrying me to the bedroom, my arms looping around his neck. Once we get there, he unbuttons his shirt. I start working on his pants.

"Take off your clothes unless you want me to tear them off."

I do as he asks. The two of us undress, and like a man obsessed, he seals his mouth to mine. My tongue tangles with his. My hands weave their way through his thick hair. His hand dips down between my thighs connecting with my already wet center.

"You're dripping, pretty girl." He dips two fingers inside of me.

I moan when they curl inside of me hitting me in just the right spot. He sucks on my neck and my ear, and the entire world feels as if it's aligned again. Nothing has felt right over the last couple of days and finally I have balance. Everything feels the way it should now that I am back in Holden's arms.

"I will never sleep in this bed again without you." Holden stops fingering me so he can back me onto the bed. I move to the middle where he cages me in. "Never again. I hated being away from you."

Then he's already notching the head of his cock with my entrance pushing inside of me inch by perfect inch. I groan. I think he does too. The moment is so beautiful, I already know I never want it to end.

"Mine," he murmurs, dipping his head down to kiss me.

"Yours."

"Say it again, Briar. I'm needy as fuck for you right now. I need to know you're mine, baby."

His words are like gasoline on an already out-of-control fire. Holden Banks is ravenous for me like I've never known.

"Yours, baby, never letting you go."

My words spur him on, and he pumps his hips faster, the sound of his skin slapping against my skin echoing in the room around us. I watch him take everything he needs from me while I unquestionably hand it over to him.

Two more deep thrusts, and my back arches as I shatter. Pulse after pulse, my limbs shake as pure ecstasy washes over me.

"Fuck, I'm coming," Holden grits out. The carved muscles of his abs tighten and tremble until he collapses over me.

I close my eyes, savoring the feeling of his skin against mine, our bodies joined with our baby boy in between us. There is so much joy in my chest, love overflowing through my limbs.

We clean up and get dressed again for work. Once we're both ready we head downstairs. I sit down on the couch to fasten the tiny buckles on my heels.

"Stay there."

"Holden?"

"Trust me, baby. I'll be right back."

I watch him walk into the kitchen in his dove gray dress pants and a crisp white button down. I've never seen anyone more beautiful in all my life. I smile, feeling a little confused, wondering what he's doing.

He sits down on the coffee table opposite me, leans over, and hands me an envelope.

I frown, heart pounding as I wonder what on earth could be inside.

"Open it."

My gaze drifts down to the envelope and I slowly pull out a piece of paper. My eyes focus on one word in the center of the page before reading anything else.

Vancouver.

Two plane tickets to Vancouver.

"Holden," I gasp, my heart pounding hard in my chest.

"I know you miss your mom, and I know once the baby arrives it's going to be a lot harder to travel. I spoke to her and she's excited to see us."

"You're coming too?"

"I hope that's okay with you."

I stare back at him, my hand drifting to the stubble on his face. "But, Holden, you're afraid of flying."

"I'll do it for you."

My chest tightens, and my teeth bite into my bottom lip. "You'll get on a plane for me?"

"I'd rather get on top of you, but yes, I'll do anything for you." He smirks, looking pretty pleased with himself for being cute.

"I know." Tears well in my eyes. "You've been nothing but the best."

"I was an idiot, and I hurt you. It wasn't my intention, but I still made you doubt how I feel for you, Briar. This is my way of showing you how much I love you. I want to fix things between us and make them right. I wanted to do something to show you how much you mean to me. I will get on a plane for you, baby. There's nothing I wouldn't do. I need you to know how much I fucking love you."

The ache in his voice makes my heart bleed in my chest. Tears blur my vision. "I love you too, Holden. So damn much. You are already my whole world. It's you, me and Slugger. The only two people I'll ever need," I say, my hand drifting over his jaw. "I can't believe you're taking me home."

"I'd do anything for you, Briar. My life now revolves around you."

"Holden—" This man. He always says the most perfect things.

He hooks a finger under my chin, tipping my face to his. "I can't sleep anywhere but with you. Never again, yeah?"

"It kills me to sleep anywhere but with you," I murmur.

Holden levels me with a look full of promises and resolution. "I won't ever allow it to happen again. I'm yours. Tell me you're mine."

"I'm yours."

His eyes close, and he rests his forehead against mine. "Move in with me, Bee."

"I already live with you, remember?" I sass, because I know what he likes.

"You know what I mean. Call your landlord. Cancel your lease. I want you and the baby with me... in my house."

"I haven't signed the agreement yet."

"Thank fuck." He smiles, wiping the tears from my eyes with his thumbs. I fight back a smile and wrap my arms around his nape. Our mouths touch, and I hold him as tightly as I can.

We kiss and kiss, relief and joy buzzing through us. Being without Holden felt as agonizing as losing a limb.

We are meant to be together.
Holden and I loving each other for as long as we live.
"I love you," I tell him.
"I love you the most."
I breathe him in.
I am home.

TWENTY-NINE

SHE CALMS MY SOUL AND SETS IT ON FIRE
AT THE SAME TIME

Holden

Briar is keeping me company as I paint the nursery, but looking at her in her faded jeans and sports bra is really tempting me to take a break. She looks cute as hell. Her tiny frame and a belly that looks like she swallowed a watermelon. I'm not sure how she can get any bigger.

It's spring in Reed Point and Slugger will be making his appearance very soon, which is why I'm feeling the pressure to get this room finished.

"What are you looking at?" I catch Briar watching me as she folds a stack of tiny newborn sleepers.

She raises her eyebrows. "Nothing."

"I don't believe you." I set my brush down on the tray, wiping my forehead with the back of my forearm. "Like what you see?"

"Definitely," she says, eyes wide. "The blue is the perfect shade."

"I wasn't talking about the walls." I shake my head, sitting down on the carpet across from her. "But they do look incredible if I do say so myself."

The day after Briar came home from Daisy's, I'd told her about the eviction notice and my plan to purchase the house. I think it helped her to understand what had been going on with me at the time, why I was so distracted. Waiting to hear whether my application was approved felt like torture, but a few days later I got good news. My parents offered me a loan for the amount I was short, on the agreement that I eventually pay them back.

Briar and I were together when the call from the bank finally came in. It was such a relief to know that we could stay in the house that feels like home to both of us. We could start planning our future, setting up a nursery for Slugger. I had an appointment the following day to sign the papers, and I asked Briar to come with me. I needed her there to sign the paperwork since her name was all over it. I wanted this house to be *ours*, so I added her name to the deed.

When she was given the papers to sign and realized what I had done, she refused. She said it was too much. But I insisted. I told her it was just a matter of time before everything I owned became 50 percent hers when I eventually asked her to marry me. And I am *going* to ask her. Briar made it clear that she didn't want a proposal because she was pregnant, so as much as it has pained me not to ask her, I'm waiting until after our baby is born knowing it will mean more to her.

I finally got her to sign the paperwork for the house after convincing her it was something I needed her to do for our family. It came with no strings attached. I watched her go through the contract signing and initialling where needed, and I've never been happier in my life. It was the beginning of our life together.

After that, Briar and I settled into an easy routine. We've

spent as much time together as we could while still making time for our friends. We went to her doctor's appointments together. We picked out furniture for the nursery together. We even went to Vancouver together two weeks ago.

Getting on the plane was as difficult for me as I thought it would be, but the blow job Briar promised me when we landed helped me through it. I white-knuckled it the entire flight, drank two or three G&Ts, and when we landed in British Columbia, I said a prayer. Briar was the exact opposite, reading one of her romance novels and sipping tea the entire flight, but her hand was always somewhere on me, in my hand or on my thigh, calming me. Briar calms my soul and sets it on fire at the same time.

As soon as we got to Briar's mom's house, I was thankful we took the trip out. It was a beautiful thing to see her family fawn all over her. We spent an afternoon flipping through Briar's baby book while her mom and her brother reminisced about every one of Briar's milestones. Her family was so damn welcoming. On our last day, Briar took me to her favorite restaurant on the harbor and then we walked the seawall. The three days we spent in Vancouver were a whirlwind and a little bittersweet for Briar. The next time she sees her mom, she'll have a baby of her own.

"We need to decide on a name, Bee. You're due any second."

Briar's due date is in two weeks, but the doctor warned us that she could go into labor anytime.

"I think we're at a standstill. Do I have to remind you that you've vetoed every single one of my suggestions?"

"In my defense, you named your cat Bear. Not sure you have the best track record."

She picks up one of the freshly folded onesies and throws it at me, scowling. I catch it with a laugh and then lean in closer, pressing my mouth to hers. I splay my hand over the top of her belly just as Slugger's little foot kicks against my palm. It makes me smile every time. "I think he wants us to pick a name."

"Maybe we wait until we meet him?"

Maybe it's time to tell her that when it comes right down to it, I'll go with whatever name she chooses. I could never say no to her. But where's the fun in that? I'd rather give her the gears for a little while longer.

I lean away from Briar when Bear struts between us, all attitude with her big, fluffy tail in the air. There is no denying the fur ball has grown on me. I've even given her full reign of the house.

"She's *my* cat, you know," Briar reminds me as I stroke the length of her back, making her purr.

"I don't know, looks like she has a new favorite."

"She hasn't forgotten the can of tuna you gave her this morning. Bribery is a sneaky tactic, Holden."

"Whatever you need to tell yourself." I smirk.

"I hope you took your pill this morning." She leans forward, stroking Bear's head. "You are going to pay for those cuddles."

"She's worth it. I can't say no to this face." I shoot Briar a wink. "Tomorrow I'll set up the crib and I'll help you put everything in its place."

Briar's eyes are soft. So soft it looks like she's on the verge of tears. I'm not sure it's normal for a pregnant woman to cry as much as Briar, but it's cute as hell. She feels big emotions. It's one of my favorite things about her.

"Tell me what's going through your pretty little head," I whisper.

She closes her eyes with the prettiest smile. "I still sometimes can't believe it's true."

"That we're having a baby?" I ask, pressing a kiss to her jaw.

"Yes. We were only supposed to be roommates," she says. "Now look at us. In love and with a baby on the way."

"So in love."

"The most." Her tears are instant.

"We were never going to be just roommates, pretty girl." I shift to the side and motion her to sit between my legs. She rests her back against my chest. "I would have found a way to make you stay." I say into her hair, running my hand over the soft skin of her belly.

Briar takes my hand in hers, bringing my knuckles to her mouth and nipping them with her teeth.

"I love you, Holden."

"I love you too. Come on, my pretty girl. Let me help you up."

I give her my hand, slowly pulling her up off the floor. She suddenly flinches, pressing her hand to her side.

"You okay, baby?"

She inhales then exhales a sharp breath. "Yeah... I'm fine. I was probably just sitting too long."

"Promise?" I ask, my stomach still free falling.

"I promise."

The pain in her side is forgotten when she sits on the back porch, and I bring her lunch and a glass of lemonade.

THIRTY

I WAS BORN READY

H olden

A missed call and a text from Briar while I'm at work the next day has me rattled. *Call me as soon as you can.*

What the fuck? I excuse myself from a meeting and go back to my desk and call her.

"Baby, are you okay?" I push through the door of my office, exhaling a grateful breath when she answers my call.

"The pain is back. It hurts, Holden." There's agony in her voice.

"Where are you? I'm coming to get you. I'm taking you to the hospital." I stuff my laptop into my work bag, grab my jacket and jog down the hall to let my boss know I need to leave.

"I'm at home," Briar says. "I left work thinking a warm bath and some rest would help but it didn't."

Has she been in pain all morning without telling me? My heart drops to my stomach.

"You're going to be fine, baby. Stay there. I'll be there in 10 minutes. Understand?"

"Yes." I hear her suck in a breath. "I'll wait for you."

I burst through the doors to the parking lot in a full-out run now. Could this really be it? Could Briar be in labor? She still has 2 more weeks left in her pregnancy. Is it too early?

The doctor told us she could go into labor early the last time Briar had her routine check, but I think I just assumed early meant a few days. Not April instead of May.

Fuck. I should have made her go on maternity leave last month. I knew she was getting tired, long days at work were getting to be too much for her. Plus, we've been doing so much in the evenings to get the nursery ready. Briar was adding tiny star decals to the wall behind the crib last night until 10 p.m. before she finally collapsed into our bed. I told her I would do them for her, but she had this vision in her head of exactly how she wanted them.

Briar's sitting on the edge of the couch in the living room when I rush inside our house. In an instant, I'm crouching to the floor in front of her pressing my hands to either side of her belly.

"Hey, pretty girl. How are you doing?" I look at up her, tears glistening in her pretty green eyes. "What's happening, Bee? Do you think you're having contractions?"

"I don't know, but I think I should see a doctor."

"Let's go out to the truck, okay? Tell me anything you want me to bring to the hospital."

"Hospital?" she questions with panic in her eyes.

"Yes, hospital, Bee. Just in case. I'm not wasting time."

She nods, agony sweeping her face as I help her to stand. I sweep her into my arms and carry her out to my truck. Once she's buckled into the front seat, I run back inside, unbuttoning my dress shirt as I go. As quickly as I can, I change into a T-shirt and joggers before grabbing the hospital bag that we had packed along with her phone and charger. I turn off the lights and lock the front door realizing the next time we're here, we might have Slugger with us. The thought sends a shot of adrenaline to my chest.

I throw Briar's bag in the back of my truck, then I climb in, checking to see how she's doing. "Briar. You okay?"

"It hurts," she winces, bent over her stomach. Her right hand grips the handle of the door so tightly that her knuckles are white.

Is this normal? If they're contractions, don't they come on gradually? Why is she already in this much pain?

With one hand on the steering wheel, I place my other on her back, reversing out of the driveway as fast as I can. I'm driving up Haven Harbor about 20 miles over the legal limit while I rub circles over Briar's back.

"We should call the hospital and tell them we're on the way." She sits back in the seat, loosening her grasp on the door handle.

These have to be contractions. That's why she's getting breaks in between the pain, right? I should be timing them. That's what I learnt in the prenatal classes we took. I check the time on the dash as I drive through town to Reed Point General.

"It'll be fine, Bee. There will be a doctor there to help us."

There would be, right? It's a hospital. There has to be a doctor available who can deliver a baby. Fuck. I love living in a small town—except for times like these, when I wish we had a big city hospital with tons of staff around to help. But babies are born in Reed Point all the time, I remind myself. They'll know what to do.

"I thought we'd have two more weeks," she whispers.

"I know, baby. Maybe Slugger just can't wait to meet us," I say, reaching over to squeeze her knee gently. "Bee, don't worry, okay? We're almost there. Everything's going to be okay."

Shit. Why is this drive taking so long? It never takes more than 15 minutes to drive anywhere in Reed Point but for some reason, it feels like it's taking 15 years to get to the damn hospital.

"It's hurting again." Briar leans forward over her stomach again and I check the time on the dash. Four minutes. It's been four minutes since she had her last contraction.

So, I drive faster, saying more prayers, until the hospital parking lot finally comes into view and I'm parking in front of the hospital doors.

"Holden, you can't park here."

"It's fine. I'll get someone to move it for me later." I round the front to get to Briar. Helping her out of the truck, I grab her bag from the backseat and grasp her hand in mine, walking Briar slowly through the hospital doors. The second the receptionist sees us, she's flying from her chair to bring Briar a wheelchair.

"I think she's in labor. I timed the pain, she's at 4 minutes apart."

"You timed my contractions?" Briar's voice sounds surprised.

"Of course I did. I read that baby book five times."

"Let's get you to see a doctor, honey," the woman says. "What's your name?"

"Briar Moore."

"And you must be Dad. Are you ready?"

"I was born ready." I fake a grin that I'm not really feeling. Now that we're here, my hands are shaking.

The woman gives Briar a kind smile then returns her

attention to me. "You can follow us through those doors and once she's in a bed, I'll get you to fill out some forms."

She wheels Briar through a set of large automatic doors, past a nurse's station to a private room. There's a bed in the center of the room, a plastic bassinet against a wall and a small bathroom with a shower on the opposite side of the room.

"This is where you'll have your baby," she explains. "Providing the doctor keeps you here and doesn't send you home."

"Send her home? The doctor can't send her home. Look at the pain she's in. She can't—"

"Holden, baby, it's okay." Briar interrupts me with her palm on my forearm, trying her best to give a small smile.

"I'm going to get the doctor on call. His name is Doctor Waterman. You can go ahead and change out of your clothes and put on the hospital gown that's on the bed."

"Okay." Briar stands as the woman slips out of the room, closing the door behind her. I throw her bag on the nearest chair and then help Briar change and get onto the bed under the blue-and-white striped blanket. There's a knock at the door a moment later.

"Hi Briar, I'm Carina, your nurse. I'm going to hook you up to a few machines while we wait for Dr. Waterman. We're going to see what's going on. Sound good?"

"Sounds good. Thank you," Briar replies before her face is contorted in pain. Her hand grips the blanket.

Carina works busily to strap a wide band around Briar's stomach with a monitor that will track the contractions and monitor the baby's heart rate. I pull a chair closer to the bed, scooping Briar's hand into mine and giving it a squeeze.

"You are in active labor, Briar. Your contractions are

three minutes apart. You will most likely have this baby by tonight. If not, it will be tomorrow."

"Isn't it too soon?" The fear in Briar's eyes is like a punch to my gut. "I'm not due for two more weeks."

"Delivering a baby two weeks early is considered near-term. Perfectly normal. I don't want you to worry," Carina says. "The baby's heart rate is 130, which is exactly what we want to see. I want you to push the red button by your bed if you need anything or if the pain gets too much. I'll be back with some ice water. I won't be gone for too long."

As Carina leaves the room, a strong contraction slices through Briar's abdomen. "Holden, it hurts so bad."

Briar squeezes my hand and grits her teeth until the wave of pain subsides and she can breathe again. "You're doing so good, pretty girl. I'm so damn proud of you."

I brush her hair from her face, stand up and press a kiss to her forehead, noticing the tears slipping down her rosy cheeks. "I'm scared, Holden. What if something goes wrong?"

I bring her hand to my mouth, whispering against her knuckles. "It's going to be okay. His heartbeat is strong."

I try to reassure Briar, but truthfully, I'm just as scared as she is. I've read the pregnancy books. I know the risks of a baby being born early. There is still so much that could go wrong.

Another contraction slams through her body, then another three minutes later and another after that. They keep coming. Briar breathes through them like she practised in prenatal classes while I rub her shoulders.

When Carina returns, she has Doctor Waterman with her; he's dressed in light-blue scrubs with a matching cap covering his graying hair.

"I hear we're having a baby tonight." He reaches for a

pair of latex gloves on the metal tray next to the foot of the bed and sits on the stool next to it. "I'm going to check to see how you're progressing, Briar. This will only take a few minutes."

A wave of panic washes over Briar's face as she waits to hear what the doctor has to say. We've been waiting here for hours for a glimpse of the man. Now that he's here, we're both on pins and needles waiting for his report.

"Baby is in position. He or she is almost here."

"He." Briar says. "It's a boy."

The doctor smiles, noticing the panic in Briar's voice. "Your baby boy is looking good. Heart rate is perfect and you're eight centimetres dilated. He's going to be here in the next couple of hours. I'll be back soon when it's time to push."

Our son is almost here. We're going to meet our baby boy.

The next two hours move slowly. Briar is in agony and exhausted but breathing through every contraction that steamrolls through her body. Just after 10:30 p.m., Doctor Waterman returns and after a brief exam, he tells Briar it's time for her to push.

"This is it, baby. Our little Slugger is almost here. You're almost there," I say into her hair, my lips on her temple.

"I don't know if I can do it, Holden." She squeezes her eyes shut and breathes through a whopper of a contraction. "It hurts and I'm so tired."

"You've got this, baby. I know it. There's no one as strong as you. You're almost there."

The doctor is talking to Carina on the far side of the room as machines beep and monitors flash next to Briar's bed. She turns her gaze to me, tired emerald eyes locking with mine, and I lean in and kiss her before another contraction interrupts the moment. "I love you. I love you so fucking much."

"I love you too."

"You can do this," I tell her, running my hand over her damp hair. "I've got you, Bee, and I'm so damn proud of you."

Her eyes search mine, until another contraction rips through her, bringing tears that slip down her cheeks. My heart is sliced wide open seeing her in so much pain. She's squeezing my hand; her jaw is clenched tight. When the contraction finally subsides, she collapses against the bed.

"I'm only doing this once," she groans. "No more babies."

A smile tugs at the corners of my mouth. "No more babies then. All I need is the two of you."

"I'm not joking. You can mark my words. We can get a dog or another cat, but no more babies."

I laugh because she's cute as hell. It wouldn't matter to me if it was just the three of us. I'd never need anything more. Just Briar and our baby boy together under one roof. I fucking love just thinking about that.

I offer Briar water before another contraction hits. Followed by another. And another until Dr. Waterman and Carina are in position at the foot of the bed.

"Let's have this baby, Briar. I'm going to get you to start pushing," he says. "Holden, you can help her hold her leg up while Carina has the other. When I tell you to push, Briar, you're going to push for as long as you can. Okay?"

"Okay," she whispers, her eyes locked on the doctor, who has folded the blanket up to her waist. I brace one knee while the nurse holds her other. Briar glances up at me and whispers, "I love you."

I'm in complete awe of this woman. She's strong and brave and she looks like a complete goddess.

When another contraction hits her at full force, Dr. Waterman tells her to push. My strong girl bares down, bringing her chin to her chest, and gives it everything she's got. When she runs out of energy and air, she expels a giant breath, collapsing into the bed.

She pushes again a few minutes later. And again. For the next 20 minutes, the room seems to spin and go silent. Briar keeps pushing. The doctor keeps encouraging her. I hold her knee because it's the only thing I can do while I pray. All I can hear is the adrenaline coursing through my body.

And then a sharp cry fills the air, and I glance down to see my baby boy in Dr. Waterman's hands.

A beautiful baby boy.

My Slugger.

THIRTY-ONE

LITTLE MAN

B riar

The smile on my face has been there since midnight, when we welcomed our little man into the world.

He was born on April 25th. Holden's dad's birthday. If that was a sign of the man he would become, it was a good one.

Hours have passed, and because he was born in the middle of the night, we've had the luxury of it being just the three of us. I've napped for 20 minutes here and there and tried to get him to latch on but mostly, I've been taking millions of photos. I'm soaking up this quiet time in this tiny room in our little bubble before our friends and family arrive to meet our little boy.

God, I'm exhausted but I'd rather sit here and stare at this perfect little angel. Our son. I've heard people say that everything changes the moment you see your baby for the first time, that the world tilts on its axis, that love takes on an entirely new meaning. I never doubted it, but I never really *understood* it either—until now.

Now, as I watch his tiny chest rise and fall, as I memorize the way his fingers curl instinctively when I brush his palm,

I know. This love isn't like anything else. It's just bigger—it's deeper, more consuming, more terrifyingly wonderful than anything I've ever felt.

A tear slips down my cheek before I realize it, and I let out a breathy, overwhelmed laugh.

"You okay?" Holden's voice is gentle, warm.

I nod, shifting slightly so my son nestles closer against my chest. "Yeah. I just…" I swallow, trying to find the right words. "I get it now."

Holden's gaze lifts to mine, his expression softer than I've ever seen it. There's something in his eyes—a quiet awe, maybe, or just the same overwhelming love that's currently flooding every inch of my body.

"Yeah," he murmurs, voice rough with emotion. "Me too."

Holden is squished into the hospital bed next to me gazing down at Slugger nestled in my arms. He's wrapped in a swaddle with little baseballs all over it, a tiny hat with a knot on the top covering his light brown hair. All 5 pounds of him. He already looks so much like Holden, it makes my heart burst. The slope of his tiny nose, the pucker of his full lips. He even has a little frown that reminds me of Holden's expression when he's in a deep sleep. He's the sweetest little thing in the world.

Thankfully, he's healthy. After being in my arms for only a minute, he was whisked away by the nurse for evaluation. She explained that she needed to check his heart rate, temperature, and breathing in case he needed additional oxygen support. Twenty minutes later he was back in my arms.

"What should we name him?" I ask, staring down at him with teary eyes.

"I thought we agreed on Slugger, but if you've changed

your mind, now's the time to tell me." Holden brushes a finger over our son's bottom lip.

"He will always be our little Slugger, but I was thinking about Hayes Holden Banks. He would have the same initials as his daddy."

Holden wipes at his eyes like he has been all night.

"I love it." He catches my gaze before leaning into my mouth. He kisses me soft and long, sending a shiver up my spine.

"Really, you do?" I ask when we break the kiss.

"I do. He looks like a Hayes."

"He looks like you." I run my fingertip over his tiny nose.

Hayes is asleep, his perfect face tranquil. Barely eight hours old and he's already got me wrapped around his finger.

"You should sleep, baby. You know today is going to be non-stop visitors, you're going to need to get some rest while you can."

I know he is right. Holden had texted everyone we know about Hayes' birth 20 minutes after he had arrived. I should close my eyes. Holden would take good care of him. He always will.

It doesn't matter, though, because just as my eyes are fluttering closed, there is a knock on the door and Daisy and Tucker peek their heads in.

Family.

Hayes' family.

This little boy is going to be so loved.

Holden's family shows up soon after, his mom's eyes full of unshed tears for her first grandbaby as she peers over Hayes sleeping in his Daddy's arms.

We're all a mess of smiles and happy tears.

My life is beautiful.
And it's only just begun.

HOLDEN'S EPILOGUE

EIGHT MONTHS LATER

Holden

Hayes stuffs a fistful of pureed sweet potato in his mouth then squeals in delight.

"Tastes good, doesn't it, bud?" I ask, grinning as I watch my little man sitting in his highchair.

"Da Da," he says, offering me the spoon he refuses to use because he'd rather use his hands.

So far, at eight months old, Hayes is happy, sweet and bright, mischievous and curious. My handsome boy is the cutest thing in the world, even when he's covered in sweet potato. He has my chestnut hair and his mom's bright green eyes and easygoing personality.

When he's done, I wash his face and hands with a washcloth while he squirms. "We need to get you cleaned up before Mommy murders me. You're going to a wedding. You need to look your best."

"Little dude eats like his dad," Tucker laughs from where he's sitting on the couch next to Jake. "Like an animal."

I just shake my head at him. Nothing can ruin my day today.

In less than an hour, I'm marrying Briar. The ceremony is taking place at a manor just outside of Reed Point, on a terrace overlooking the ocean, then we're having the reception in one of their ballrooms. Tucker is my best man. Jake, Grayson, and my brother are my groomsmen. They're all here with me in the groom's suite while Briar and her bridesmaids get ready in a room down the hall.

So far, with the exception of me failing miserably to get Hayes down for his nap, the day has gone smoothly. He's been distracted by all of the people and the energy in the room. My little man is as excited as me. I'm finally marrying my favorite person on the planet.

My dad walks over to Hayes and picks him up from the highchair. He holds my son in his arms and gives him a kiss on his chubby cheek while I fetch his suit. Over the past eight months, the two of them have created quite the friendship. A bond. My parents and Barb see Hayes often, even taking him for sleepovers so I can have his mom all to myself.

"Time to get dressed, Hayes-y-haze. You're going to look so handsome." I bought him a miniature version of my dove gray suit so he can match his daddy. Once he's dressed, I snap a photo of him for Briar. I've already sent her over a dozen today. Yes, I'm that guy—thankfully, my fiancée thinks it's cute.

Today is an especially special day for her. Not only are we getting married, but it's also New Year's Eve, the day she was adopted by her stepdad. I worried it would be too much for her—an emotional anniversary, a reunion with her mom and her brother who flew in for the wedding, a wedding ceremony and reception. Plus, a very busy baby. But she promised me she'd be okay. It's her favorite day of the year. She also wants me to love New Year's Eve just as much as her, so she refused to back down on the date. Briar has managed to change my mind on December 31st as well as a list of other things over the last 12 months.

It blows my mind to think that a couple of years ago I thought I might not want children. Becoming a dad is one of the best things that has ever happened to me. I smile every time I think about the day Briar told me she was pregnant. It seems imaginable to me that I ever thought I could live this life without Hayes and my girl. When I think back to my life before my little man, it feels incomplete. There's no other way to explain it. Hayes is my future. And soon, I hope to give him a brother or a sister.

I've learnt to relax a little. I'm no longer the wound-tight neat freak that I was before Briar moved in. The house feels like a home now, with Hayes' play-mat in the center of the living room and the highchair next to the kitchen table. There are toys spilling out of baskets beside the couch. Bottles drying on a rack next to the kitchen sink. Sure, it feels a little chaotic sometimes, but every room I walk into reminds me that our house is full of love and life.

The only thing missing is to make Briar my wife.

I proposed to her the night we brought Hayes home from the hospital. We were sitting at the coffee table eating Thai food. I had Hayes in my arms, rocking him to sleep so she could finish her dinner. The proposal wasn't fancy or a big, grand gesture like she probably reads about in her romance books, but we had shared so many memorable moments around that little wooden table, divulged so many secrets, that it felt right. The second I got down on one knee, Briar started to cry. When I slid the oval solitaire ring on her finger, she gasped. Nothing had ever felt so right.

Hayes giggles and hides his face in my neck as we walk downstairs to the terrace where the ceremony is taking place. He missed his nap, which means he'll either fall asleep after dinner or throw a fit. I'm praying he goes with the first option. When it gets to be bedtime, Barb offered to take him back to their house so that Briar and I can enjoy the rest of the night.

I take my place at the alter with Tucker and the guys on my left and wait for Briar, my heart bursting. I look down the aisle, lined with candles in glass cylinders and fresh orchids, for my first glimpse of my bride. When the violinist starts to play Pachelbel's Canon, and she comes into view.

My eyes are glued to her as she walks down the aisle on the arm of her brother wearing a simple white dress, elegant and flowy. Briar is breathtaking. She puts all other brides to shame. Her long, blonde hair is swept back over one shoulder with a glittery clip, and in her hands is a bouquet of white and soft pink roses.

She strides towards me, a confidence in her step that is so perfectly Briar. She knows who she is. She knows I have eyes for no one else but her. I am hers. Till the day I die.

The moment Hayes sees his mom, he lets out a squeal, his bright smile showing all four of his teeth. When he smiles, he looks just like his mom. A tear escapes before I can wipe it away when he reaches for Briar. If he could walk, he'd be off like a rocket.

I adjust Hayes on my hip, remembering to breathe, as Briar makes her last few steps towards me and our son. She looks at me like I'm the only other beating heart in the room and mouths the words, *I love you*. I mouth them back to her, understanding exactly what I have and how lucky I am. Love runs through my veins like a river.

When Briar reaches Hayes, she takes his hand in hers and brings it to her lips, kissing his chubby palm. We're both a crying mess when I hand Hayes over to her brother.

Briar places her hands in mine, and our eyes lock. Everyone else in the room fades away.

"Your boys missed you this morning," I whisper.

My heart pangs when she vows her love for me. Briar cries when I repeat the same vows back to her. My hands are in hers as the minister talks about commitment and love and growing old together. Then we're slipping rings onto each other's fingers and we're pronounced man and wife.

Everyone cheers when I take Briar in my arms and kiss the life out of her. We only break the kiss to come up for air. I'm always trying to catch my breath around this woman.

"I love you, Mrs. Briar Banks," I tell her.

She smiles. It ruins me.

"I know, baby," she says softly. "I love you too."

My lips meet hers in a long and lingering kiss, and when I pull back, she looks up at me, eyes glistening. It feels like in this moment the entire universe conspired to bring us together.

"I want more babies with you, Bee."

"We can have five or six," she says.

I take her hand and the two of us face our friends and family ready to begin our new life together.

Forever begins now.

I like the sound of that.

I KICK OFF MY SHOES AND THEN TAKE OFF MY TIE AND DRESS shirt, tossing them on the chair. I find Briar in the bathroom in a plush, white hotel robe, leaning towards the mirror taking off her makeup.

I step behind her, smoothing my hand down her neck. It

only takes a gentle press of my fingers to make her head fall to the side, making room for my mouth to suck on her skin.

"Holden," she whispers. "I'm almost done. The hair stylist must have used a can of hairspray. I'm not sure I'll ever be able to brush it all out."

Even as she objects, she pushes her ass into my already hard cock. Her breathing is shallow, lust in her eyes when they meet mine in the mirror.

"Here, let me." I motion to her hairbrush on the bathroom counter. She hands it to me and then removes the diamond barrette in her hair.

I carefully brush the silky strands of her blonde hair, section by section, until it falls in long, smooth waves down her back. She leans back slightly, her eyes closing in quiet contentment, a peaceful smile curling at the corner of her lips.

"Feel good?" I ask her.

"Mmm... so good," she whispers as a shiver runs down her spine. The sound of the bristles gliding through her hair is the only sound in the room.

Carefully, I work through the tangles, watching her shoulders relax as if the weight of the day—the emotions, the vows, the enormity of it all—has finally settled over her. Brushing just the ends, I'm careful not to pull too hard, working through the soft waves. With each slow stroke, she sighs.

When I'm done, I set the brush down and run my fingers through her now-smooth hair, letting the strands slip through my hands like silk. Then I lean down, push the robe over her shoulder and press a slow, lingering kiss to her bare skin.

She grinds her ass over my cock, as I gather the back of her robe, lifting the material until it's up over her ass. Her breath shudders when I run a finger down the seam of her soft cheeks until my hand is between her thighs. It only takes a second for her to grant me access, and she widens her legs.

"Holden," she moans, dropping her head back to rest on my chest.

I look in the mirror at her face tilted upward, the incline of her neck, her mouth parted in euphoria as I reach around her and find her clit

"Stop toying with me and fuck me," she breathes, as I play with her slick entrance.

"You need to be quiet or we're going to have to stop. We're in a hotel and we have neighbors."

Her teeth press a divot into her bottom lip, and she nods. "I can be good. I promise."

Her eyes flutter open when I unbuckle my belt and unzip my pants. Pushing my pants and my boxers down my thighs, I run the head of my swollen cock up and down the seam of her ass. She braces her hands on the counter, going up on her toes, and tips her ass up to allow me easier access.

My beautiful girl likes it most when I fuck her from behind.

She shimmies, trying to pull me in, but I wait, watching my cock tease her incredible ass. Right now, I just want to be as deep as I can inside the bliss of her heat, for as long as I can.

Trapping her between me and the counter, I catch her eye in the mirror. Our eyes stay locked as I sink inside her in one long thrust, until my balls meet her perfect heart-shaped ass.

Holding her hips in place, I stay where I am, every inch of me buried in her tight, wet channel. When my body begins to shudder and the need to rock my hips back and forth is too much to fight, I pull out to just my tip then slide back in.

Everything else evaporates the minute I'm joined with Briar. It's just me and my girl, and all I can think about is how badly I need her. The groan that leaves her lips tells me she needs me in the exact same, carnal way. A bone-deep, earth-shattering way that only deepens every day that we are together. Even now, I find it hard to believe that this woman is mine. In my heart, I've always known it.

I burn for Briar Moore. She is fucking beautiful, and I want to worship her every day of my life. Her back arches, and she pushes her ass into my pelvis, taking me as deep as she can. She feels like a fucking dream.

"That's it, baby girl. Use me." I grind my hips, moving my hand to cover hers where it's gripping the counter, the diamond ring I gave her against my palm. "Come for me, Bee. I'll follow you over like I always will, every day of your life."

The feel of her hugging my bare cock is almost too much to bear, but I'll wait as long as I need to for her to get off.

She whimpers. She's close. I fuck her, and she tightens around me.

"My wife," I say.

"My husband."

"Mine," I say, needing her to hear it.

I push into her again and again, sliding my hand around her body until my middle finger finds her clit, rolling it in circles.

My eyes are on hers in the mirror when she loses herself completely, clenching around my cock as her orgasm tears through her. I slam into her once more before I'm coming deep inside her, my balls constricting. Once I pour every drop into her, I collapse against her back, enjoying the feeling of being inside her. It takes a few minutes before I'm ready to pull out, and then I turn her in my arms to kiss her softly.

Briar's arms wrap around my neck, the two of us in a post-sex bliss. She pulls back a little to look up at me. "Take me to bed, Holden. You've worn me out."

I love this woman.

I have never felt such a need for another person in my entire life. When I think about forever, I think about her and our son and our future together. She has given my life meaning.

She drags me into the bedroom, slips off her robe and watches as I pull back the plush white comforter. Lying on my back, I pull her on to me so she can rest her head on my chest. I run my fingers through her hair. "Remember when you told me you didn't believe in soulmates?"

"And look at you making me eat my words," she murmurs, flattening her palm over my heart.

"I love you the most," I say before she lifts her head, eyes hazy, and I kiss her with everything I have to give.

"I love you with all four letters." Then she gives me that smile that will always make my heart skip a beat.

A smile pulls at my lips as Briar rests her head back down on my chest. I don't know how I got so lucky to marry the girl of my dreams.

Some people are worth the risk. I'm just glad I took a chance on the right girl.

BRIAR'S EPILOGUE

FIVE YEARS LATER

Briar

The smell of churros and popcorn fills the air as I tighten my grip on Hayes' hand. His little fingers, slightly sticky from cotton candy, curl around mine as we weave through the bustling crowd. Holden walks beside us, carrying our daughter, Harlow, on his shoulders. Her pigtails bounce as she excitedly points toward Sleeping Beauty's Castle in the distance.

"Mommy! Look! It's the castle! Just like in the movies!" Harlow squeals, her voice full of awe.

I smile up at her, my heart swelling. "It's even better in real life, huh?"

She nods so enthusiastically that Holden reaches up to steady her. "Careful, Princess," he teases, flashing me that grin that still makes my stomach flip, even after four years of marriage.

Ahead of us, our best friends and their kids—18 of us in total—walk together, the kids laughing, talking a mile a minute about which ride to go on next. The dads are already strategizing in that way they do, debating Genie+ times and the best way to tackle the park without too many meltdowns.

"Alright, game plan!" Jake announces. "We do Fantasyland first for the little ones, then split for the big rides."

"Don't forget Dole Whip," Birdie chimes in, tossing her mom, Everly, a knowing look. "It's tradition."

"Oh, I would never forget Dole Whip," Ev say dramatically, making her 14-year-old laugh. I still find it hard to believe that Birdie is a teenager.

The kids cheer as we make our way to Peter Pan's Flight, the four strollers parked nearby like some kind of parental army base. While the dads keep the younger ones entertained, Holden and I steal a moment to ourselves.

"Can you believe we pulled this off?" he asks, glancing around at our chaotic, beautiful group. "Four families, ten kids, and we're all still standing."

"Miraculous," I agree, watching as Holden leans down to help Harlow fix her Mickey ears. The sight of my husband —the man who started out as my temporary roommate and pretend boyfriend, now a father to our two little loves— makes my heart ache in the best way.

"Ready, Mommy?" Hayes tugs on my hand, his green eyes filled with excitement.

"Ready!" I say, squeezing his fingers.

As we step onto the ride, the laughter of our friends and children surrounding us, I realize this moment—right here, in the middle of the chaos, in the middle of Disneyland—is pure magic.

As the ride begins, the ship tilts forward, gliding over the miniature London below. Hayes gasps beside me, his tiny fingers gripping mine tighter.

"We're flying, Mommy!" he whispers, his voice filled with wonder.

I smile, soaking in the joy on his face. Next to us, Holden has one arm wrapped around Harlow, who lets out a delighted giggle as we soar past twinkling stars. For a moment, the world outside disappears, and we're just here —suspended in magic, in laughter, in love.

As we step off the ride, the rest of our group is waiting just outside the exit. The dads are wrangling the strollers while the moms are handing out snacks in a well-rehearsed assembly line.

"Next stop?" Tucker asks, lifting his son, Theo, onto his shoulders.

"Teacups!" the older kids shout in unison, making all the parents groan.

"Oh no," Jake chuckles. "Not again. You're on your own for that one."

"Come on," Everly teases, nudging him in his side. "You survived last time."

"Barely." He gives his wife a playful glare before leaning down to kiss her forehead. "But for you? I guess I can risk it."

As we make our way towards the teacups, the midday sun casts a glow over Main Street, U.S.A. The scent of sweet waffle cones drifts from the ice cream parlor, mingling with the distant melody of a barbershop quartet. There's an energy in the air—the kind that only a first time to Disney-land can create—when you see your husband's face light up seeing it for the first time.

Grayson walks ahead with Sierra and their daughter, Sadie, whispering and giggling like co-conspirators. Their other daughter, Stella, is in a stroller shooting a bubble wand into the crowd.

Behind me, Tucker and Daisy push their younger kids, Rosie and Jack, in a double stroller, while Daisy negotiates with their older two, Evie and Theo, about whether they *really* need another stuffed animal. Jake and Everly, the last of our group, are wrangling West, who is covered in chocolate from a half-melted Mickey bar.

"You know, I'm proud of you for getting on the plane," I say to Holden.

He raises an eyebrow. "I'm not sure I had a choice when you came up with this whole idea to get me to Disneyland."

I sigh dramatically. "Call me the dream maker. Just making sure my husband gets to see the one place he's always wanted to go."

"I love you, Bee." Holden tangles his hand in mine as we reach the teacups. "Tell me the truth," he whispers. "Did you ever imagine this would be our life?"

I glance around at our little tribe—the people we fell in love with, the children we brought into this world, the friendships that have only deepened over time.

"Maybe not exactly like this," I admit, watching Grayson chase Stella, both of them laughing. "But I wouldn't change a thing."

He squeezes my hand, smiling. "Me neither."

"This is where friendships are tested," Grayson mutters. "Who's actually willing to get on one of these things with the kids?"

"I'll take one for the team," my husband says, lifting a hand.

Tucker grins. "Well, if you're suffering, I guess I have to as well."

I watch Hayes run to the ride with Holden, while Harlow, who's three, curls against my hip, her fingers gripping the fabric of my shirt.

Unlike her brother, who thrives on speed and adventure, Harlow prefers to take everything at her own pace. While

Hayes runs full speed ahead with every experience, Harlow observes first, carefully deciding whether something is worth her time. She's sweet, affectionate, and adores her daddy—but she also has a quiet stubbornness like him too. If she doesn't want to do something, no force on earth, including bribery with Mickey-shaped treats, will change her mind.

When the ride is over and Holden manages to wobble off with Tuck and the four kids they brought on the ride with them, he takes a moment to center himself.

"That," he manages to say, "was a terrible idea."

"*That,* Dad," Hayes corrects, jumping up and down, "was awesome!"

"Now princesses!" Harlow squeals.

Hayes immediately makes a face. "Princesses are *boring*."

Harlow's little brow furrows. "No."

"Yes."

"No!"

Holden chuckles, ruffling his daughter's hair. "If my girl wants princesses, then we'll find princesses."

She grins, satisfied, and I feel that familiar sense of gratitude—because this? This messy, chaotic, love-filled time with my family and best friends? It's everything I've ever dreamed of.

"I love you, babe," I say, going up on my toes to press a kiss against Holden's lips. "Your kids are the luckiest."

He laughs, kissing me one more time. As we make our way toward Tomorrowland, with our best friends beside us, our kids bubbling with excitement, and the afternoon sun stretching golden across the sky, I take a deep breath and let it all sink in.

This is everything I ever wanted.

Maybe even more.

.   .   .

THE END.

CURIOUS WHAT LILY HAS COMING NEXT? GET
ready to fall hard for Deal Breaker—book one in the brand
new Deep Cove Millionaires Club series, following four hot
brothers who do hot things you're going to love. Book one is
Ford's story—a steamy, small-town second chance romance
with a broody CEO, a secret baby, and enough slow-burn
tension to fog up your Kindle and it's available now

Read Deal Breaker now and meet Ford + Landyn

TO FIND OUT OTHER RELEASE NEWS AND WHERE YOU CAN FIND
Lily, follow her on instagram, @authorlilymiller and on her
website. Make sure to sign up for her newsletter too.

WWW.AUTHORLILYMILLER.COM

ALSO BY LILY MILLER

HAVEN HARBOR SERIES

One Good Move

Play For Keeps

Never Say Never

Wish You Would

BENNETT FAMILY SERIES

Always Been You

Had To Be You

Heart Set On You

Crazy Over You

DEEP COVE MILLIONAIRES CLUB

Deal Breaker

Rule Breaker

ACKNOWLEDGMENTS

It's always hard to say goodbye to a series I have lived, breathed and slept for almost two years of my life. A cast of characters who have filled my days and nights.

The men of Haven Harbor came to me while writing my debut series when I realized I wasn't ready to leave Reed Point. I had written Grayson Ford, the witty, best friend of Beckett's, into the final book of the series and when readers began asking me if Grayson would be getting a story, I couldn't ignore them. Hilarious, sweet Grayson needed his own happily ever after!

I have to thank my beautiful friends in the book world for supporting me and sharing their love of my books. Every share, mention and edit mean the world to me. I hope you know how much you mean to me.

My editor, Carolyn, fills in the missing pieces of my stories. We've worked on eight books together, known each other practically our entire lives and raised our kids together. I am forever grateful for the hours she puts into making my books better.

My cover designer, Kim, never disappoints. Also, our eighth book together. It's hard to believe.

My PA, Kait, keeps my life organized. My newsletters would never be sent off on time without her.

My PA, Anita, runs my events so smoothly. I would be a mess without her by my side.

Briquelle of Briquelle Kayanne Photography for taking

the cover image of my dreams. Lindsey and Alex for allowing me to use your image. The way Alex is holding her jaw, the kiss, and the fact that they are getting their own real life happily ever after is magic!

Mandy Durnil and Melissa McGovern for your insite. Phoebe and Jordan for being a huge part of my team. The four of them never let me down.

My friends, Emily, Carmen, Mary, Brandee and Leah love me the most.

My family, Emme, Miller and Daniel love me the hardest.

I can't wait to announce soon what's coming next. To hear about my new spicy, small-town series coming soon, make sure you're subscribed to my newsletter.

I love you all,

Lily xx

AFTERWORD

Thank you for reading! If you loved the story, I'd be so grateful if you left an honest review—it helps more than you know. Your time and thoughts mean the world.

Want to stay connected? Join Lily's newsletter to get the latest updates, special sales, audiobook news, and first looks at new releases.

Lily Miller Newsletter

ABOUT THE AUTHOR

Lily Miller lives in Vancouver, BC with her husband—her real-life book boyfriend—and their two daughters. When she's not writing love stories full of heat, heart, and happily-ever-afters, you can usually find her in the kitchen cooking, sailing the Pacific Ocean, or with country music playing in the background.

A lifelong romantic, Lily has been hooked on happy endings since she was a kid, and now she channels that passion into writing small-town, contemporary spicy romance that celebrates love in all its messy, swoony, unforgettable forms.